THE ALEXANDROS EXPEDITION

The Alexandros Expedition

PATRICIA SITKIN

Boston: Alyson Publications, Inc.

Published as a paperback original by ALYSON PUBLICATIONS, INC.
Copyright © 1983 by Patricia Sitkin. All rights reserved.

Typeset and printed in the United States of America.

First edition, first printing, November 1983.

ISBN 0 932870 35 X

THE ALEXANDROS EXPEDITION
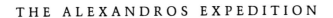

1

March 21, 1979 — Palat, Tariq: The squat, dun-colored building that was the prison's hub was the most ancient structure still in use in Tariq. A primitive, attenuated sphinx carved into its sandstone facade had gone blind and clawless with time. The building's uses had never varied: for countless generations it had been the site of the eye-gougings, boilings, flayings and dismemberments by which the country's rulers protected their position and amused the populace.

There were more modern prisons in Tariq, built since the harbor at Palat had begun to silt up and the town to shrink to a village, but this one had been much used in the weeks since the revolution. The disadvantage of its less sophisticated personnel and facilities for interrogation — there was no electric power at Palat — was more than balanced by its distance from population centers and inaccessibility to the media. It was a convenient depot for prisoners whose disappearances needed to be managed with tact.

The rusty metal door inside the archway just beneath the sphinx's single breast swung outward, and the tall, big-boned Englishman and the little Russian were pushed through it into the cobblestoned street. An angry, guttural chanting, its source unseen, enveloped them as they were led toward the public square. The larger man, touched by panic, watched his companion. Mikhail's square face showed only its usual easy composure — he might be on his way to an embassy affair, one that would surely bore him.

"It has to be the ugliest language in the world," Simon

7

said, trying to match the Russian's aplomb and succeeding at least in keeping his voice even.

"It's hardly euphonic, I must say," Mikhail began in his excellent English. The short-haired guard with the low forehead and the thick, muscular one — Mikhail called them Cretin and Muscul-man — prodded them along with their American-made machineguns, and knots in the rope around Simon's ankles hobbled him at each step. "Appropriate to the occasion, though. I think we're meant to be unnerved."

Muscul-man pushed too hard then, sending Mikhail to his knees. He stood, dusted himself off and continued as if the guard were an impropriety best ignored. "Imagine using those sounds to speak of love."

"Or soothe a baby." Simon thought of his own, the first, born a few days after his arrest, perhaps never to be seen or soothed by him.

One leg of Mikhail's grey prison trousers came unrolled and threatened to tangle itself with the rope at his ankles. He stopped, held up his hand to the guards and pointed at it; Cretin nodded permission, and they all waited as Mikhail rearranged himself. They had worn their own clothes until this morning when they had been made to change into prison uniforms. These were all one size, and Simon felt constricted in his, while Mikhail's sagged round him like a half empty sack.

They had shaved, though, and Mikhail had carefully combed his blond curls. "Got to maintain our image for the wogs."

"*What* did you say?"

"Wogs. I shouldn't like it to get back to Mother Russia, but it's a word I've come to understand."

Mikhail's matter-of-fact racism shocked Simon a little. Otherwise, the political gulf between them seemed only a trickle beside the ocean that separated them from the savagery of their jailers. Neither had yet suffered more than a sharp push, but the prison walls echoed through the days with cries from other prisoners, some only children.

They set off again but more slowly, the guards recognizing now that their steps were constricted by the hobbles. This shouldn't be happening today, to either of them. The hawk-faced old man who had prosecuted, judged and sentenced them had set April fourth for the flogging. That was a fortnight

8

away, days that might bring an end to this government of atavism and vengeance.

Mikhail, a junior official in the Soviet embassy at Persarum, had been left to tidy loose ends when the others were called home. Some wag had left a bottle of vodka in one of the files, and discovered by a cleaning woman, it became Exhibit A in Mikhail's trial for public drunkenness. Simon had pushed his luck too far, continuing to send material to his London editor despite increasingly urgent warnings from less vulnerable European colleagues. They had been convicted on the same day, by the same judge, of the same charge, but Mikhail had been sentenced to fifty lashes, Simon to thirty. Both had fared better than the American arrested a few days later and charged with spying. He had already been shot.

Tariq's new rulers were using each as surrogate for a country that had bet on the wrong horse. No intelligence agency in the world had thought the overthrow of the Emir possible. His army, air force and secret police squads were smaller than those of the Shah of Iran, but larger in proportion to Tariq's population, which was ground down by poverty, illiteracy and fear.

The Emir's nerves had made the difference. A few bloody popular demonstrations alarmed, a half dozen or so explosions near the palace shook, and the gunning down of a cousin on the streets of Persarum quite devastated them. He and his family, taking three planes from Tariq's air force and as much of the country's portable wealth as they could carry, had scrambled off to Argentina. Always timorous and apprehensive of a military coup, he had begun years earlier to pinch off any shoot of leadership in the security forces, so their attempt to carry on government in his name was brief and bred largely from inertia. Within days, officers and men, swaying to the prevailing wind, had scattered or joined the street mobs in erasing the old regime.

The reins of government fell loose. Members of the fragmented coalition of middle-class intellectuals, communists and socialists which had begun the revolution reached out to pick up those reins but too late. They had been grasped by the mullahs, supposedly on behalf of the people — eighty per cent Shiite Muslim, seventy per cent illiterate. The holy men were totally inexperienced in their use, but they liked the feel of power and held on tight.

9

The economy was reduced quickly to shambles, but, with that flash of brilliance sometimes given to political amateurs, the mullahs found a substitute for comfort, almost for subsistence: it was anger. That was present already and thriving — at the Western powers, which had kept Tariq subject to a capricious tyrant; at the USSR, which had paid lip service to the revolution while sending arms to the Emir; and, as always, at the infidel, the Sunnis and those who could read and write.

The mullahs preached revenge and were rewarded by the fierce devotion of four out of five Tariqis. The others, those who complained at the closing of the secular schools, the forced imprisonment of their wives and daughters in the chador, and the increased size and power of the secret police, were learning to keep silent.

Men appeared in the street and spat at Mikhail as the four neared Palat's central plaza. They entered it through a small northern gate, the mob parting to let them through, oozing back together and rumbling like one huge, viscid animal. Simon had thought the Tariqis a pretty people at first, now they ringed him and Mikhail, their white teeth flashing in golden brown faces as they shouted hatred at them both. They were lined four or five deep, completely around the square. Men and boys must have been trucked in from miles outside Palat; the village could house only a fraction of this lot.

The square held itself aloof from the din that filled it; it was a soothing monochrome in beige, turned pinkish in the sun, its contours softened by centuries of erosion from the sea and desert winds. Buildings here were free of the posters and murals one saw everywhere in Persarum, showing Western flags dripping blood, Tariqis tearing Western political figures asunder.

A citified-looking group — Western trousers worn above their sandals — brandished a Russian flag in Mikhail's direction, tried to set it afire and failed. An American one was produced, evidently for Simon's eyes and in either the absence or the ignorance of the Union Jack. Ridiculously, Simon found himself a little offended. Both flags were ripped and trampled into the cobblestones.

"They've omitted the brass band," Simon said, his voice high pitched but still steady.

"Oh, not an omission. Music is counter-revolutionary, don't you know?" Mikhail laughed lightly, almost genuinely.

10

"Simon, you look like an overstuffed scarecrow in that getup."
And Mikhail was a waif, his grey shirt flapping in the hot desert wind.

His laugh annoyed the guards. Cretin slapped Mikhail's face hard enough to leave his palmprint across it, and the crowd growled its approval, its collective face sullen with righteousness.

Muscul-man inserted himself between them and, with Mikhail out of sight, Simon could no longer control the physical show of his fear, the trembling, the cold sweat. He thought back to the days before his trial, when his greatest worry had been been about the rightist London tabloids and the circus they would make of his arrest. Simon's father was health minister to the shaky Labour government and one of their prime targets.

Two armed men, presumably police, joined their guards. One gave Simon a businesslike push, no doubt to show that his standing was official. Some such gesture was necessary to set them off from the crowd, since many of its members carried guns and a similar random mixture of Eastern and Western clothing.

Someone tall and very solid placed himself in the center of the square, his face touched and obscured by the rounded shadow of the mosque; he held a short whip with several tails. A youngish holy man with a dusty black beard moved from the crowd to stand beside him, and total, obedient silence fell as he spoke. His dialect was strongly regional, and Simon understood only random words. The spectators looked serious and satisfied.

Ever since he had been sentenced, Simon's waking nightmare had been of a public flogging he had once covered in Pakistan. The prisoner had been bound to an A-shaped wooden frame set at an angle to the ground, his kidneys covered by protective cushions. Most of the blows, from a single cane, had been directed at the buttocks. The purpose appeared to be to inflict a maximum of humiliation with a minimum of serious damage, and a doctor had been in attendance. No such amenities here.

Some boys from the crowd dragged a wooden plank with a wedge at one end from a building beside the mosque and set it at the feet of the man with the whip. Cretin and one of the policemen pushed Mikhail forward, and he walked between them, straight with bravado and stiff-legged with fright. He reminded Simon of someone — that jaunty, enduring courage. Davie. It was Davie Talbot.

They pulled the loose shirt over Mikhail's head, forced him face down upon the plank and bound his wrists to the wedge protruding from it. A second wedge was driven through the wood between his ankles and the hobbling rope twisted around it. Cretin dragged his trousers halfway down his buttocks, and the two left him.

The sound from the first blow slapped against Simon's ears, and he turned his face away. A guard pushed his head with the flat of his hand. Simon closed his eyes then, and the guard twisted his arm. He opened them. Five now, and Mikhail lay unflinching. His body began to twist against the plank at the eighth, and he screamed at the next — and the next. Simon stopped counting.

The mob was utterly silent now, reverent in its ecstasy. Mikhail's screams turned to moans, then ceased altogether.

It was finished. The policemen walked out there and cut Mikhail's bonds, then dragged him away by his wrists. He looked dead.

Powys, Wales: David Evan Talbot, reputed third son to naturalist-explorer Sir Francis Talbot, studied his reflection in the tinny bathroom mirror. "Evan," he said to it. "Not David. Evan." The face, pointy-nosed, freckled and winter pale, looked back at him from under hair the colors of weathered straw. He thought again that Francis's Norman blood must have run thin at his conception, fifteen years after that of his second brother. Evan resembled half the farmers of Powys.

He found the cigarettes he had been hunting and returned to his vigil by the telephone. The expected call would determine whether his half-formed plan had possibilities or was only an agreeable fantasy. In either case, it seemed more real than his surroundings just now: the quaint cottage he had bought a few years earlier when he thought he knew what he was about, its self-consciously rustic furniture and the damned snowscape he had been laboring over for days. That looked more like a jumble of marshmallows than the scene outside his kitchen window.

Unable to paint, Evan indulged himself with the dream, imagining it done and Simon home safe. The newspapers would certainly take notice. Even the tabloids had changed their tune about Simon these past days, their glee at a Labour party scandal replaced by horror that Tariqis would dare to lay their dusky hands upon a true-born Englishman.

Yes, and Francis would read about Evan in a new light: nothing then about broken engagements, nothing about pop singers — and perhaps even the bloody art critics might take a second look. "Art for a pastel powder room" one of the bastards had labeled last week's exhibition, Talbot's first. Bastard! His eyes crept, though, back to the marshmallows, and the telephone rang.

It was young Peter, calling as promised from the London offices of Amnesty International. "The prison staff is the same. The commandant and the guards are Shiites, so they were left alone. But everything else is different. It's no good, Talbot."

"Perhaps their price is higher, but once a pattern is established—"

"There's no pattern whatever to this government." Peter said.

"We shan't be dealing with the government, only with the commandant, and with the price he was getting for the Emir's prisoners he probably got accustomed to some luxuries he's missing now. We'll simply offer twice as much."

"How would he account to the authorities in Persarum?"

"We can help him out with all sorts of stories: scores of international spies invaded Palat, and—"

"That's not so amusing just now. We had word that they've shot the American."

Peter was trying to frighten Evan off, perhaps because he himself was out of his depth. "I may have misled you about my position at Amnesty," he had said last week over a long, expensive meal at Le Gavroche, planned by Evan as the most tactful of bribes. "I'm only a volunteer, actually, and that in the fund-raising sector." Blushing, he had plunged bravely on. "What I do best is to stuff envelopes, though sometimes I carry the mail downstairs."

Evan hid his disappointment. "They ought to be bloody grateful to have a genuine barrister clerking for them. I hadn't expected you to set a rescue expedition in motion, only to get me some information. About the prison in Palat, for instance, and its staff. I've been doing some boning up about Tariq, and I understand that, historically, there's been nothing and no one that couldn't be bought."

Charily, Peter had agreed to dig for information at the Amnesty secretariat and to call Evan this afternoon. What he had found had made him more chary than before. "I don't like it at all," he went on. "They won't let our observers inside the country now, and the consensus here is that the mullahs are going to make the Emir look like Father Christmas."

"There's nothing firm yet, Peter — may never be. What I should really like to see, though, is a map of Palat and a diagram of the prison. Amnesty had people there a couple of years ago, I know."

"But I don't know where to look. It was only chance that I learnt about the staff. There's a mad Italian journalist who visits us when he's in London, and he'd just been to Palat hunting some 'disappeared' schoolchildren. He's gone off now to Chile or some other nightmare place, and I just don't know—"

Peter would try, though. Evan, older, had been kind to him at school, and there was a debt — tacit but not small. Evan turned to social pleasantries, eager to ring off now and call Hamish.

Two rings, then "Saunders here" in the husky tones of the old friend whom he hoped to make his co-conspirator. Evan made himself known. "Davie." Some fluster there; perhaps the November lover, the man whom Simon had disliked, stood beside him.

"Are you alone?"

"Quite. The least bit rattled, though. I've been speaking with Christine." Simon's wife. "She was being all bright and brave, you know, and then the baby began to cry. Christine as well. I didn't know what to say."

"Nor do I. I've some ideas, though, about what we might *do*. I should like to see you—"

They agreed to meet the next evening at Hamish's flat. He had sounded relieved, almost eager at the hint of action.

Even his father's expeditions began as fantasies. Like them, this one was taking on form and substance, a crew enlisted, transport and timing projected. Evan studied the cruise brochure once more. Professional antiquaries, its planners seemed oblivious to contemporary realities. The ship would dock at Palat, Tariq, nearest harbor to the celebrated ruins of Artemion, on April first — three days before Simon was to be flogged.

Palat: "A single pebble is adequate to wipe the anus," an Iranian holy man, Khomeini, had written — either just before or after his rulings about the consumption of sodomized horseflesh. He had been mistaken. This mullah stood within inches of Simon now, and the stench of feces from his unwashed robes and body was hardly bearable.

At his bidding, the guards began to pull at Simon's shirt. He clutched it to him, and the strained fibers parted from his neck to his waist. Muscul-man drew it forward and off over his arms and made as if to lead him to the center of the square. Something odd was happening, though. The man with the whip executed a kind of dance step, near to a series of pirouettes, the crowd rumbled its appreciation, and he left them through the south gate. Four boys wiped the mingled blood and urine from the plank on which Mikhail had lain and drew it back inside the building next to the mosque.

"Tmro," the mullah said to Simon, who regarded him blankly. "Tomorrow," he said then in his guttural, bastardized Tariqi. He pushed Simon's bare chest with his finger and made whipping motions in the air.

Of course: why only one show when they might have two? Simon fantasized striking out at one of them, preferably the holy man. His body, though, had loosened in relief at its reprieve, and he accompanied the guards meekly back to his cell.

March 22 — Palat: They would give him no news of Mikhail, though he pled with his hands to the night guards, men older and less coarse than Cretin and Muscul-man. Then, a little after the first light, they brought him a new cell-mate, a good-looking chap in his mid-thirties wearing European clothes. He was Tariqi but a type different from their jailers, with clean, longish hair and a high forehead.

"Abul." He introduced himself in Tariqi which Simon pretended not to understand. His knowledge of the language was a resource he had kept secret here. Abul, it transpired, spoke passable French and wanted to talk, though not about politics. He looked away, out into the corridor, when Simon told him about Mikhail and the American.

"Why have they sent you here, Abul?"

The man looked back at Simon. "Homosexuality," he said almost indifferently.

"My God!"

"Don't fret yourself. Truly, I am homosexual, but I have had one lover for many years. Neither of us strays."

"I was not fretting on my account but on yours. I heard that they now call that a capital crime."

"Only selectively. I shall be here for a few days for 're-education.' I made an unwise reference to my students about a former hero of the revolution who has now been discredited. But I am quite safe.

"I am a true hero of the revolution and well documented as such. I played myself in a film that has been shown a dozen times on television. Look." He bared his chest to show its scars, not unimpressive ones. "I had these from the Emir's men but was able to hold my post for several hours afterward — long enough for relief to come. I am the central figure in the largest mural on Capital Square, and everyone in Persarum knows my face."

It was true that Abul was treated differently, and Simon benefited a little from his importance. There was meat — fresh and rather good — in the breakfast rice, and sweet, thick coffee replaced the usual bitter tea.

2

London: The young barrister stood at a work table pushing copies of the monthly Amnesty International newspaper and a three-page mailer into pre-addressed envelopes. Across from him, a famous actor stapled the mailers — about the bloody excesses of the Nicaraguan dictator Somoza — while an American journalist beside him folded the news sheets.

Here in the fourth floor offices of the British sector assembled what must be the most over-qualified clerical staff in London. The mindlessness of the work was one of its attractions for the volunteers. One could think through a brief or engage in the best sort of talk without changing one's work pace. Now, though, the American was going on about inflation, and the actor, always eager to show that he could cope in the real world, had begun a recital of super-market prices and was not at his most scintillating. Peter let his mind drift to the business that had occupied it for much of the past week.

He had been flattered to be consulted by Talbot and had braved the second floor office that was Amnesty's heart, located an ex-prisoner through the files and prevailed upon him to draw the maps. Now the impetus he had taken from Talbot had gone into reverse. What the devil was he doing for the man — playing accessory to his suicide?

No, it would be best if the commandant's history, the record of ransoms paid to him and the maps simply disappeared now, undelivered. Peter slid the brown envelope that contained them under a stack of flyers about missing persons in Chile and looked up to find Talbot watching him.

One always forgot that he was rather small, probably not over five feet six inches, and not particularly distinguished looking. What drew one were the long, slightly tilted blue eyes which lit when he spoke, seeming to invite one to share some wonderful adventure.

"Peter, thanks are inadequate—"

"No thanks at all, please. I have nothing for you."

"Odd." He raised his eyebrows, amused. "You had all sorts of fine things this morning."

Someone yelped at the worktable, and Peter turned to see that the actor had somehow driven a staple into his thumb. When he looked back, the brown envelope was in Talbot's hands. "As I was saying about thanks," he grinned and turned to go, as if fearful that Peter might try to wrestle his prize away from him.

"Talbot, please wait—" Peter squeezed past the closing door and into the elevator. "What it is, there's a fine chance that you could find yourself in Roud's place, providing the Tariqis with their favorite spectator sport on April fourth."

"That's quite impossible, Peter, with the arrangements I've made."

"Whatever you arrange, there's going to be a moment when the commandant has both you and the money. And then—"

They had reached the front door, gone through it and almost into the arms of a pack of newspaper reporters. Cameras clicked, lights flashed, and a canary-haired woman with a saccharine smile sidled up to them.

These tabloids' hyenas had been tormenting Talbot for three or four years, more intrigued with his rakish social life than with his famous father's exploits. Five had grouped themselves round him now, making escape to the street impossible. "I'll wager that Margot and Sir Francis get on famously together," the woman said chattily. If Talbot didn't contradict her, she would quote him accordingly.

Talbot had charged them once, Peter remembered, and every afternoon paper had featured his snarling photograph. This time he had adopted a mien of aristocratic condescension, not easy for one of his height.

"To the best on my knowledge, Margot and my father have never met." He backed up two steps while speaking, presumably to be able to look down upon them. The group, anticipating his retreat through it, formed a phalanx between him and the door.

"What our readers want to know—" a fox-faced man began, but Talbot had caught sight of a taxi turning from the Strand onto Southhampton Street. He flagged it down with one gesture and made his break in the direction opposite to the one expected, wheeling and running for the street. The woman sprang into the lead to intercept him, slipped on black ice and went sprawling, impeding the lot of them. Talbot leaped into the tall black cab, waved at Peter and was a block away before the group on the pavement had disentangled itself.

"Well done!" Evan called through the glass divider. "Primrose Grove, number twenty-three, please, in Belsize Park. You needn't hurry now; through Hyde Park would be very nice."

Evan lit a cigarette and leaned back to enjoy the ride. His spirit lifted as always at sight of the great stone lions on Trafalgar Square. They returned his regard proudly, while behind them fountains played upward against the slow fall of large, feathery snowflakes.

He had recovered from the ambush, but it needed to be thought about. He had shaved off the beard he had worn for several years, hoping that would protect him from this kind of thing, at least for the necessary few days. How had they found him? Only Peter had known that he would be at the Amnesty building — and the switchboard operator at Evan's club. The leak had sprung from there, and he would need to stay away from the place.

A hotel? If one of the papers showed his beardless photograph today or tomorrow, no public place would be safe; they might even get wind of the cruise and expose his presence there. The wrong people, then, might easily reach the right conclusions. He must find a private lodging and make his arrangements from it by telephone. It wouldn't be easy.

They drove past Hyde Park where the great trees still held their buds clenched against the cold and came into sight of Kensington Gardens. Lavender and yellow crocuses had forced their way through the frozen ground, promising an end even to this fierce, tenacious winter. They rounded Marble Arch where Tyburn had stood, then turned left into congested traffic.

Perhaps he could stay in Hamish's flat until their flight left for Venice — unless the November chap was still there, or a new one. Hamish had never spoken to Evan about his love affairs, but Evan had learned a bit from Simon. There had been several, in the years since school, none lasting more than a few months. When one thought about it, that was odd in Hamish, with his capacity for friendship.

The taxi climbed Havistock Hill, turned left just opposite the Belsize Park underground station, then left again onto a brief, narrow street of Victorian houses coverted into blocks of flats. They stopped. Evan paid his driver and climbed the steps to number twenty-three. He pressed the bell to Hamish's flat, the second of ten, without much hope.

Hamish, despite offers from two top schools — and those in his own field, classics — had chosen a post at an East End comprehensive school. "I want to devote at least a few years to reality," he said — he had meant service — "before withdrawing into intellectual lotus land." The school was an hour from Belsize Park, and it was only four o'clock. Hamish would travel by tube, of course, having sold his car last year and regarding taxis as irrelevant to the lives of normal people.

After a decent interval, Evan pressed all nine of the other buttons, but no one came. Cold clawed at his exposed face until his eyes ran, and he was about to leave and take shelter in one of the shops near the underground station when someone small and dark appeared behind the glass of the outer door. It opened a cautious inch or two, and Evan smiled but met only neutral regard from alert brown eyes.

"I'm a friend to Mr. Saunders, and he isn't at home. I wonder if I might wait for him in the hallway here — it's very cold."

The boy, Indian or Pakistani, smiled now and held the door wide. "A friend to Hamish. Garden flat, you know, he never locks it. I shall take you there." Evan followed him down a narrow stairway, and the boy opened Hamish's door with a sweeping gesture of his arm, palm up, near to a bow.

"Thank you very much—"

"Kemal." Ho, Evan's first contact with the Muslim enemy — this one was utterly charming, going to grow into a beauty. He reached into his pocket, but Kemal shook his head. "Oh, no, Hamish is my friend as well." He was gone.

He saw the kitchen first, a view that might have interested Hogarth during his Gin Lane period. Fastidious enough about his person, Hamish was indifferent to his surroundings almost to the point of unconsciousness; the remains of a number of meals littered every surface. That and the unlocked door reaffirmed Evan's conviction that his friend needed a keeper — surprising he had suffered neither botulism nor burglary in the years since he had left his mother's house.

Evan searched quickly for signs of a second presence and found none — only one toothbrush, and the large wardrobe was half empty.

In contrast to the kitchen, the large desk in the bed-sittingroom was ordered, its squadrons of sharpened pencils ready for action against neat stacks of paper. Centered over it was the painting that had been Evan's gift when Hamish had left university. Evan had been more sure in his work then than he was now. He walked nearer to study it.

It was better than the marshmallows, he thought, remembering the hours of straining for precise detail, for delicate gradations of color. He knew, though, that if he saw it in a public gallery, he would wonder why it was there. It was a soft summer landscape in Wales with rounded hills and a wood, a stream in the foreground, a derelict country house to the back, and he had been thinking, in his jejune arrogance, of Constable when he did it.

Constable would never have conceived that wood. Was it lack of depth? No, one could imagine walking into it, but it would contain no surprises. A marzipan glade — no possibility of anything, revealed or hidden, that wasn't sweet and alive — no dead trees nor murky pools, no corpses. Even the pebbles in the stream were so clearly defined that no water creature could hide among them.

He thought back to the actual scene. There had been withered branches in that gentle wood, and the stream in August had been a brackish rivulet. God, would he never learn to tell himself the truth?

Settling down to wait, he took a paperback book from an end table. It was a novel about Alexander the Great and began interestingly; perhaps Evan would read it in preparation for the cruise. It would be pleasant to parade a few bits and pieces of ancient history that Hamish hadn't forced into his head when they were at school. His eyes began to misbehave, though, after the first dozen pages. Threatened with the usual headache, he set the book down.

A bullfinch, feather-fat and cheeky, watched him from the garden, through the sleet; the poor little devil was hungry or he wouldn't come so close. Evan found a piece of stale bread, took it outside and crumbled it over a stone pediment. Even before he was finished the bird flew down to peck at its windfall.

Hamish was being a very long time about coming home. Bored, Evan began to work at the terrible kitchen.

Palat: They came for him again in the late afternoon, and Abul was marched beside him to the square. He was not hobbled as Simon was; viewing Simon's flogging would evidently be part of his re-education.

If anything, Simon was more frightened than he had been yesterday, and there was no Mikhail for whom to keep up appearances. But some inner heat kept off the cold sweat and shivering that had seized him then.

Just before them a seven-year-old capered through the gate beside his father, his face shining in anticipation, and Simon recognized that it was his own hatred that supported him to his second appointment with the man with the whip.

But he wasn't there. A firing squad stood in his place, and, before it, against the innocent rose-beige walls of the building beside the mosque, stood six men. They were dressed raggedly in the warmer garb of the hills, young, in their late teens or early twenties except for one middle-aged chap in the center, and all were barefoot, their feet swollen and bloodied — during interrogation, no doubt.

A new mullah, greyer of beard than the last, took his place in the center of the square and spoke. Simon was picking up the dialect now and understood most of it: these were Kurdish traitors to the revolution and enemies to Islam.

The older man kept sliding down the wall to form a whimpering bundle on the ground and two policemen stepped forward repeatedly to pull him up again. The young ones stood firm in mingled defiance and disbelief — too young, all of them, to understand that everything, everything could end so quickly.

The end came for them in three volleys from the riflemen,

just after the collapsing Kurd had been propped for the fourth time, and the mob swelled forward to spit upon them or spurn them with its feet. Simon and Abul were kept there until the crowd dispersed and the bodies of the Kurds were tumbled into sacking and dragged away.

The wall where they had stood was pitted now, stained with brains and blood, its innocence gone. Simon stole a glance at Abul. The hero of the revolution appeared unmoved as, no doubt, did Simon. He probed himself for compassion and was dismayed to find only relief that his own torment had been postponed.

London: "What do you think, Hamish?" They sat, sipping whisky, the cruise documents spread on the coffee table between them.

Remembering school adventures instigated by Davie, many of them involving swimming too far, climbing too high or going too near something best avoided, Hamish was a little afraid — but excited too. Unlike the school escapades, this one had a purpose. "The timing is absolutely providential," he answered, "as if it had been set up for us."

Replacing the typewritten itinerary, Hamish saw a letter of confirmation: it was for one cabin, Hector Seven. Shaken, he hid behind the brochure, which pictured a tall, tan and white ship on incredibly blue waters. This aspect of Davie's plan hadn't entered his head at all — only the two of them, in one cabin, sleeping, dressing, undressing, Davie's body within arm's reach of his. Minutes before, as Evan worked at the kitchen sink, Hamish approaching undetected, had needed to fight down an impulse to touch his light, longish hair. He had often done that surreptitiously when they were at school, and the hair had been a soft yellow, silk between his fingers.

"Why a cruise?" he fenced and realized that he had just contradicted himself. "Isn't there a faster way?"

"This isn't just any cruise but a Cobb's cruise, swarming with professors of history and archeology — I reckon you'll know some of them — and world-famous. No one ever questions a Cobb's passenger or sniffs at his luggage, and that's going to be very important. The trick is going to be to get Simon out of Tariq, not just from the prison.

"As for faster ways, there's no airport within a hundred miles of Palat, and airport security is said to be paranoiac throughout the country. Anyway, Hamish, with the Easter holiday coming you'll only miss two days' work."

God, didn't Davie remember at all? As if it were just the timing that troubled Hamish.

That autumn of their last year at school, Davie had studied himself into a constant headache, trying to raise his marks to the level asked of him at home. His reward was to have been inclusion in his father's winter expedition up the Amazon. A letter from Sir Francis had arrived late in November, just after the victorious school report, and Davie had read it with the set smile with which he covered his losses.

"It's no good. There's no place for me this year."

"Perhaps next year," Hamish said, hating the man.

"Perhaps." Davie turned from him and then turned back, flashing the white, thin smile. "No. Never. What it is, Hamish, what it really is — Francis doesn't like me." He made a face at, Hamish knew, his stature, his coloring, his school failures, all the qualities that made him, in his own mind, less than other Talbots. "I understand it. My brothers are so different, so, oh, good at everything, don't you know? Sometimes I wonder where they found me."

Everyone wondered. Hamish's mother, feeling Hamish slighted once by Talbots, had repeated some gossip about Davie's parentage — not to demean Davie, whom she liked, but to dissociate him from a family whom, in her inverted snobbery, she disdained. At times Hamish chose to believe her, regarding those other bulky, black-haired Talbot men as draft horses, sharing none of the grace and charm he loved in Davie.

"Well, look at me." Hamish had looked until he thought his chest would burst, and his fingers had reached out to smoothe the creases from the perplexed forehead. Davie didn't recoil, and control deserted Hamish altogether; he kissed his friend fully and tenderly upon the lips. Davie recoiled then, all right, his eyes wild with horror, and Hamish had wished he could stop ever having been.

The pretense that it hadn't happened was relatively successful. The stunned friendship picked itself up and survived, but differently, the two managing their comings and goings so that they were alone together as little as possible. Safe, comfortable Simon became both a buffer and a link between them, and each spent more time with him than with the other.

Hamish looked again at the itinerary. "April first. The three of us will fly home, then, from the next port."

"Actually, not. The next four ports are Muslim, and the Turks are trying to keep diplomatic relations open with Tariq. They might even ship Simon back. No, he'll need to stay with us until we're in Greece."

"*Then* we'll fly home."

"Why need we? We'll have paid for the whole cruise, and it sounds rather fun."

Fun. And torment. The pain of the old, one-sided love affair had encased Hamish in a kind of carapace that protected him from other heterosexuals. Oh, he had friends, a few good ones like Simon whom, for some reason, he couldn't imagine touching in that way, but his sexuality was expressed with men of his own sort. He had been half able to convince himself that he was in love with some of them, but then David would reappear, and his lovers would seem suddenly cheap or effeminate or puerile.

Hamish stood and began to pace the room.

"You might freshen our drinks, while you're up."

"Ought you to have a second? Christina told me you'd been ill." An ulcer. Davie looked better now, though, than he had in the autumn, the gaunt look gone from his cheeks along with the beard.

"Oh, not a problem now, I'm on a new medication, quite marvelous. I could pickle myself in whisky to no effect." Hamish added to their drinks, tossed his own off and began pacing again.

"I'll be left with none of the time I'd planned for preparation," — Hamish fumbled — "this year's classes are especially demanding."

Davie sipped and studied him. "Hamish, I don't think you're all that keen." The tight smile appeared. "It's all right, you know, and perhaps I was being self-indulgent — it could have been quite nice with both of us, the cruise and all. Really, though, one can manage — or botch — the thing quite as well as two."

Hamish suddenly didn't believe him. "Tell me about it."

"Palat's no more than a village, you know — here's the map — and the prison is only a ten-minute walk from the dock. I'll go there while the tourists are bused to Artemion. . . ."

Who, then, would watch over and, if necessary, rescue the rescuer? Self-possessed, worldly, effective David — he was capable of the wildest idiocy as well. At school he had somehow come into possession of a largish cube of hashish with which the three had planned to experiment.

They had climbed through the bathroom window and into the attic, which they had used before as a sort of clubhouse, but this time Simon had missed his footing on an ancient rafter and, clutching the hashish, fell through the plaster, down straight into the housemaster's room. Davie had leaped after him through the great tear in the ceiling, had taken the brown tablet from Simon before the master could gather his wits. Then he had swallowed it.

"Why?" Hamish had shrieked at him minutes later, feeling his skin go clammy and watching his pupils devour the irises of his eyes.

"He'd have seen it."

"They caught Scott and Farquar with some last year and barely slapped their wrists."

"Simon won't have the prefecture next year if he's caught." He hadn't had it anyway — too much imagination in Simon for that job.

Hamish and Simon had forced Davie to vomit up the hash, but he had been ill and disoriented for hours and had clung to Hamish like a child. It hadn't been precisely the stuff of which Hamish's dreams were made but it was the nearest he had come to it.

"Enough," Davie said now with the pleasant composure that, in him, symptomized bruised feelings. "If I might impose upon you for a bed until the flight leaves for Venice—"

Hamish swallowed his laugh — six days, and the bed-sittingroom was hardly larger than a ship's cabin. "Shut up," he said. "You know I'm coming with you." And, with that commitment, a great jumble of doubts seized Hamish.

Palat: They had stolen his clothes yesterday when he had gone to the square and they had not replaced the prison shirt that had been torn from his back. The days were warm enough, but Simon's throat was scratchy from the chill of the night before.

"Vous avez froid," Abul said to him proffering his blanket — he was fully clothed beneath it.

Abul had brought the blanket with him from Persarum,

and it looked relatively clean, but minutes before Simon had watched him kneel upon it to pray to whatever devil it was that they all addressed. *"Non,"* he said and, after an interval, added a cold, *"merci."* He huddled himself for warmth on the bare, harsh mattress, turning his back on the Shiite.

London: "I've given myself a new name," Davie told Hamish, folding the maps he had been explaining. These were amateurishly hand-drawn and did not inspire confidence. "It's Evan now, and you'll need to remember it until we've got Simon back. The Talbot's common enough and can stay."

"Evan." Hamish tried it out, liking it; it suited his friend's piquant, Celtic face better than the David, which was worn as well by another, older Talbot, one of the draft horse breed. But the change increased Hamish's feeling of unreality. Did real people, not in books, actually engage in the kind of adventure they planned? And if they did, would real people stand the least chance of success? Perhaps because of his single but significant peculiarity, Hamish clung to the ordinary and distrusted acts and places outside its bounds. "Why," he asked, "why the change?"

"If it gets known that I'm on the cruise, we'll be joined by reporters from all the damned tabloids. Difficult to play James Bond with those hanging round our necks."

James Bond — oh, no. "Is it that bad?"

"I'm hot press since my affair with Margot."

Margot? David must mean the pop singer, recently divorced. "Good God! Have you had one?"

"Actually not. We're not even 'just friends.' I spilt my drink on her shoe in a nightclub a few weeks ago, spoke to her long enough to apologize, and the press took it from there. Very nice for my image with Anne. After all the brouhaha, she changed her mind and doesn't care to be Mrs. Talbot after all."

"So that one's off." It was Evan's third collapsed engagement in as many years. "Are you sad about it?"

"Not at all. Relieved. I don't know why I enmesh myself — and girls — in positions like this. I have an affectionate impulse and, before I know it, I've proposed to someone. When she accepts, I feel trapped."

Hamish searched for something wise and comforting to say but, embarrassed by the pleasure Evan's words had given him, was unable even to look at him directly. He stood. "Best

27

begin dinner, I think, or we'll both need your anti-pickling medication. Sausage all right? With mash?"

Evan looked dismayed, and Hamish remembered that he cooked for himself in the country and loved dining out when in London.

"Afraid not. Your sausage had a peculiar smell, and I chucked it when I tidied the kitchen. So I owe you a dinner. There's a new little French place — no, you wouldn't like that. Rule's. I shall take you to Rule's."

"That's awfully posh, isn't it? What if you're recognized?"

"I'll ask for a private room. Telephone?"

"In the hallway." Posh *and* expensive. While Evan rang the restaurant, Hamish studied the contents of his wallet — he had left himself less than fifty pounds with which to finish the month.

"When you thought I wasn't so keen," he told Evan later, "I was being Scottishly concerned about raising the price of my ticket."

"Oh, that — we'll work something out later. They're booked and paid for now." They weren't, Hamish knew, and knew as well that the "working out" would require dogged persistence on his part. Evan showed neither the parsimony nor the extravagance that Hamish had seen in other rich young men — he was simply indifferent to the presence or absence of money and faintly bored by any reference to it. "I need to know, though, what you think of the overall plan."

"I had one question earlier," he began, as cautious now of sending Evan off without him as of joining him. "If Tariqis are so susceptible to bribery, why didn't Simon's mother give it a try?" She had been allowed to visit him in February, shortly after his arrest.

"Wrong place, wrong time. He was in Persarum then with a shining new prison staff, the commandant son of one of the mullahs and an aspiring politician. Simon's arrest was still fresh news then, his picture in all their papers. So many new enemies of God and Islam have been discovered and done in since that Simon must be almost forgotten."

"Have you spoken to any of the Rouds about this?"

"Not even a hint." He leaned forward, the long, narrow eyes intent on Hamish's. "Truly, Hamish, I believe we can do it. But to raise false hopes with his family. . . ."

They shared a small, rather dark room at Rule's restaurant off the Strand with an elderly couple whose conversation showed both to be nearly deaf. Their Italian waiter's English was limited to foods and wines. He resembled Hamish a little, Evan thought, with his dark, curling hair and a classical cast to his features, but he was merely handsome while Hamish was beautiful. Why? A slight vacuity to his face, perhaps, no sign of the calm strength apparent in Hamish's. He had a fine, slender rump, though, and swung it provocatively as he left them.

Hamish, sipping the last of the wine with which Evan had plied him, was oblivious. The dinner had been excellent and tamely British enough for Hamish's taste; he looked very content. That part of Evan's plan which would be least palatable to him had still to be explained, and Evan had been hoping for an hour for a question that would lead into it.

"Davie — Evan — let's say all goes well. We have him, we're outside the prison — on the street. Simon's appearance is hardly run-of-the-mill, and, as you said, his picture has been shown there. What if he's recognized?"

"He'll have an adequate disguise. I mentioned that you and I need to do a bit of playacting our first days on the ship."

"I thought that was in aid of avoiding reporters."

"Only partially. Simon not only has to get through the streets of Palat and past the harbor police but past the crew and the cruise people as well. They ply their trade in those waters and mustn't be involved. We're going to pass him off, just long enough to get him into our cabin, as another passenger — as you, in fact."

"And how do you plan to accomplish that?"

"I'm not terribly happy about this part. As it stands—" Evan looked directly into his friend's face. "As it stands, I'm afraid that you and Simon are going to have to run the gauntlet in drag."

"In — oh, Jesus, no!" He had gone pale, not pink, which was bad. Hamish was open about his homosexuality, but masculinity was important to him; his carriage was almost assertively male.

"If you can come up with something equally effective, I'll be delighted."

"It's asinine. A skirt and dancing slippers will hardly help Simon, of all people, to meld into a ship's company—"

"No dancing slippers. Chadri, those things the Shiite Muslim women must wear. The Tariqi one is more strict than the others, all in one piece, and only the eyes show. I'm having two made, and—"

"And how the devil are two Shiite Muslim women to pass as Cobb's passengers?"

"They're not. The ship's company is to think that you and I have been up to peculiar fun and games in Palat. We've got to put on the sort of show that will prevent much surprise when—" Evan ought to have chosen his words before, the slang ones might offend Hamish, while the formal seemed cold, almost clinical. "When two homosexuals in local drag reboard the ship at Palat." Hamish looked not only distraught but angry. "I'll do most of it, I'll be the outrageous one — oh, look, Hamish, it's only for three days. Afterward, with luck, you'll be a hero."

Hamish tossed off the rest of his wine. The waiter reappeared, and Evan ordered brandies; they remained silent until he brought them. Hamish sipped and composed himself.

"I suppose you're right; I can't think of another way. Right about Simon, anyway, but why must I wear the bloody thing?"

"Height difference. Simon's to board as you, you as me, and he is to you as you are to me. Were I suddenly to become four inches taller than you, we shouldn't pass at all, even with the shock value of the chadri."

"I see." Hamish watched the old man help his fragile wife from the opposite table, and Evan traded his full glass for Hamish's half-empty one. "It's rather good, actually. Sorry to have been so damned negative."

It was going to be all right, going to be fine. "Not negative, conservative. A virtue in this business." Evan raised his brandy snifter and touched Hamish's. "A toast to conservatism."

3

Venice, March 29: The American doctor sat at a table in St. Mark's Square surrounded by postcard vendors and scores of obese pigeons; he sipped Campari with distaste. "This stuff is awful, Milly, I'd forgotten how much I hate it."

The voices from the table behind him rankled too. "Do you see, Hamish? It's the Guardi and the Canaletto made flesh. The Doge's palace really *is* that heavenly pink, and the horses made for Alexander still prance above the church." Etonian vowels flowed forth from somewhere beyond Max's left shoulder.

"Mm." The versatile British monosyllable was almost a growl.

" 'Mm?' Don't you like it? Isn't it everything I promised?"

"Of course I like it; it's quite magnificent," the growler muttered irritably. "Only, Evan, *must* you keep on this way constantly?" The voices fell to indistinguishable murmurs. Queers, Max judged, one twittery and one sullen.

"I think the boys at the next table are fellow passengers," Milly said softly. "Their hand luggage is Cobb's canary yellow. I don't think I've met either a Hamish or an Evan before; they sound like characters from an ethnic comedy."

Max couldn't see them without turning around, which he preferred not to do. "They sound like flaming faggots, too."

"One might be gay. The Evan. His shirt is open almost to his navel; he's wearing a necklace and a heavy gold earring through his right ear. I think that's what that means. Or is it the left?" She was carrying on in that defensive, chatty way of

31

hers. "The other is got up quite normally and is very, very handsome. He looks sweet, too, rather like that statue of Hermes holding the infant Dionysus."

Ordinarily, her chatter was not unamusing, but Max's memories of the previous evening were fresh. "How's the stomach?" he asked.

"Settling." She was drinking, of all things, a Coke, and presently finished it. "It was that damned duck pâté last night."

"It had nothing to do, I suppose, with six martinis before dinner."

"Not six. Anyway, Max, you forgot to order dry martini cocktails, and the first was only vermouth. English gin is weaker too." Max raised his eyebrows at her and she looked away, pretending to study the domed church. "I thought there were four horses. Two must be out being cleaned or something."

She had vomited repeatedly on the flight from Luton to Venice, the third such episode in the past month, each one increasing Max's uneasiness. That was not, he admitted to himself, for Milly — her health was good, her temperament basically serene — but for himself. Her drinking reflected upon him, upon his control over their life together.

"I hope tonight won't bring a repetition."

"Oh, drop it, do. I was terribly excited about the cruise — celebrating."

"If you continue to celebrate so soundly, you could miss out on a good part of it."

He had overdone it. Her mouth was drooping at the corners, the first symptom of a sulk that might go on for hours. She smiled at him, though, suddenly and brightly. "Look, we still have an hour before boarding. Let's explore the Doge's palace."

They left their table, dodging pigeons and passing the young Britons at the next one. The dark-haired boy, Milly's Hermes, smiled tentatively as they passed. Max nodded and was assessed by narrowed eyes from the ordinary, rather impudent face of the other.

"They match their voices."

"Not really," Milly said. "The patrician tones come from the gamin type, the cranky Scottish burr from the beauty."

Inside the palace, Milly stopped to study a painting in the

first room. "I don't think the ship will wait long if we're late," Max urged. "We'll come back some day; let's just try for an overview right now."

"Just let me see who—" The diagram identifying the paintings was inaccessible, surrounded by Venetian schoolchildren. "I think it's a Titian."

"Tiepolo, actually." The boy with the earring was suddenly beside them. "The difference in their blues simply shrieks at one."

"Oh, thank you." Milly's smiling acceptance of his condescension rankled Max.

"It certainly doesn't shriek at me," the one called Hamish said kindly. "It's quite glorious, but I shouldn't know it from a Rembrandt." He turned and tried to herd his smaller friend onward and away from Max and Milly, but the Evan appeared determined to take up with them.

"I see we're shipmates," he said cheerily, waving a flexible wrist toward Max's carrying case.

Max tried to steer Milly in another direction, but the four were caught and forced closer by a surge of children that pushed them into the next room and the next. Max was getting his overview more rapidly than he wanted as forty ten-year-olds stampeded them past and under rich painted landscapes, sumptuous robes and fine bare limbs.

"Let's stop and let them pass," he said. "I'd like a better look at that last ceiling."

"Why is their teacher rushing them so?" Milly asked, obviously irritated at the tutorial mismanagement as well as the chocolate stains some grubby hand had left on her sleeve.

"A pity, really," Hamish said, watching the students and their speeding teacher with a look of professional interest. "They looked so interested, but she—" The reason for their pace became apparent as the four tried to return to the room with the fine ceiling. Two new groups of students pushed and jostled each other through the doorway, amicably urged on by their teachers.

A little girl fell down just past the door and had her hand trod on. Hamish brushed past Max, cut through the clot of children like a diver through water and had her disentangled from the rest and in his arms before the first sobs broke out. "There," he said tenderly, "I know it hurts. There."

Max squeezed through to them, intending to check the

hand for injury, but she drew it away from him and hid her face in Hamish's shoulder. The teacher appeared, the sobs ended, and Hamish was relieved of his burden which smiled at him adoringly as it was led away.

"It's a way he has with women," Evan said to Max. The doctor's vague dislike began to harden, and he looked down without expression at the smaller man. Evan docked his head and touched his forelock in mock deference.

"Will all the cruise be like this," Hamish asked wistfully, "hurried past all these superb things with no time to see them?"

"Oh, no, my dear," Evan gushed. "All the rest are guided tours, and I understand that Cobb's absolutely coddles one—"

The group exploded into a mahogany-paneled room of heroic proportions, and Max took Milly's arm, putting distance and a score of school children between them and the two young men. It was the hall in which the doges had held court, and Max peopled it briefly with a keen-faced, cruel-faced nobleman and his canny followers, avid for power and beauty. The doge's throne was usurped then by a young Italian teacher whose theatrical gestures brought howls of laughter from his pupils.

"Max, we *could* miss the ship," Milly said, more concerned now with future than with present glories. "It's going to be hard to get out." They followed an exit arrow under a small archway and into a narrow passageway to find themselves suddenly, startlingly alone and contained by silence. "Good lord, it's the dungeon; we *are* trapped!"

Another arrow appeared in the dim tunnel, and they followed it past cold, bare white-washed prison cells toward a hint of daylight. That, they found, came not from the hoped-for doorway but from a grilled window which looked out wistfully on sun-baked pastel walls and balconies cascading with bougainvillea, punctuated by a pretty little canal. They were standing on the Bridge of Sighs from which the doges' defeated enemies had taken their last view of the city and of life.

To their relief, the next few steps took them back to the square. "Which way is the harbor?" Max asked, disoriented by the bright sunlight. Milly thought she remembered, and he followed her lead a little dubiously until the ship came into sight. Narrow and graceful, the Alexandros towered above them, her flags, the blue and white Greek one and the Union Jack that identified her with Cobb's, billowing in the light sea breeze.

They boarded with a panting British schoolboy onto Heracles Deck and were halfway up the wide, gold-carpeted stairs to their own cabin on Hector Deck when Max remembered the landing tags. He turned back to replace the two numbered plastic discs, which would show them present and accounted for, on their hooks beside the cruise desk. As he did so he nearly collided with a red-haired woman in her mid-twenties, long-limbed and singularly lovely. His smile was returned by another so bright and friendly that it lit the moment.

The warmth of the encounter followed him upstairs. "I heartily endorse your choice of cabins, old girl," he told Milly. Hector Six was small but fresh and clean. "I'm going on deck to have a drink and watch Venice sail away. Want to come?"

"I think I'll forego the drinks tonight. I'm going to hang your suits and a few of my things before the wrinkles set. Go on, Max, and I'll come up when the ship begins to move."

A radio speaker on the desk between their bunks began to sputter, and a woman's voice announced from it, "Will passengers holding landing tags numbers 66, 67, 70 and 71 please report to the cruise desk at their earliest convenience?" The tone was tinny, the accent Thames-side and the expression indifferent.

"I'll bet they're still in the dungeon," Milly said. "Pass me that coathanger, please."

Max sat on his bunk and watched her unpack, glancing from time to time out the porthole at the still unmoving harbor. "We're ten minutes late sailing. I wonder—"

"Will Mr. and Mrs. Geoffrey Cartier and Mr. and Mrs. Arnold Dare report immediately to the cruise office?" The voice from the speaker was no longer tinny but pure ice. The instrument of a presence with whom to be reckoned.

"I'm glad we were on time, Milly said. "The Cartiers and Dares seem to have gained instant notoriety. Let's go on deck."

Palat: The bloody Shiite was praying again, his hair curling towards Mecca and the hole in the corner that served them both as urinal, his socked toes toward the corridor. Five times daily all of them did that, and one could see its effect on their morals. He scrambled up now and folded his blanket. "*Aujourd'hui*," he said, "*j'ai peur.*"

Today! Simon's fear swelled with each march to the square — how many now? First Mikhail, then the Kurds, the "prostitute" who had refused the chador — she had died before they were half done, but they had finished the eighty lashes anyway and then put a bullet into her senseless body. The boy thief then, and later two women who might actually have been prostitutes.

On each occasion, Simon had been told with gestures that this show was to be his own, and, while his mind questioned, his body never lost its gullibility. He had not screamed yet nor wet himself nor otherwise disgraced the faraway playing fields of Steppingford, largely because his loathing for the savages had grown apace with his fright.

During their first year at school, Simon and Hamish had read Tolkien's *Lord of the Rings*, aloud for Davie's benefit, and Simon had failed to fall in love with it as promised. "I don't like Mordor, and I don't like the orcs," he had told Davie, who'd been enchanted with it all, sketching scenes from it as they read. "Nothing in nature is purely evil, as they are."

Simon had been mistaken; Mordor was here, the mullahs its terrible wizards, their followers its orc mob.

"*J'ai peur*," Abul murmured once more, but not fearfully, only thoughtfully. He was safe, not because of his revolutionary heroism — Simon had seen many heroes fall in the days before his arrest — but because of his religiosity.

Abul walked to the urinal circling as widely round Simon as possible. He probably thought that Simon's dislike of him sprang from his admission to being queer. It would be edifying for Abul to learn otherwise, but Simon was very hot, too tired to talk and unable to remember the French word for homosexual.

At Sea: The cabin-mate whom she had yet to meet must be what Lindsay's father would call an odd duck. Lindsay closed and replaced the yellow canvas case, identical to her own, guilty about her involuntary prying and a little apprehensive about its results.

Feeling a new series of sneezes approaching, her handkerchief a sodden mass from the previous one, she had opened the case, flinging its contents aside in a hurried search for the box of tissues packed somewhere inside. The first book, a paperback, was the same color as the thriller Lindsay had read on the airplane, the next three had hard covers as did the school texts she had brought along, and she had realized her mistake only when she saw what was revealed beneath them: a small, snub-nosed pistol of the sort one saw in old gangster films.

In mindless haste, she replaced over it a Bible, a diary, a purple tome entitled *Cast out the Chaff* and the paperback; that was *Save Our Families* by Gwen Noyes. More anxious now than embarrassed, she wished she had examined the gun. Was it loaded or—

Of course. The cruise people had asked her to fill out a form regarding her choice of cabin-mates, and Lindsay, eager for the taste of as many new cultures as possible, had opted for an American — they must have provided her with one. She had read that some American women, alarmed at crime in their cities, carried and were trained in the use of firearms — foolish perhaps, but not necessarily ominous.

Lindsay found the tissues, gave her nose a refreshing blow and stretched herself out on the small bunk. She should, she supposed, have taken advantage of the afternoon stop in Venice, but she had been awake half the night, too excited to sleep on the train taking her from Wakefield to Luton, and she was learning to gauge her strength in order to get the most from the expensive, long-anticipated cruise, a Christmas gift from her parents.

They had never indulged themselves with such a tour, the family having taken the less expensive Cosmos or Thompson ones every other year since Lindsay had been eight or nine. They had been half-apologetic for this extravagance, telling Lindsay that they wanted her to escape the seemingly endless winter at home and to conquer the cold that had hung on since last November.

What they really hoped, she knew, was that the cruise would end what they imagined to be Lindsay's languishing over a broken engagement. Their imaginings were endearing but wrong. Over the holidays, she had been spiritless if not dismal, but that from the long cold and a large, wild class of comprehensive school nine-year-olds, not from the end of a small love gone cold.

The unregretted fianceé had been even further from her

thoughts today, for Lindsay had caught herself at an old pastime: watching and assessing men near her own age. Disappointingly few had yet surfaced on the cruise. At Luton, Lindsay had seen the homosexual pair; one was startlingly handsome, and the other looked amusing, but they had each other's undivided attention. The small Cornishman then, who had sat across from her on the airplane had been kept well in tow by his large, imposing mother.

Her interest had been sparked once, at the customs shed in Venice. The man just ahead in queue was alone and presentable: pleasant features on an alert, cheerful face. D. Wilder was printed on the yellow tag dangling from his camera. He didn't notice Lindsay at all, which was not surprising — her size, voice and coloring were not against her, but they weren't with her either, unless her purpose was to avoid attention. The entire cruise might pass without Wilder discovering that Lindsay was aboard the Alexander.

Or perhaps not; now that she thought about it, she had seen fewer young single women than men. Only, in fact, the obese American librarian with the unfortunate nervous giggle — oh, God! That would be the cabin-mate, of course; the cruise people would put them together because they were the same age and neither smoked. Seventeen days of that laugh and fundamentalist religion as well—

The door swung open, and quite a different woman strode through it — a smashing creature, tall and straight, with rich red hair, golden skin and features as symmetrical as an American film star's. "Hello," Lindsay said, rising. "Was Venice nice? I'm Lindsay Wilson."

"How lovely!" The shining smile held so much welcome that Lindsay wondered briefly if this could be an old but forgotten acquaintance. No, she had not seen her cabin-mate before at Luton, on the airplane or anywhere at all. "I mean that your name is lovely, not Venice. Lindsay. So very English. I'm Sharon," she went on, as she opened one of the suitcases the cruise people had laid out on her bunk and began to unpack it, talking and smiling still. "I'm a Campbell, but not from Scotland. Florida, where it's warmer. As for Venice, I don't like Italy very much at all. There are beautiful things, of course, but the dirt and" — the smile became confiding and a little sad — "the way those men leer at you."

Only leers? Lindsay, here with her parents at fifteen, had

received a sound pinch. It wouldn't do to tell Sharon, but she had been more flattered than otherwise.

"Perhaps Venice looks cleaner from a distance," Lindsay said, drawing a sweater from her yellow canvas bag. "I'm going on deck to see."

"If you'll wait just a minute, Lindsay, I'll come with you."

Lindsay sat down again reluctantly, rested now and eager to begin exploring the ship. "We might have a glimpse of the cruise celebrity," she said, making conversation.

"Oh my! Is there one?"

"Frank Culver, the tennis player, is here; at least his name is on the passenger list."

The smile disappeared for the first time. "I despise the man."

"Why, Sharon? He sounds rather nice — one of the few players who can lose as graciously as he wins."

"He lives with a woman not his wife." Oh, dear, so did half a dozen or so of Lindsay's friends. Sharon pushed her emptied suitcase under her bunk, and Lindsay set off with her for the upper deck, thinking wistfully now of the plump librarian.

Palat: Today's was to be a new kind of show and again not Simon's. A wooden pole had been driven into the ground in the south center of the square, and several piles of egg-shaped rocks of varying sizes were arranged in a half circle before it. Beside the pole stood a boy of fifteen or sixteen with close-cropped, spiky hair and a simian forehead — and the rancid holy man. The boy would be today's sacrifice, no doubt, and — Simon shuddered — evidently by stoning.

Silence fell when the mullah turned his face to the crowd, which was larger than usual but surprisingly quiet. A crime had been committed against Islam, the revolution and the boy beside him, he declaimed, and the devil who had done it was now in the square. The boy had been raped and was to name his attacker, who would be dealt with according to law. The victim's nostrils were clotted with matter, and he appeared retarded, particularly after he stepped outside the circle and began to scan the crowd, his mouth gaping in puzzlement. The holy man took his shoulders, not gently, turned him in the desired direction, and he pointed at — Muscul-man, who was standing beside Abul.

The mullah grasped the boy's shoulders again, pinching

the right one hard, and Simon, who had been near hysterical laughter at the guard's predicament, understood then what was going to happen. Abul didn't. He showed no alarm until the pointing finger touched his chest.

Even then he showed more repulsion than fear. "This is idiotic. I have never seen this filthy boy, and I should vomit if I had to touch him—" He was ignored, and Muscul-man and one of the policemen took his arms. Abul tried to dig his feet into the ground, but they dragged him to the pole and fastened his wrists above his head to a metal ring set into it.

Abul, head down, hair hiding most of his face, flung himself violently from side to side, the pole shifting slightly with his body. He stopped suddenly and raised his head, tossing his hair back, his handsome face afire not with fear but with rage. "Carrion," he shouted and spat squarely into the face of the mullah. "You carrion fanatics have destroyed the revolution!"

Several young men armed themselves with stones and hurled them. They aimed at the lower body, but Abul's abrupt fall ended their sport. The pole had been driven through a few inches of packed sand but not into the bedrock beneath, and Abul's struggles had loosened it. It toppled after him as he threw himself forward and to the left, and a stone from the first volley smashed into his right temple as he fell. He lay unmarked and unmoving then, his sightless eyes reflecting the light from the setting sun.

The disappointed mob was silent for a moment, then surged forward, grasping stones and letting fly. A creature near the forefront yelped and was led away, teeth broken, lips streaming blood. Soon the hero of the revolution was completely hidden beneath an irregular mound of rocks.

4

At Sea: "If you plan to wear that shirt to dinner, I shall dine here in the cabin."

"No, it's served its purpose. From the looks we had walking round the deck, I reckon everyone has placed us now. I was cold as the devil as well. Is this going to be too garish for you?" Evan held out an orangey-brown tie with small flowers on it for Hamish's inspection.

"It's all right." It wasn't, really. Hamish felt no guilt for his nature — his fatherlessness or his genes or whatever it was that determined such things had left him no choice in the matter, and he had the gifts of acceptance and respect from his mother and friends. But he would have preferred a stretch on the rack to the ridicule that the coming days promised.

His spirits had survived the flight. They had sat beside an elderly woman who knew either nothing or everything and who had been quite pleasant even before they helped her with her luggage. At St. Mark's Square Hamish had allowed himself to be amused at Davie's game almost to the extent of joining it. Then the Americans had arrived with their Cobb's hand luggage, and he had wanted to disappear.

On deck just now, Davie — no, Evan, he must remember to think Evan — had put on the sort of performance that caused Hamish to shrivel when he saw it even from strangers. All those eyes had followed or avoided them, carrying their messages of amused, patronizing forbearance, distaste or, less painfully, outright hostility.

Hamish had been looking out over the railings at Venice,

dramatically silhouetted in the sunset, when Evan, having finished unpacking, appeared beside him. He was carrying a woman's handbag, and Hamish had feared for a moment that Evan would kiss him then and there to the audience of 280 fellow passengers with whom they would be closely confined for more than a fortnight. Instead, he had indulged in an orgy of wrist flapping and resounding girlish chatter liberally punctuated with "dearests." Where the devil had he picked it up?

His dress now was flamboyant but not outrageous. "Might we tone it down tonight at table? We shall be dining, breakfasting and lunching with these people for some time."

"Hamish. I think it's rather fun. Don't you find it amusing at all? The people who hate us are the sort we should hate anyway."

"It might not spoil things for the others to perceive us as human as well as homosexual. Some of us actually are." That had been a cheap shot, and Hamish was immediately sorry.

"Oh, Jesus, that's it, of course. You're so damned human, in the best sense, that one forgets—" Evan never blushed but went pale so that his freckles stood out as if painted onto him. "No one would guess, you know, and that's why I need to put on the show—" He was floundering, and Hamish decided to rescue him.

"You were right. We had to put it across. I think my sense of humor has atrophied."

The sweet, grateful smile pierced Hamish through. "It's done now, and I *will* tone it down. I want you to enjoy the cruise. Once we've got Simon, it ought to be very nice indeed. I was reading about Alexander the Great recently, and it was interesting."

Evan was trying to please. He hated to read, and Hamish had needed almost to drag him through history at school. "I like *that* shirt," he said. "Ten minutes before dinner — will you have another whisky?" They had bought two bottles for the cabin at the duty-free airport shop.

"Go ahead. I think I prefer wine at dinner, and I oughtn't — My God, Hamish, I've just realized. My stomach hasn't hurt for days, not since you agreed to come. You're fine medicine for me." His hand, light on Hamish's shoulder, set up the old thrilling, terrifying vibrations. God, didn't he remember at all?

White-covered tables ornamented with wine bottles and

the vivid reds and greens of anthurium filled the long dining room on Achilles Deck.

"Your cabin?"

"Hector Seven." A woman wearing the yellow Cobb's uniform showed them to places marked with their names. Three Greek waiters stood near the wall; one had been on deck during Evan's performance, and he whispered to the others. They all laughed aloud and stared knowingly at Evan and Hamish. This time Hamish found himself more angry than embarrassed; no doubt all of them claimed ancestors who, in Pericles' time, would have taken pride in homosexual friendship.

Hamish looked away from the waiters and at the two young women being seated on his side of their table for eight. Evan would be please; the one on the end was a beauty. Or possibly he wouldn't — she was quite tall, and he disliked being towered over. The other was small, her face redeemed from plainness by clear, shining grey eyes.

They introduced themselves, and the little one, Lindsay, murmured something pleasant about Luton. The tall one cut them dead! It seemed a reaction beyond the ordinary to their masquerade, and Hamish searched his mind for when, where or how one of them might have offended her. She behaved as if Evan and Hamish weren't even there, speaking nonstop to Lindsay in tones of honey. The avid smile she wore made her less attractive, seeming to consume rather than light her face, wrinkling the flesh round her eyes and exposing too many small, feral teeth.

A man with sparse white hair and a great deal of eyebrow seated his wife and himself, and more introductions went round. "Sarah and Reg Ffowkes-James." The faces were civilized, the accents posh and — oh, God, that maroon and grey striped tie! Steppingford — and a prefect as well. Hamish pushed Evan's foot with his under the table, but Evan continued the conversation he had begun with Lindsay, and his accent, ungarnished for now with effeminacies, was registering on the Ffowkes-Jameses.

A man wearing that tie on an occasion like this would be the sort of old boy who would keep up on the doings of every class for the past fifty years. Were he to recognize Evan and associate him with Simon — Sarah turned towards her husband, and Hamish saw her lips form "Talbot?" Both studied

Evan with elaborate unconcern. Hamish got his attention at last with a solid nudge, and his eyes followed Hamish's to the tie.

"Dearest," he gushed, turning to Hamish, "I was telling Lindsay about that frightful do at the Doge's palace—" His voice had climbed half an octave, he had done something to his hair tonight so that it resembled a haycock the worse for weather, and the damned earring swung back and forth as he spoke. Sarah's mouth turned up at the corners, her green eyes sparkling with amusement. "I think not," she whispered to Reg. Evan had known what he was about.

The American couple they had seen in Venice took the two remaining places, across from Evan and Hamish, just as the starters arrived "What are they?" Hamish asked Evan.

"Dolmas — stuffed grape leaves. You'll like them."

Hamish forked one tentatively. It was filled with rice, but the seasoning was too exotic. He contented himself with the lettuce and drank the resin-flavored wine.

They might have fared worse for dinner companions, Max supposed, seeing the honeymoon couple nearby who shared a table with four children of assorted sizes but uniform shrillness and their besotted parents. Where had he got the impression that British children were well-mannered? But his luck and Milly's had not, apparently, been of the best.

Milly's Hermes, across from Max, stared moodily at the fish course, the Twerp of course beside him. "It's only sole, you know, just what we have at home. But very fresh, very nicely cooked," the Twerp encouraged.

"It's got bones and a peculiar sauce," Hermes answered tragically.

"It's a Greek ship, Greek cooks. Try and remember that your ancient heroes ate food cooked other than in the British manner."

"For the most part, they ate porridge." Hamish growled, and the Twerp turned away to address himself to his other neighbor, a small girl with dun-colored hair and a smaller voice — her lips moved, suggesting speech, but Max heard nothing. Hmm. A proper English Mouse.

Beside the Mouse, a bright spot — the Gazelle, the red-haired girl from the stairway.

The woman beside Milly had been straining for a glimpse at Max's placecard. "I see that it's Dr. Ross," she announced victoriously. She would be in her mid-sixties, Max guessed, and wore beauty like an old, very comfortable garment; her every gesture both regal and theatrical — the Diva.

"Oh, Max, please. Every third passenger is Dr. Someone."

"Really," the Twerp drawled. "What a scrumptious opportunity to have one's ailments seen to. We must take advantage, mustn't we, Hamish." Sympathy for Hamish, who seemed glummer than ever, grew in Max.

"Do you realize we're all berthed in the same corridor?" the Diva observed. "I think Miss Shaw likes to experiment — last time there was no fixed seating."

Milly produced the desired response. "You've taken the cruise before?"

"This one only once, two years ago, but it's our seventh trip with Cobb's."

Her husband regarded her with benevolent amusement. No one would wear so shabby a tie with that handsomely tailored suit unless it meant something. This must be the Old School Tie.

Sharon's bright brown eyes, which had been roving the dining room through the first two courses, lit now on something that interested her, and she excused herself charmingly, leaving them for a young man at a distant table.

"I'm wondering if that could be Frank Culver," the Diva said, observing Sharon's find.

"I believe that man's name is Wilder, actually," the Mouse said gently.

"An alias, perhaps." Sarah, like Milly, evidently enjoyed drama. "The boy's life was threatened, you know, by a Muslim terrorist group after he played a benefit match for crippled Israeli children." The Old School Tie gave her a patient look, but his eyes, meeting Max's, twinkled. Why not an alias for the passenger list then?

Wilder-Culver seemed surprised, then pleased at the Gazelle's attention. She returned quickly to her own place, though, looking worried and distracted and not at all pleased.

Their lambchops arrived with the ubiquitous french fries, and Hamish regained his friend's approval by clearing his plate. The squealers at the next table had finished their dessert

45

and departed, and Max listened to the low British buzz and the higher, more staccato American sounds that filled the dining room.

Reg had been speaking to the Twerp. "I positively will not set foot in their country. We ought to have closed our embassy when the Americans and Russians left theirs. Ridiculous to try and woo those fanatics."

"What was that?" Max asked. "I missed—"

"Oh, Reg is angry that we're stopping at Palat and won't go ashore," the Diva told him.

"I wish I could agree with you." A little sadly, Max discerned that the smile with which the Gazelle swept their side of the table was calculatingly endearing. "But I think the press has been terribly unfair to those people. The Tariqis are doing their best to purify their little corner of the earth, to rid it of sin and greed, and they should have our help, not our interference."

"Don't you feel, though, Sharon," the Diva said loftily in her whisky contralto, "that their methods of purification are sometimes the least bit intolerant?"

"I—" Sharon lowered her eyes to her plate and then raised them flashing, the new smile resembling that of an embattled Amazon. "Yes! They are intolerant of those who break the law of the Lord. Our Christian prophets, and we have a few, even today, are muzzled by the whimpering for tolerance that we hear from the press, from the weak and the evil. It's tragic to think that in all the world it's only two Muslim countries that are actually trying to apply the commandments of Christ Jesus."

Max changed his mind — no gazelle here. This was another Born Again, the fundamentalist sort whose rebirth would seem to have set its ethical development back several millenia.

"I'm afraid the Christianity of torture by flogging escapes me," Reg said gently, turning once more to the Twerp, who, with characteristic civility, stared down at his Greek pastry, "which is what they threaten to do to our young journalist, Simon Roud. Brilliant boy, he attended my old school."

"That was another media lie." Now Sharon leaned forward, intent, her lips protruding over the white teeth. "The man was drunk in public. He knew the law and was simply

46

flouting it, expecting the West to bring out its wog sticks and sail to his rescue. The Tariqis had no dignified alternative to punishing him as they would have punished anyone else."

Hamish, who had spoken little but drunk a good deal of retsina, went wine-colored. "That's not true," he blurted hoarsely. "He respected those people, never drank alcohol in Muslim countries."

"How—" Reg began.

"Hamish, dear," the Twerp said through a mouthful of pastry, "I understand there's to be dancing in the lounge tonight. May I speak for the first one?"

Max, having managed not to choke on his wine, watched the speechless reactions of his table companions. Sharon looked from one boy to the other with loathing, while the Mouse surprised Max, covering her mouth with her napkin to hide the laughter evident in her pretty grey eyes. Hamish stared fixedly at an anthurium flower as if, bee-like, he hoped to busy himself inside it, while Reg alone studied Evan directly now and with interest.

The boys did not dance together after dinner; Hamish disappeared altogether while the others climbed the stairs to the Lounge of the Sirens on Hector Deck. Wilder-Culver, the possible tennis virtuoso, appeared beside them and murmured something to Sharon. "Thank you, but I don't dance." She did, however, give him the toothy smile.

"A stroll on deck then?"

"That might be pleasant." The young man was going to have a surprise when he learned what that elegant package contained.

Reg, who had held open the lounge door for the women, stepped back for an instant beside Max. "Do you know," he asked softly, "why fundamentalists never make love standing up?"

"I can't imagine."

"Afraid others will think they're dancing."

"Ho! That calls for an after-dinner drink. Would you and Sarah join us?" The four sank comfortably into the deep lounge chairs, and Max ordered brandy all around. Milly changed her order to ginger beer.

Twerp had cornered Lindsay and now showily twirled her about on the dance floor where a four-piece Greek band held forth enthusiastically. The dancers were few: a boy and girl

47

whom Reg explained were Colonel Cobb's protegés — each year he awarded scholarships and a free cruise to two promising archeology students — the dismayingly youthful ship's doctor with one of the cruise girls, the honeymoon couple, Lindsay and Twerp.

Milly began to speak of London theatre, and Sarah let drop that Reg was business manager to one of the major companies. Max and Milly were as impressed as she could have wished.

Sharon's stroll on deck had been short; Wilder-Culver reappeared alone and took Lindsay from Evan as the band paused between songs. They made a pleasing couple, Max thought, Lindsay's trim little figure reminding him of Milly's before two children and many martinis.

Evan passed and saluted them as he left the lounge. "What a pity," Sarah said. "The other is such a lovely boy; his smile simply melts one."

"What's a pity?" Reg challenged. "Hamish's is a perfectly satisfactory way of being. Our ancient Greeks knew that."

"That's true, of course," Sarah propitiated. "I refer only to his choice of partners. Little Evan is a bit much."

Milly, still abstinent, sipped at a second ginger beer. "I don't know — there may be more to Evan than first appears."

"There could hardly be less." Max grinned at Sarah.

Reg was thoughtful. "I agree with Milly. The young man works too hard at being an ass — and only at particular times."

Drinks finished, they retired to their cabins and Max stretched out on his bunk. Milly threw his new silk pajamas at him and surveyed Hector Six with satisfaction. She was high with sobriety and anticipation, and Max regarded her undressing with an interest he had not felt in months.

Her shoes were off now and a stocking — he lay watching her and feeling a little high himself, relieved to find that new places and people still stimulated him despite entrapment in his work. He had been a little concerned about that, especially when he found himself quite unable to abandon his black doctor's bag. It had accompanied them to London in one of the suitcases and rested now beneath his bunk; Milly had been annoyed at having to jettison a couple pairs of shoes and extra handbags to make room for it.

"What was that tonight about Evan?" he asked drowsily.

"Evan? He's a Talbot, all right, but not an Evan."

The dress was gone now, and Max gazed at her breasts,

showing through the slight bra, not so erect as they had been but still firm and rounded. "What does that mean?"

She gave him the Mickey Mouse smile which showed that she was uncertain whether she would or wanted to be taken seriously. "That's David Talbot."

"Who?"

"Sir Francis's son, the one who paints."

"And whose romantic adventures are featured in the tabloids. What on earth makes you think that?"

"I wandered down to Sloane Square a couple of weeks ago, when you were sleeping off your jet lag, remember? I told you about seeing an exhibition of his work."

"I remember. You liked it, but the critics didn't."

"They said they were too pretty. Some of them were, I suppose, but there was real promise — a combination of discipline and sensitivity."

"I wouldn't say that this Talbot is distinguished for either," Max teased.

"Anyway," she went on doggedly, "I saw his photograph. He was bearded, but—"

"A beard makes a lot of difference, Milly. And that kid's problems, according to the newspapers, are totally different from this one's."

"Ah, but Evan's would be a perfect disguise for someone like that, wouldn't it? Who wanted to get away where he wasn't known? And, Max, he does overdo it."

"Oh, God. And Alec Guinness was sitting two rows ahead of us at the Aldwych Theatre last week." Milly had been certain it was he and quite unabashed to learn at the interval that it was merely another theater-struck American. She disappeared into the bathroom. Max had probably hurt her feelings again, but this flight of fancy could cause more embarrassment than the Aldwych one, and he wanted to ground it.

"I think you're wrong, dear. Wasn't it Sir Francis and one of his sons that we saw on Sixty Minutes last year?" he remembered triumphantly. "They were huge men and both dark-complected." He had undressed and was enjoying the calming roll of the sea; the bunk was very cozy. "Hurry to bed. It's great, feels as if you're being rocked in a giant cradle."

She was back, having applied the night cream with the pleasing smell, too happy to be offended and hunting something. Max knew what it was.

"You're probably right; I *do* romanticize. Where the hell is my nightgown?"

He had hidden it under his pillow. "Come look for it over here."

At Sea — March 30: Max must remember to keep the door to the bathroom closed; one could hear through its wall everything that was happening in the next cabin. He listened idly as he shaved.

"Pass me that shirt, would you please? No, dearest, the blue one."

"Evan, if you dearest me once more, I shall be sick — if possible, directly into your suitcase." The ship, having rocked comfortably through the night, was pitching more sharply now; Max's shaving kit fell to the floor. "Ohh. I'll probably be sick in *any* case."

"Deservedly — for your dreadful puns. I *am* sorry, though. I'm sorry about dinner last night as well — what I said, you know."

"No need — good job you thought so quickly. Absolutely imbecile on my part — ohh."

"Not well at all, are you? Perhaps breakfast—"

"Oh, David, please not." Davie! Milly and her damned intuition — Max made up his mind at once not to tell her. The success would only serve as a springboard for her next leap to a wild conclusion; besides she wouldn't be able to keep the secret from the others, particularly if she were drinking again. If the boy in Hector Seven craved privacy enough to resort to a ploy like this one, he deserved to have it.

"Think about something else, then," the ci-devant Evan continued. "Think about calling me Evan. You must, you know."

"Evan. You're not Welsh. Where ever did you find it?"

"It's my second name."

"You told me the E was for Edward."

"I lied then, thought it rather silly when I was small. Mum was taken with an actor of that name before I was born and inserted it in revenge for the David — didn't care for my uncle. I think our names are good — so very noticeable, like false noses."

"I should say we're quite noticeable enough."

"All right. I promise to aim for inconspicuousness — at

50

meals, anyway. I like those people too, except for that red-haired bitch."

"The American doctor? You tease him shamelessly."

"He seems eminently teaseable. I quite like him, though. He reminds me—"

"Of your father. His height, complexion, those heavy features—"

"Strong, Hamish, not heavy." Regarding them in the bathroom mirror, Max was not displeased. "I think Max's are Jewish, while Francis likes to think of himself as the image of the Conqueror's Lieutenant. But you're right, they're certainly similar. And that air of command — not assertive, simply there."

"I suppose doctors get that from ordering people about all the time. But I can't picture you carrying on before your father that way."

"Perhaps I have an urge to, and I'm taking it out on poor Max—" One of them closed the bathroom door, and Max heard no more.

He had been flattered to hear himself likened to the distinguished Sir Francis, but he was not altogether converted. While the frou-frou had been false, as divined by Reg and Milly, Evan's solicitousness of Hamish and those admiring looks he cast upon him were—

Max was annoyed suddenly at his own bigotry. Where had he, a liberal by choice and breeding, contracted the homophobia he had just discovered in himself? Whatever its source, he disliked it and would conquer it. He combed his hair, regarding the firm line of nose and chin. Heavy be damned! Strong.

He returned to Milly, who looked up at him from her bunk, wan and unmoving.

"You're not dressed. Hurry up, I'm famished."

"Go on to breakfast," she said limply. "It's not fair after all yesterday's abstinence, but the thought of food shrivels me."

"Have a dramamine." He reached under his bunk. "You see? The Black Bag is justifying its presence already."

Hamish felt a little better. He had made his way to the Lounge of the Sirens, only a few steps from the cabin, and sat there on a small divan sipping sweet, milky tea. The large room, which would be the ship's social hub, the site of its lectures and

51

dances and tonight's cocktail party, reminded Hamish of his mother's sitting room with its green plants and its comfortable furniture. He was almost startled every now and then to discover that the windows looked out not on her garden in Finchley but on the Adriatic, navy blue with patches of choppy white. That distant line to the east must be Albania. He felt a moment's curiosity as to what might be going on beyond it, then needed to look somewhere else and quickly — the undulating coastline had brought back his nausea.

The lounge was nearly deserted, most of the ship's company at breakfast below in the dining room. Hamish thought briefly of joining Evan there, but just then the ship executed another excruciating maneuver over and through a heavy swell, sending a tropical plant to the floor and a pale passenger running past Hamish to an exit. Others began to drift into the lounge, most of them appearing in uncertain health.

An obvious exception was the small, fortyish blonde woman who marched briskly to the great coffee urn at the lounge's center and placed a stack of lavender papers beside it. She wore the yellow Cobb's uniform and must, Hamish decided, be the Miss Shaw whose imperious voice instructed them over the loudspeakers. Her manner too was formidable, and Hamish hoped that she would never find occasion to call *his* name and number.

The American woman, Milly Ross, took coffee from the urn and moved cautiously over the unsteady sea-colored carpet in Hamish's direction. "Seasick?" she asked him.

"A little."

"Me too. I'm hoping to effect a cure with these." She sat beside him on the divan and proffered a tube of dramamine. Would you like to try one, Hamish?" He accepted a tiny white pill and downed it with the tea without great hope. Milly had taken two of the lavender papers from beside the urn and gave one to Hamish.

"Orders of the day," she said. "They tell me Miss Shaw prepares these in her spare time, which must be between two and four a.m. What a terrifyingly competent woman!"

Mealtimes were listed, and dress was suggested for tonight's cocktail party and dinner. The passenger list was amended: Mr. and Mrs. Gordon Thrim to be added, Mr. Frank Culver to be subtracted. "Max will be disappointed," she said, drawing a line on her own list through Frank Culver's name. "He's a tennis enthusiast."

They read on. Two passengers had lost their boarding tags in Venice and were anonymously scolded. Someone had failed to turn in his passport and was ordered to report to the purser's office at 0900. Times and topics of lectures were listed last.

"Ah, Professor Hodgkins will be doing Crete."

"Do you know him?" Milly asked.

"I've heard him speak," Hamish replied. "He's very good indeed and approachable as well, unlike Dr. Cameron, for instance. Cameron is brilliant but — oh — rather removed from it all." In their two years of association, the eminent scholar, who had praised Hamish's work in the classroom, had never recognized him outside it.

"Cameron. He's the first speaker, doing Liaboam."

The breakfasters began to appear, cheerful and hearty. Hamish watched Evan progress with feline grace across the tilting lounge. He carried a sketching pad — and the wretched handbag. "Oh, here you are. I'm going on deck for a bit."

"Aren't you staying for the lecture?" Milly asked.

"I think not. It's simply beautiful up here and shouldn't be wasted. Hamish, someone's tidying our cabin now. May I leave this with you?" He tossed the handbag down beside Hamish and was gone. It lurked there like a small, dangerously filthy animal until, desperate to tame it, Hamish flung his muffler over it. He glanced about distractedly, and his eyes met Milly's. She was smiling at him, beginning to laugh. It was the right kind of laugh, and he joined her.

"Actually, I suppose it's quite useful; he's got all our papers in there and our drachmas and dinares. I'd simply misplace them."

"Kind of an *enfant terrible*, though, isn't he? You're very patient with him."

"I ought to be. He's an extraordinary person." Hamish felt defensive. He liked Milly, though; she was a comfortable age, his mother's.

"You've known him a long time, I imagine." She stopped, her attention drawn to a woman who had taken the seat just across from them. The newcomer kept her eyes fixed on the floor, her mouth a parabola of discomfort. "Excuse me, Hamish."

He watched her walk across the lounge, reminded of Gillian Roud, Simon's mother. He conjured his friend and counselor of countless school holidays as he remembered her best, digging in her garden on a spring day, one ample cheek usually mud-smeared. Milly was smaller, thinner, but the features and carriage were very similar, as was the calm, unpretended interest in others.

Having dispensed a dramamine to their fellow sufferer, she returned. "You and Evan were school friends?"

"Yes, from first form onward." Hamish seldom let pass an opportunity to speak to anyone of Evan; it was a weakness, perhaps, but harmed neither of them and provided him with one of the few pleasures of their complex relationship.

"What school?"

"I doubt you'll have heard of it." Milly looked faintly rebuffed, but that was getting too near. "Not Eton," he smiled at her. "Anyway, I was a scholarship kid — out of a state school, you know — and I had never stayed even one night away from home."

"It must have been hard for you."

"Without Evan it would have been awful. He'd got sent away to prep school when he was seven — a dreadful one, an expensive, pretentious kind of Dotheboys Hall. He was twelve years old when he came to school and a battle-scarred veteran." Literally; he was still marked by a caning he had taken when he was eight. "He was the smallest boy in the school when we began, but there was something very tough and durable about him."

"Gamin."

Hamish looked at her, astonished. Oliver and the Artful Dodger some of the masters had called the pair of them. "He's very posh, though. His family—" He caught himself. "Evan decided, anyway, that I needed taking care of and took me on. He fought several boys who mimicked me during the first days."

"He won, though he was so small?"

"Oh, no. He always lost. It stopped them, though; they liked him, and he could make them laugh."

"That's rather sweet. Evan was the soldier, I gather, and not the scholar."

"That's right. Evan has got dyslexia — word blindness," he explained.

"I know. I taught English literature until last year. They see the letters scrambled—"

"Left-handed usually, or—"

"Right-handed with a left-handed parent." They grinned at each other, savoring their discovery of a shared interest. "Is there much of it in the UK?"

"It wasn't always recognized. That's what happened to Evan at his prep school. He had a very high IQ, so they decided that his bad reading came from laziness or defiance. He was always being caned."

"Did his parents know? And tolerate it?" Milly looked appropriately shocked, even disgusted.

"No one ever was thrashed in my school." Hamish defended his island against her unspoken thought. "But, yes, his mother knew. She would get all tearful and vow to take him from school, but, when they spoke to her there, they could always talk her round."

"She sounds a very silly woman."

"I'm afraid she was. Dead now, drowned last year in a sailing accident—" Oh, God, now he had done it; that had been front page news even in the Guardian. Hamish watched Milly for signs of recognition: none. It was all right, the Talbots were a British phenomenon and unlikely to be written about in the American press. He continued. "They knew about dyslexia at our school, and Even was never thrashed there. But it was too late."

"Yes. If one doesn't get to them early, they can never really enjoy reading; it's even physically painful."

Max appeared and sat down beside them. The lounge had filled; latecomers were opening folding chairs to sit at the back. The pitch of the ship worsened, and Hamish planned his route to an exit.

5

Palat: They came for him early, before noon, and certainty jolted through Simon: this show was to be his own. Something inspired a rare laugh from Cretin, and Simon, following his pointing finger, saw that he had wet himself. He had felt nothing.

They motioned for him to stand, and he pushed himself to a sitting position, but his legs would do nothing at all. Cretin took one arm, Muscul-man the other, pulling him to his feet, but the legs collapsed, ending in an awkward tangle beneath him. Simon saw and heard but did not feel Cretin kick one of them; he stepped back to aim a second kick, but Muscul-man restrained him, and both men left his cell.

The right leg rested at a nasty angle, and Simon was trying to straighten it with his hands when they returned with the commandant. The three knelt round him, poking and prodding — Cretin pinched flesh from Simon's thigh between blackened fingernails until the blood came, but Simon felt nothing. They pulled him to his feet again, the legs collapsed like overcooked spaghetti, the commandant swore at the guards, and they all went away.

The tall, very thin man who returned with the commandant must have been a doctor of sorts. He brought a small hammer with which he hit Simon's knee again and again in an unsuccessful attempt to produce the reflex jerk. Others appeared later with a stretcher and rolled Simon onto it.

He was carried across the prison yard and into another

building that was part of the rectangular complex, then lifted onto a mattress covered by a sheet. Two guards Simon had never seen removed the wet trousers and washed him, covering him afterwards with a kind of hospital gown. Something like a large black bird of death appeared when they were gone and took his temperature. From the posture and shuffling Simon guessed it was a very old woman, though he saw only two tiny black eyes peering from under the heavy cloak. She gave him a blanket and left water on a small table beside his bed, then vanished.

"Roud." Mikhail lay prone on the bed just to his right; Simon began to weep.

"You're alive."

"Not altogether." His voice was thinner than a whisper, and the face he turned towards Simon was saffron, almost translucent, skin stretched tight across its bones. The savaged back was bare, and a fly fed from it.

"There's a fly on you," Simon cried, "just between your shoulders."

Mikhail only lay there. "Perhaps you could shoo it off, Roud."

Simon couldn't reach and, in trying, almost fell off his bed. "I'm sorry — my legs don't work."

Mikhail appeared to have gone off — he was silent for a long time, his eyes closed. Then the slight, disembodied voice sounded again. "Simon, I'm so sorry. Did they beat you?"

"They've hardly touched me, only keep taking me to the square each day, saying it's my turn. It's always someone else, though. This morning when they came for me, the legs went out. I think it's all in my mind — there's some medical word for it."

Now Mikhail *had* gone off; the rise and fall of his breathing was so light Simon could hardly be sure it was happening, and the fly still sucked at his back. Hysterical paralysis, that was the term, he thought almost indifferently. The black-cloaked creature had placed a piece of shelf paper beneath his water jug, and, rolling it up, Simon was able to reach out and frighten away the fly.

At Sea: Evan set the sketching pad down on a deck chair and leaned over the railing; his earlier impulse to draw was totally lost in the unpleasant surprise he had given himself. It had been a wretched thing to do to Hamish, and where such an impulse came from, much less got acted upon, he didn't know. He could quite as easily have slung the handbag over his shoulder and brought it up here to the deck which he had almost completely to himself, the ship's company having gathered downstairs for a lecture.

Last night as well. Evan could have created the necessary distraction by dumping wine over himself or someone else and needn't have humiliated Hamish as he had done, but he had used the first words to pop into his head. And why had they been the first? He closed his mind against an answer he didn't like.

He would make it up to Hamish, who had already sacrificed too much pride. Odd, the intensity of old friendships, Evan thought, as he remembered this one's half-comic, half-melodramatic beginnings.

It must have been their first week at school, each thinking that he alone was new and strange and vulnerable. Hamish, just out of a house filled with women, had been under siege. He talked like a girl then and had made a fine scapegoat for the uncertainty of the others.

Simon, already with the voice and height of a man, had held himself aloof at first from their teasing, then one day began to orchestrate it. He was a clever mimic and had four other boys roaring with laughter at his imitation of Hamish. Hamish had pretended that they weren't there at all, though Simon's face was inches from his. Hamish became suddenly to Evan the essence of everything brave and breakable, Simon the craven breaker. Hoping to hit and run, Evan had punched Simon in the mouth.

Simon's bulk was deceptive; he was very fast, and Evan's next sight of him was from on the ground. The four witnesses had disappeared; Hamish, stoical about his own abuse, had been crying his head off; and Simon's eyes were popping in dismay.

"You ended my budding career as a bully," Simon told Evan years later. "I knew I was being a bastard to Hamish, but they were egging me on, and there was a kind of perverse fun to it. Then you.

"There you lay, smaller than my little brother at home, making me feel no end heroic, of course. You'd fallen with your head bent to one side, and there was so much blood." The slightest misfortune to Evan's thin, pointed nose always produced quantities of it. "I was afraid I'd killed you, and I couldn't remember any prayer at all."

It was Simon's guilt at first that made him their protector. Then he and Hamish, amiably jockeying for first place in almost every school subject, had found how much they had to talk about, and Evan had tagged along. Simon's marriage had changed nothing; Christina accepted and almost blended into the sixteen-year-old friendship.

Two long, muscular arms appeared suddenly on the railing to Evan's right. He suppressed a start, continuing to look out over the blue-black swells of the Adriatic.

"Hello, Talbot."

Evan raised his eyes reluctantly; the face was faintly familiar, not pleasantly so.

"You've forgotten me. Dirk Wilder, formerly of the *Sun*."

Bloody Christ, a hyena! "Formerly?" Evan asked, striving for polite indifference.

"Yes. I suppose the old rag has never been in the best of taste, but last month they plumbed the depths. I was assigned to do a series on a child rapist, and my editor insisted on the kind of detail that could only inspire imitators. I chucked it."

Evan strained for a response. "Sensible."

"Not altogether." This face was better bred than the others but wore now the same shallow, avid look. "I'd already booked this cruise, and now I find myself a bit strapped."

All right, Evan must have a week at most. "If you need a loan—"

"Ho, you *do* hold us in low esteem. No, I don't blackmail. I need a story, though, very badly just now, and I've been handed one. It's unlucky to refuse a gift from the Fates."

"It's sensible to postpone taking it when they're holding out a better gift," Evan drawled. "I can promise you a very good story indeed when the cruise is done."

"What? You're engaged again," the boyish voice baited. "No, I forgot. You've come out of the closet to be with beautiful whats-his-name. Sir Francis has given his blessing, and the services will be held—" Holding himself still required an effort Evan couldn't sustain much longer; he felt sweat forming on his forehead faster than the cold sea wind could dry it.

Wilder must have read murder in his face. "Sorry," he

whined, "*that* was in bad taste, I suppose. But I can't wait until the cruise is ended; I need something by mid-April. I can write it with your cooperation or I can simply call in what I've seen from our first port."

"All right. I can give you your story within the week," Evan calculated. "On April 6th you'll have something unusual. What you are seeing now is, as the Americans would say, a scam, and, if you write about it, not only will you look a fool when the cruise is done and I become myself again, but you will spoil the scam. There will be no story at all, then, do you understand?"

"I think so. I need surety, though. A bird in the hand—"

"I'm going to meet someone, someone far more news-worthy than I. For several days, you will be the only journalist in a position to know and write about that meeting."

"Great!" That, for once, had been just right. There was a naiveté to these spinners of scandal — they evidently came to believe in the world that they had spun. Wilder's eyes were wide as those of a child in a sweet shop. "Not — Margot?"

"Definitely not Margot. That was a scam by your people. I'm afraid that's all I'm in a position to tell you."

"I understand — I've simply got to wait and wonder. Oh, good *luck*, Talbot!" He clapped Evan across the shoulders and left him.

Neutralized now, this unsavory fellow might even be useful. No longer displeased with himself, Evan retrieved the sketching pad and began to block out a seascape.

Just as Dr. Cameron stepped onto the small lecturer's platform that had been the bandstand the night before, the ship took a lurch that sent him sliding across it. Untroubled, he set his feet well apart and reached for an elusive microphone. A hole an inch or two in diameter at the elbow of his old sweater showed itself as he adjusted the speaker. Cameron had changed little in five years, though the hole was larger than Hamish remembered it.

"Ladies and gentlemen," the Oxford scholar lilted Scottishly, "I have been scheduled to speak about the archeological site at Liaboam, but a few words about contemporary Tariq may be in order. I understand that several people have opted out of Sunday's tour, and I address these remarks particularly to them.

"First, Cobb's arrangements in Tariq were made before the proclivities of its new government became apparent. Our taking advantage of services already paid for will in no way enrich these fanatics."

The Scottish mind, Hamish thought, amusement momentarily displacing his nausea.

"Which brings me to the second point. For several days all of us will be guests in a Muslim country and in close contact with its people. I should like to remind you that the fundamentalist religiosity of Tariq's ruling clique bears no more resemblance to the teachings of Islam than that of Spain's inquisitors or Salem's witch-burners to Christianity."

An approving murmur and one "Hear, hear!" arose from his audience, but all was not agreement. A tall figure rose from a seat near the center and made its way slowly and deliberately to the front, past Cameron to an exit. "That's a blessing," Milly whispered to Hamish as Sharon slammed the door behind her. "I was afraid she was going to ask for equal time."

"And," the Scotsman continued, "lest we indulge ourselves in too much righteous superiority, it should be observed that the savagery which we see now in Tariq is at least in part the reaction of a battered people, battered, to be sure, for centuries by its own rulers but more recently with the collusion of the Western powers, our own governments, who chose to protect the position of those rulers."

This brought some raised eyebrows, but the ship then bucked cooperatively, spilling plants, ashtrays, even a lamp, and easing Cameron's transition from politics to archeology. The interruption covered Hamish's dash from the lounge.

He spent the rest of the lecture period sick in his own cabin and heard the second talk, by Ewing of Cambridge, over the cabin speaker, prone on his unsteady bed. Evan came in.

"Time for lunch."

"Oh, my God."

"None of that. You need ballast. We'll take the buffet rather than the set lunch, and you can choose quiet, soothing things." He helped Hamish get up and pushed him along to the line at the aft end of the lounge.

The buffet was all too colorful and more unsettling than the coastline of Albania. Hamish glanced at Evan's plate and then away; Evan, his cheeks pink from the sea air, his eyes bright with appetite, had taken everything. Hamish chose two water biscuits and a *blanc mange.* The second was firm, chewy almost tasteless and precisely the right thing. "I think it's a new wonder drug," he told Evan and returned for a second.

The third and fourth lectures were comfortable expositions to the cultures of Crete and Mycenae. Hamish learned nothing new from them, but he liked having his memory freshened and almost greedily anticipated standing on the actual sites.

"Rather awful," he told Evan as they dressed for the cocktail party, "I've hardly thought of Simon all day. It's rotten of me to be liking all this so much."

"It isn't. *So* glad you're fit again." Evan put his arm round Hamish's waist, pressed it briefly, then returned to the business of knotting his tie. He was so innocently and easily affectionate, like a nice puppy.

At dinner Milly was not as pleasant as she had been during the day. As the meal progressed she became strident, like an American tourist in a bad television play, and repetitive. It was evident that she had taken more than her share at the cocktail party. Hamish tried to attend politely to her, but Max and Sarah began a discussion he wanted to hear—

"David," Milly called peremptorily. Hamish looked back at her and saw, as he had feared, that she was looking directly at Evan. Damn his stupid babbling of the morning! "David," he heard again.

At Sea — March 31: She couldn't fool herself this time. Her stomach pitched uncertainly as it had done yesterday, but the pitching was accompanied now by pounding in her chest and throbbing in her head. Milly lay on her bed, able neither to rise nor to sleep. She would be a shambles until midafternoon, and much of Crete would pass her unobserved and unexperienced.

"How do you feel?" Max was dressed, looking eager and handsome in the collared velour she had bought him for the cruise.

"Much as I deserve." She had anticipated and, unexpectedly, silenced him.

"Coming to breakfast?"

"I think not. Get me an aspirin and a glass of water, will

you please, on your way out?" He did, and he left her.

She had squandered much of the previous day but something worse nibbled at the edge of her mind. She had been a fool at dinner, no doubt, and embarrassed Max. Just how wasn't important and couldn't, needn't be remembered; such losses were usually recoverable. She had more than two weeks to regain her image with Reg, Sarah and the young people.

Tonight she would listen. She would ask Sarah questions that would indulge her taste for gossip, Reg about the dramatists. She would learn Lindsay's interests and even hear Sharon out; she would find out what Hamish taught and where. And Evan—

Oh, no, she had done more than play the fool, she had done harm, terrible harm to someone, and the certainty of this, almost mystical, sickened her.

She must reconstruct the evening as clearly as she could manage and not allow her mind to fall into its usual pattern of evasion. "It was the booze." She forced her brain to shape the thought and the ugly word that she disliked hearing. It was not her fragile digestive tract nor her sensitive sinuses. "It was the booze."

It made her stupid. She had regaled Sarah with the glories of the Royal Shakespeare Company's *Coriolanus* — as she had done the night before, only more briefly and coherently and before she had learned that Reg was part of a rival company. The young people, who had been interested in her conversation earlier, turned away and began talking in different groups.

That started, as usual, half perceived in a series of blurred *déjà vus*, a nastier symptom. She stopped being interested at all in the others, wanting only their attention. And began to show off. Oh, God.

She had decided, she remembered now, to show that she was more there than the rest of them. She had called to Evan twice as David, authoritatively laying her superior perceptions out upon the table for all of them to see. She forced the scene from the back of her head to the front and was reassured.

Sarah had been close to the denouement of what must have been a very funny story: the entire aft end of the table had exploded in laughter just after Milly's second "David." She had met Hamish's horrified and disenchanted eyes, read their message and clammed. Not so bad, that one — only he had heard.

Near the end of the meal Sharon, who had pointedly ignored the boys throughout the previous evening, had done an about-face and turned her sweet, rather hungry smile onto Evan. "What do you do, Evan, what do you work at?" she had asked, peering around Lindsay.

"I'm not working just now." His eyes, intensely blue, went flat under elevated brows, and he turned back to speak to Lindsay. It had been a practiced, definitive snub and, against Sharon, totally ineffective.

"What did you do last?" Sharon persisted, the smile now showing what must be every tooth in her head.

"Something I may not continue," he said coldly. "It has never been well received." He tried again to turn away.

"Oh, but you must," Milly had cried. Not flaunting superior knowledge, merely eager to encourage Evan, she had sunk from egocentricity to cretinism. "So few contemporaries have your control and discipline — most seem to feel that they can simply throw paint at a canvas and rely on the genius of the viewer to pull it together. It's only that you haven't decided what you want to say as yet; when you do, you'll say it beautifully."

Everyone had heard that, and Milly now tried to sort out their reactions. The most painful had been Max's foot coming down heavily upon her instep. Sarah went taut as a hound on the scent, careful not to look at Evan, who regarded Milly with a sick, defeated smile.

"So you're a painter," Sharon began. "I knew there was something familiar—"

"Lindsay, would you dance with me, please?" Evan asked and whisked her so quickly from the table to the lounge that none of them heard her consent.

The whole table knew now, thanks to Milly, that David Talbot was on the Alexandros. Given the delicious quality of that sort of secret, half the ship would hear it before the day was out; Milly had destroyed the privacy for which the boy had made so desperate a bid. She wallowed in self-disgust.

Well, it was done, and nothing would undo it. Milly could, at best, try to manage herself so that nothing like it would happen again. There was only one way to ensure that:

no drinks tonight, no drinks at all. The thought was not awful, not even uncomfortable. Why had it taken her so long to admit that it could be necessary?

Then suddenly Milly knew: it was the fear that she must give up all alcohol, not only tonight but forever. It was the vision of all the years stretching before her barren of the sweet comfort, the warmth, the special life that resided in liquor. It needn't happen. Gin was worst — no more of it, ever. And she would take nothing, not even beer for the duration of the cruise.

Later, at home again, she might allow herself to experiment, she relented. But she would watch herself to see how much she could handle without becoming an aggressive, ego-imposing sponge.

Their steward, Georgi, a slight, dark-skinned boy with golden curls, rapped at her door, bearing a tray with two croissants, orange juice and coffee. "Dr. Ross asked me to bring."

"Thank you, Georgi." She ate, forcing herself at first, then enjoying the flaky, buttery rolls. The day was *not* ruined. Milly laid out her lemon yellow blouse, a favorite.

Palat: The doctor came to see them. He took Mikhail's temperature and began to swab the scabbed back, but Mikhail stirred and moaned. The tall man grimaced, tossed the swab away and pulled back Mikhail's eyelid for a moment, then sucked in his cadaverous cheeks so that he resembled more than ever a sick bird of prey. His attention to Simon's legs was perfunctory, but he frowned at the thermometer and listened for a long time at Simon's chest. He turned then to the room's third occupant, the boy thief whose right hand had been cut off and who only slept, ate and cried.

The commandant appeared before he was done dressing the truncated arm and the doctor, much taller, spoke down to him as one might to an inferior but very dangerous dog. "This man is dying." He indicated Mikhail.

Simon had thought Mikhail was recovering, and he fought back the too-easy tears that could betray his understanding of Tariqi. Mikhail had slipped back now into the comatose state in which he had spent most of yesterday, but at the first light, just an hour before, he had been alert and cheerful.

"We *will* get out, Roud, and you and your Christina will visit me in Moscow. I'll show you that it's not all blizzards and austerity. There's a small place near the Metropole Hotel, no better shashlik in the world—" And, at the thought, Mikhail had even picked at the breakfast rice.

"I'm not in a position to advise the people at Persarum," the doctor continued, "but, were I you, I should call them and suggest that he be sent home as a 'humanitarian gesture' for the few days he has left. The Russians are not going to take this passively."

"They can tell the Communists he was murdered by another prisoner — the American, maybe." The words, spoken at the knit in the doctor's tie — he hadn't troubled to raise his eyes to his face — were dismissive.

"That would be clever — had he been knifed or merely battered to death. But the Russians will expect his body to be returned, and that will tell them when and how he died. Also, I should think that a prison murder would reflect slightly on you."

"Mm." The commandant picked his nose thoughtfully, his brows contracting. He would, Simon thought, call his superiors at Persarum. "What about the Englishman? When will you have him walking?"

"He's better staying as he is just now. Your Englishman is developing pneumonia."

"Will he recover?" The flabby face on its thick neck went sharp and anxious.

"With proper care and medication."

"You're to see that he has it," the commandant spat.

"I'm afraid, since I'm allowed to visit these people only twice weekly, that is beyond my control."

"You're to come in daily, then."

"That will change nothing. The man needs nursing care, more than a daily visit."

"I'm going to tell you something that maybe I oughtn't." The murky eyes rose to the doctor's face, and the tone changed to one of wheedling. "The Englishman must not be allowed to die; I was told when he arrived here that he was to be treated carefully and not to be flogged at all. It seems that the son of an ayatollah executed one of his wives in London — for cause, mind you — and the damnable infidels have charged him with murder. Those in Persarum hope to arrange a trade."

Oh, Jesus, he was safe! He disguised his astonished out-cry, still wise enough to keep his single resource secret. Even if the Home Office refused to deal with them, Simon was safe — they had no concept of Western justice and would expect the mullah's murderous offspring to be punished if Simon was harmed.

"Look, I'll place one of the guards here as nurse, and—"

"It had best be one of the brighter ones — he's got to be capable of counting out four antibiotics daily or the trade with London will be in corpses. I'll send Ahmad here with some capsules, and you yourself must see to it that the Englishman takes them."

The pneumonia, a comfortable ailment he had survived as a child, troubled Simon not at all; he felt wonderfully safe and free.

"What about the boy? Can I put him with the others now?"

"Where is he going? Into Block Three with the students?"

"Students?" The menacing manner returned briefly but was discarded. "There are no students, I don't know what you're talking about. The boy goes into Block One with the regulars."

"My God," the doctor murmured in French. "It would have been kinder to have killed him."

"What?"

"The stump isn't healing well, he must stay here longer."

They left separately, the tall man disdainful but wary. Three flies sucked at Mikhail's back now. Without thought, Simon slid from his bed, walked to Mikhail's and shooed them away.

Crete: Had it come even a day earlier, Evan's unmasking could have ruined the whole plan. Now, though, a disclosure in those papers that had repeatedly associated him with Simon could not happen before they had come to and gone from Palat. And Milly's revelation need not damage the still-critical part of his disguise, that with which he had so repelled Hamish just now at breakfast.

Why, then, was he feeling so untidy in his mind? Why was the ulcer beginning to misbehave as it had not done in weeks? He had, perhaps, overdone it this morning, flaunting the stupid handbag despite Hamish's evident misery. Again.

He grimaced and, impulsively, dumped the contents of the fawn-colored handbag out on his bunk.

He slid the old passport that he had claimed lost into a zippered compartment of the Cobb's carrying case; its replacement was held in the cruise office along with those of all the other passengers. He broke the wad of Turkish dinares into smaller bundles and arranged them inside the black recesses of the chador, encountering the Luger pistol; that, he reminded himself, must be loaded tonight.

Hamish returned from the deck as Evan flung the empty handbag under his bunk. "We won't be needing that again."

"I'm dismayed, of course." Hamish didn't smile.

"One can see that you are. Next you'll be wanting me to shed my earring; simply no satisfying some."

"After last night at dinner, I can't see a purpose for it. They all know who you are." Hamish turned away, studying the cruise manual.

"Who, perhaps, but not what—"

Hamish turned upon him, grasped his shoulders and pushed him down into the small single chair. "Charming," he said, his Grecian nose pinched white, his eyes hot and hard on Evan's. " 'Who but not what.' What you are pretending to be, what I am, is not an it. He and who will do very nicely."

"Good God, you didn't let me finish—"

"I oughtn't to have let you begin — any of this. Your carrying on this morning was ridiculous, redundant, and as you bloody well know, humiliating to me." Evan felt the relief of a guilty child subject to a long-deserved tongue-lashing. "How would you feel if I kept up a constant parody of, oh" — he studied Evan distractedly — "short people."

Evan wished that Hamish would hit him, hard and in anger, but he heard his own voice, controlled, almost superior. "I think you're forgetting what's going to happen tomorrow. A piece of rather bizarre behavior has got to be made to ring true."

"I don't believe it's going to happen," Hamish challenged. "Your plan has more holes in it than Cameron's sweater." He sat down on his bunk, though, waiting to be convinced again.

"It's time to review, then." Evan pulled a suitcase from under his bunk, opened it and drew out the second chador. "Best check this for length right now." Hamish stood reluctantly and had it held against his shoulders. "It's right, shows just enough shoe. Pack it in your hand luggage — I've put the longer one, for Simon, in mine."

"You *want* our shoes to show? Surely British oxfords won't add to our authenticity."

"We want them to do when you re-embark. Two completely authentic-looking Muslim women might not be allowed to board. In Palat, you'll go barefoot; I've brought some brown tint for your feet."

"Where is all this supposed to happen? And won't we look the least bit off wandering the streets of Palat with our shoes in our hands?"

Hamish was only irritable now, and Evan was pleased with his growing practicality. "There's an abandoned naval barracks beside the prison. We'll keep the carrying cases there, and you and Simon can change clothes inside it afterwards. As for getting through the streets, you'll find when you put this thing on that you could hide a Land Rover under it. You'll simply sling the cases, shoes and all in them, over your shoulders and wear the chador on top."

Hamish's irritation had vanished; he nodded, thoughtfully nibbling a fingernail. "If we can get inside this abandoned building, so can anyone else. The cases could be stolen while we're in the prison."

This was the point at which Evan had hoped to abandon specifics. "Actually, Hamish, you will never be inside the prison. You — and the Luger — will stay in the barracks with the money. We've got to have a simultaneous exchange or the commandant could find himself a good deal richer and in charge of three British prisoners instead of one. There's a pattern to these things."

That must have sounded knowledgeable, if vague, and Hamish seemed satisfied. He would raise the devil if he learned the full plan too soon; when the time came, he would be too hurriedly occupied to question it.

Evan would hand over half the money when his offer was accepted, would direct Simon to Hamish's hiding place, then stay beside the jailers for the half hour that would easily see his friends back to the ship. He could assure himself this way that Simon was not pursued and himself serve as surety to the prison commandant, whom he would lead, finally, to the hidden half of the ransom.

It had been done before, the prisoner bought, the courier

69

later freed — the sticky part was Tariq's new and complicated piety. As Peter had warned, Evan might find himself playing Sidney Carton.

I'm just beginning to think it might work." Hamish gave Evan one of the old smiles, his eyes soft as a deer's but warmer, a twist of humor to his mouth. "Sorry, Evan, about the tantrum. Can't you stretch your creativity a bit further and come up with a way to get yourself back on the Alexandros — that day, from Palat?"

"Not without us all being caught; the harbor police will keep count of the number disembarking and re-embarking, and you've seen Miss Shaw with those landing tags."

"Yes. She watches them in but not out. I'll bring yours ashore the next day at Antalya." Hamish was repeating that for the fourth or fifth time, like a child chewing over a safe, known arithmetical combination.

"I'll be at the quay, and we'll board together — not in drag, I promise."

Hamish was trying, unsuccessfully, to close the zipper of his yellow canvas bag into which he had crammed the chador. "That won't do. Take it out, and I'll fold it for you." Evan compacted the thing, and the zipper slid easily into place, Evan's hand brushing Hamish's as he secured it. He saw Hamish flush deeply and looked away — Jesus, it was still there.

"One more detail, Hamish: that chap who tidies the cabin, Georgi, mustn't see Simon, of course. You're to keep that sign on the door, the one that says someone is sleeping, at all times."

"He might come in anyway — by afternoon or so."

"Not into Hector Seven. He was here when I got back from breakfast just now, bent over the trashbin, bum conveniently extended. I pinched it flirtatiously, and he took off at a canter."

"God, Evan, you're wasted in the arts." Hamish sank back on his bunk, helpless with laughter. "Only think what you could do in the secret service." He extended an arm, and Evan rose and moved towards him.

Miss Shaw's voice sounded, metallic over the speaker. "Disembarkation will begin at 9:45."

The ship shuddered slightly, and Evan changed direction, opening the door to the corridor. "They've dropped anchor.

Look at this, Hamish — it's only 9:30, and they're queued up the stairs and well into the lounge."

"It is quite unnecessary to queue for disembarkation. The buses will not depart until ten hours." There was an edge to Miss Shaw's voice.

"Best queue now," Hamish said predictably. Evan closed the door.

"Not quite yet — we haven't discussed one detail. In the event that you need help after I've left you, after you're both on board, I suggest you go to Reg. I think he placed both of us that first night at table and made the connection with Simon — he's been watching us since like a friendly computer trying to reckon what we're up to."

A happiness near euphoria filled Evan, and he let his arm rest across Hamish's shoulders. Hamish stood and moved away.

"My queuing instincts can no longer be denied."

The line moved down the stairs and onto Heracles Deck, past Miss Shaw, who regarded it with displeasure — it blocked access from the cruise office to areas of the ship where she had business — to the bulletin board, from which each of its members removed a small plastic landing tag, down the gangplank and off to the parking area at the end of the quay where six Mercedes buses waited.

Milly caught Evan's eye while they were still on Heracles Deck and gave him a sheepish smile. He wasn't angry at her and had no difficulty returning it; her interference had been kindly meant. She had only been acting true to her breed, that of his mother who had alternately indulged and betrayed him from his first memories to her death along the tricky shore she had promised not to sail.

"Smokers to the back of the bus." A cruise girl, the dark, pretty one, motioned them onto Bus Five.

"Sorry," Evan said. Hamish had never smoked. "I no sooner hear that kind of thing that I'm perishing for a cigarette. Shall we separate? You'll have a better view."

"I'll sit with you."

Sarah and Milly were across from them, their non-smoking husbands sharing a seat towards the front. "We lepers," Sarah said, struggling with her lighter.

Heraklion, as they rode through it, presented a prosperous

contemporary face, its streets filled with pretty people in Western dress, its store windows with displays more colorful but not unlike those at home. Buildings became scarce; they passed small, well-kept farms preened with rototillers and an occasional miniature tractor. "Amazing that we're only two days from home," Evan murmured to Hamish. "Look at spring." Fruit trees blossomed delicately, and scarlet poppies dotted the roadside grasses.

They turned off the paved road into a disappointingly ordinary gravel courtyard and stopped; they were at Knossos. The last bus arrived and unloaded, and 280 Britons, Americans and Canadians were taken inside utilitarian hurricane fencing along with their six local guides to find themselves suddenly, dramatically faced by the painted pillars of the Palace of Minos.

"Odd," Evan said, "the pillars are thicker at the top than at the base."

"You with the artist's eye. I shouldn't have seen that if I hadn't read about it." Hamish grinned at him, cheeks pink, eyes shining; he was having a fine time after all. "They're tree trunks set upside down. Ah, here's Hodgkins."

Hamish had introduced Evan to the professor at last night's cocktail party — a nice man, something of the teddy bear about him. He stood now below the hennaed pillars, his son Robin beside him. The boy, fourteen or fifteen, held his father's notes. For an adolescent, he was unusually at ease among adults and seemed pleased to be of help to his father.

"Three thousand years ago," Hodgkins began, and the ship's company pressed closer to catch his words, "while cultures to the south revolved round their hubs of mysticism and death, these people were celebrating life and made some astonishing strides in improving its conditions. I speak not only of their plumbing, which, as you will see, has yet to be equaled in much of the world, but of gaiety, comfort, the creation and enjoyment of beauty. These qualities of Minoan life—"

Hodgkins spoke and moved with the enthusiasm of an actor born, and Evan found himself attending, even interested — not at all like school.

They broke, at random, into six groups then, each following one of the young, local guides through the intricate maze that had been the palace. "This was the queen's bedroom," announced the young historian who led Evan's group, her flutelike English accented but fluent. "Please look at the bathtub." It was terra cotta but otherwise looked Victorian and rather comfortable. "It's still useable. The wall painting over it is not restored; what you see is the real, the incredibly ancient thing." It was vibrant — Evan touched it when no one was looking and found himself in the midst of his first antiquarian thrill. He determined to read about what he was seeing, however his dyslexic eyes behaved.

Hamish, who probably knew more than the guides, had gone to feel the place out for himself. Evan caught sight of him unexpectedly, standing high on an eastern wall and looking out over the valley beneath the palace. His face was rapt and open, the dark hair curling away from it ruffled lightly by wind from the sea. His beauty caught at Evan's throat like a barb and twisted there with sweet, sick pain.

It was very bad, worse than he remembered it being at school. Why had Evan done this to himself? What trickster, hidden deep inside him, had thought up the game he'd insisted on playing and lulled him into believing that he could escape its consequences — and that of the hours and days of physical nearness to the old, the first beloved? His arm, where he had let it touch Hamish earlier, tingled with yearning.

The guide was pointing out an amphora now, whole and large enough to have housed Ali Baba and a couple of thieves. Though Evan continued to walk behind her, he had lost the thread and barely heard her voice.

He had made love to women and not disliked it. From the first, though, and that had been very early, he had found sex more satisfying with men. When he was fourteen, he had begun to dream carnally of Hamish — and to wake ashamed. He had wanted the friendship to stay as pure and good as the friend. He had been shocked later to discover a bit of the barnyard in Hamish — and then briefly excited. He had known always, though, that to love his friend even once would make the other kind of love hateful to him.

The guide had brought them full circle, and they queued once more for the buses. "Your turn by the window," he told Hamish. His stomach felt as if it had at last succeeded in digesting itself. Evan popped a green capsule into his mouth and swallowed it, he thought unseen.

"I thought it was better."

73

Not unseen. "It is. I'm only being precautionary." They had warned him that it might begin to bleed; then he would be quite immobilized tomorrow, and it would all be for nothing. Evan tried to empty his mind and fill it again with things outside himself.

"You're dead pale."

"Perfectly fit, honestly. Tell me about that archeologist — Sir Arthur Evans — who restored the palace."

"Well, he's anathema, you know, to the purists. For all his magnificent work, they think he committed sacrilege when he had those pillars painted red and some of the wall paintings restored in color. The colors are right, though, just as they were. I think they add tremendously to the spirit of the place. I really felt I had caught it — been shot back in time, you know. I was playing Theseus."

"I caught it too for a bit." The pill was beginning to help, and the voice of his friend soothed. "I'd like to read about it."

"I'll read the briefing from the cruise handbook to you tonight; it's quite well done and puts it all in historic perspective." They fell silent, watching the countryside slide past.

Evan ordinarily was captain to his mind, monitoring its contents as Miss Shaw did passengers, but his command was escaping him. Memory of Simon's words about Hamish's lovers crept into his head and rankled there — then, oddly, comforted. None had endured longer than Evan's engagements. Evan kept his own homosexual affairs brief and emotionally aseptic, but that was for the sake of discretion; one would expect Hamish to seek a permanent companion. Perhaps it was for Hamish as it was for him: there had been no one before or since with whom he felt so right, so alive and comfortable at the same time.

To return from nearly three weeks of that to the sterility of surface relationships, begun from duty or lust or convenience, was going to be hard to bear. For the first time in years Evan let himself chew over the seductive, the impossible alternatives. A long-term, clandestine arrangement? Disguise would go against every grain in Hamish. To live together openly, as friends and lovers? Evan remained a Talbot, albeit an undistinguished one, and to bring this humiliation down upon Francis was unthinkable. A quick, safe affair, perhaps — oh, God, the trickster was back, and Evan had almost opened the door to him.

Hamish was going on now about Theseus and Ariadne. His telling was clean and clear as water, but Evan found himself attending only to the graceful, expressive hands of his friend and wanting to touch them. Tonight, in Hector Seven, only the two of them, Hamish reading to him cool, soothing things from the next bunk, both tense about what must be done in Palat in the morning — it would be sure to happen. And if not tonight, the ones to follow. . . .

Perhaps none would follow. Without fear, almost with relief, he imagined himself jailed in Palat and kept to fill Simon's place. Or somthing more final. Ho, they called that a death wish, and it wasn't at all the kind of equipment that ought to be taken to Palat. The chances were that Hamish and Evan would be back on the Alexandros either alone or with Simon, whose departure would still leave them a week to themselves. He must find a way to distract himself.

Little Lindsay? She was a wonderfully responsive dancing partner, like gossamer to his touch, and she seemed to have been spared the coy silliness that spoiled so many women. Evan had been disturbed to see Wilder take her up; the facade of his accent and appearance hid the jackal within, and he would, Evan supposed, be attractive to women. He thought he could like Lindsay very much and she him; they might come to a casual shipboard arrangement that would save both of them from trouble.

6

Palat: The antibiotic didn't arrive, only new chaos. Simon heard it begin and then watched the prison yard in horror from the slitted opening between his bed and that of the boy thief. The boy stood on his bed and watched too, then scuttled beneath it, curling himself into a tight, shivering ball. Simon saw the guards leave the yard and hurried back under his sheet.

Mikhail, thank God, had slept through it, but he woke when Cretin and Muscul-man burst in. In sweating haste, the guards stripped the top sheets from the beds and bundled the bandages and medications from the cupboard, snatching even the thermometers and water tumblers from the nightstands beside them. They left then without a glance at the three patients.

"What the devil—"

"I think there's been another revolution, this time the right kind. They're going to send us home, Simon." Yesterday that calm, sleepy smile had comforted Simon; then he had recognized, sickeningly, its euphoria. That, he had read, was one of the symptoms of kidney failure.

They lay and waited, and the boy continued to cower beneath his bed. The door creaked and, of its own weight, swung outward a few inches — the guards had left it ajar. The boy, pressed close against the wall, crept toward it on his knees and his single hand. He froze at the sound of voices raised outside and dove back into shelter.

A grizzled, gape-toothed face appeared in the doorway.

76

"The doors are open," it croaked. "The Kurds are coming. Get out, get out." The child surfaced once more, his mangled arm held to his chest; he crept again along the wall to the door and out.

"Simon," Mikhail said, "you're to go now too. Only get me some water, and I'll be fine. The Kurds are our comrades, don't you know?"

Simon knew Mikhail's thoughts about the Kurds. "Nonsense. I'll carry you."

"Where? How far?" No euphoria now, his voice was sharp and hard. "There's no time for English romanticism, Roud. Have a look at us both. The border is forty or so kilometers away. You're ill, but alone you just might get there."

"Let's try. Please." Simon knelt beside the other bed, and placing Mikhail's frail arm around his neck tried to raise him to a sitting position; the arm slid helplessly down his back.

"Please don't," Mikhail gasped. "Water now, only water."

Simon would get the water first, then rest a little; he was dizzy when he stood, his fever must be climbing. He could bind Mikhail's wrists together then with a strip of sheeting, place the arms round his own neck like a loop and support the rest of him with an arm under his knees so that the poor back would be free of contact.

Simon reached an adjoining cell block where water leaked from a tap, only to find he had brought nothing in which to carry it. Street noises, very loud to penetrate in here, followed him back to Mikhail.

"Do you hear them, the savages? I must have been mad to try and send you out there," Mikhail said. "You must not go now, they'll tear you to pieces."

The only container the guards had left was the urinal beneath Mikhail's bed. Simon took it to the water tap and washed fluid from it; it was pinkish yellow and thick as blood.

He held Mikhail's head in the crook of his arm and pressed the urinal to his lips, and Mikhail drank. "Not champagne," he murmured, "but I think you've brought me some of your fine whisky from Scotland." Simon kissed the hot, dry skin of his forehead — somehow he would get the two of them out of Mordor.

At Sea: The afternoon at the Museum in Heraklion had been a chain of small vivid delights, quite in contrast to the ruined morning during which Sharon had sermonized from one end of the Palace of Minos to the other. After lunch, the red-haired Sharon had gone to visit friends who were vacationing there, and Lindsay had spent nearly five hours with Dirk and away from the confining presence of her cabin-mate. She returned to Hector Four filled with kindly resolve.

The smile was there to meet her and the smell of cheap face powder, hard to account for since Sharon wore no makeup. The smile was not, Lindsay had begun to suspect, for Lindsay. Not that it was insincere. Sharon's world contained two entities: audience and adversary, and those around her were perceived not as individuals but random fragments of either set.

"What a lovely dress!" she said of the Marks and Spencer jersey Lindsay had decided not to wear. Now, her conversational obligation fulfilled, Sharon could begin the evening homily. "I don't understand how you can force yourself to dance with that Evan."

"Oh, my religion is different from yours," Lindsay equivocated. "Dancing is acceptable."

"I mean how can you bear to be touched by that *kind* of man?"

"I like Evan," she answered pleasantly, resolve holding. "And he dances superbly."

"Do you know what he is, what he and that other man are to each other?"

Oh, *honestly*! Lindsay, hurrying to dress and escape, tore a stocking, one of only three pair she had packed. "I might guess, but I don't know. I think that's a private matter and only the concern of Evan and Hamish." Damn, she had sounded as righteous as Sharon, who looked put down and a little hurt. Lindsay hated cruelty and could at least listen to the poor girl. Perhaps a different tack—

"You began to tell me about being reborn this morning, Sharon, and we were interrupted. You were eighteen, you said."

"Yes. I had just entered college. I hated it there, and God spoke to me." Lindsay had at least put her on a more positive line of thought; Sharon's face shone, her eyes fixed and luminous. "He said that the school was evil and I must leave it. He would show me a path."

"Did you hear His voice?"

78

"I heard no sound. The words appeared, clear and separate, as if my mind was a piece of paper and they were being written upon it."

Lindsay put down her hairbrush and turned to face the girl, suddenly interested, almost fascinated. Whether or not such things actually happened, it evident that Sharon believed what she was saying.

"I met Gwen then, and she was the path."

Gwen? Lindsay remembered the book, then, which Sharon had tried to lend her: Gwen Noyes. "She's a prophetess, Lindsay, she truly is. God has spoken to her too. I worked with her for a year, and then my own time came. God told me to go into the world and spread His message. I've been traveling ever since, trying to do that."

"Did the message come to you in words too?"

"Oh, yes. He told me that to tolerate sin is to sin, that His law is unchanging. He will give the world a little more time to stamp out sin, and then the cities of the deviates and those who smile upon them will be destroyed, as were Sodom and Gomorrah."

Sharon's communicant sounded more satanic than divine to Lindsay. She found herself strangely embarrassed, as if Sharon had removed all her clothes and gone parading around the cabin without them. "That's — interesting," she dissembled. "I was to meet Dirk in the lounge — oh—" she glanced at her watch and then lied, "five minutes ago."

"Would you mind if I came along?"

Lindsay would mind very much, but what on earth could she say?

Lindsay sat at table beside Evan wearing her usual muted colors, and he needed to listen closely to hear what she was saying over the more assertive tones of the others. But there was a quiet radiance to her, if one chose to see it, and beside it Sharon's prettiness was as overstated as her smile. Hamish understood what Evan was up to — he even expected it — and directed his conversation toward Milly, who was sober tonight and listening more than she spoke.

Evan asked Lindsay to dance as they left the table, and, upstairs in the lounge, Wilder watched them with the expression of a dog who had just had its dinner stolen. He approached them purposefully between songs, but Evan proposed a stroll on deck and herded Lindsay from the lounge before Wilder could reach them.

"I'm afraid you haven't taken very strongly to Dirk."

"Just now both of us are hoping for undivided attention from the same woman."

"It's more than that, I think."

"It isn't personal. My experience with those of his — profession — hasn't always been pleasant."

"He isn't with the *Sun* any more, you know. He's freelancing, hunting material on this cruise."

He was indeed; Evan would need to think about his answer to that one. For now, nature was on his side. They leaned over a railing to watch the moon's path ripple toward them, gold on obsidian. An occasional wave broke phosphorescent in the distance, and it was just cold enough to make Lindsay shiver in her light frock.

"Take my coat." He used the jacketing maneuver to pull her close, and their brief kiss was rather sweet. She moved away, though, with finality.

"No more of that, thank you very much." She knew who he was, Evan thought, and was being cute. "Not that I disliked it. What I shouldn't like is to find myself a tabloid statistic."

"Oh, that. But I haven't proposed." She laughed. "I might propose an occasional cuddle, though."

"I don't do that — anyway, not on such short notice." Predictable, he concluded. They always opted for marriage — with a Talbot. He had expected more from her and was disappointed.

"How much notice would you require?"

"More than you could give, Evan. I know what you want, and I'm not it."

Not so typical — his interest revived. "That's nice; it's more than I know. Tell me, please, what I want." She was silent for a moment, studying him, and he tried to look at her seriously, as if her answer would be important.

"You want what you're pretending — but nicely, in a different way to the pretense. You love Hamish." He gasped audibly and turned from her. "I'm sorry. I'd no right to say that, and I've hurt you."

"Not hurt, only surprised. I thought you had seen through our game."

"Is it a game? I watch people, and I find your care, your

consideration for each other — well, almost beautiful. Few of us love so kindly."

She was as direct as her eyes, perfectly sober and looking at him as if she cared very much — evasion, perhaps, but no lies. "Hamish and I have been friends more than half our lives — I suppose I *do* love him, but there's no affair, nothing physical between us."

Lindsay's darkening blush showed itself in the moonlight. "Oh, Evan, I've got this dreadful habit of bursting out with the first thought that comes into my head — and it's usually wrong, as this was. I'm so sorry." She had wanted to give; Evan put his arm round her shoulders and pressed them lightly, he hoped comfortingly. She felt small and vulnerable there.

"Please, Lindsay, no need. Why ought I be annoyed at your taking precisely the impression I tried to create? A tribute to my acting skill." Frighteningly, it was not his acting that had given him away. "I'd no idea my performance came off so well — small wonder Wilder thought he'd found a lively story." That hadn't been quite fair, but Evan was glad he had said it — Lindsay would be thrown more into Wilder's company in Evan's absence and should understand the kind of man he was.

"Dirk." She chewed on that for a moment as if she didn't like the taste of it. "So that's the sort of story he's hunting."

"He's agreed to give this one up in exchange for a better. I've had a reason for all this frou-frou, you know, and soon I'll be able to tell it to you." Feeling Lindsay press closer under his sheltering arm, Evan realized that he was lying after all.

"Lindsay."

"Mm?"

"What you said at first — about Hamish and me. There's some truth to it." He had never said it aloud and had now astonished and silenced himself. Lindsay didn't move away, though, and smiled up at him.

They were no longer alone. Sharon was suddenly, brashly beside them; they moved apart but slowly and deliberately by tacit agreement. "Oh, here you are. It's nicer than the lounge, so cool."

She placed her large forearms on the railing beside Lindsay's and stared out over the water. A bizarre girl! Evan countered her dreadful manners with bad ones.

"It *is* cold," he said. "May we dance once more, Lindsay?"

"Oh, let's do. Good night, Sharon."

They left the red-haired woman looking back toward Crete at the moonset and went downstairs where they danced until the musicians put away their instruments. Hamish was asleep when Evan returned to Hector Seven.

Ephemae, Turkey — April 1: He was dreaming a fine dream. The entire palace at Knossos had been restored and painted in vibrant primary colors, and he and Evan were learning the bull dance on an elegant tame bull.

"Hamish!" Evan was pressing his shoulder now, looking distraught. "There's some trouble. I'm sorry to waken you, but I must have the maps — where—"

"In the desk drawer." Evan unfolded the detailed map of the Mediterranean countries and spread it out on his bunk. "What's wrong?"

"I've just come from the cruise office; they're going mad down there trying to rearrange everything at a moment's notice. We're docking at Ephemae in Turkey, not at Palat."

"Why?" So it was not going to happen — Hamish's disappointment had the force of a blow. Only now did he realize how certain he had become that Evan would pull it off.

"The mullahs seem to have lost touch with reality altogether. They had some Kurdish women stoned to death in the hills above Palat because they weren't wearing the chador. The Kurds are coming down with swords and antique rifles and anything they can find, raising absolute hell, and the Shiites are loading their machine guns and putting on their white martyrs' robes. Colonel Cobb contacted Miss Shaw on the ship-to-shore and suggested that the place might not be the happiest of harbors today. Ah, Ephemae. Here it is."

Hamish rose to study the map. "So we're at full stop."

"No, now, look at this. Ephemae is — it can't be more than twenty kilometers from the border. Palat is less than forty from here. Cobb's is busing everyone nearly that distance to the digs up here at Artemion." He pointed out a dot in southeastern Turkey. "It *can* be done!"

"With everyone shooting at everyone?"

"News reports get exaggerated. If it looks like a battlefield, we'll turn back, but a little confusion might actually help us. We've dropped anchor; I'm going to try to get ashore and look for some kind of transport — and a driver who isn't

82

too well-informed. Get dressed, Hamish, and have some breakfast—"

"I'm coming with you — we agreed to share risks."

"No risk here at all, and I'm best doing this alone. They might ask for passports when I hire the car, and you can't get at yours." He folded the map and placed it in the canvas bag along with the two smaller, hand-drawn ones.

"Where's the money?"

"The chador's got all kinds of inner seams; I've tucked most of it among them."

"You won't go without me?"

"I couldn't if I chose, and I don't. Bring me a croissant or something from breakfast, will you please?"

"Where will I meet you? When?" Hamish hadn't thought they would be separated so soon, that he would need to think for himself. His fear now was of botching things.

"There's a small park at the end of the pier. I'll meet you on the far side of it in — oh, give me forty-five minutes. If I'm not there, wait." He touched Hamish's hair lightly and was gone.

Two croissants were left in the basket when breakfast was done, and Hamish pocketed them; Reg saw him and raised his thick eyebrows. "Planning a picnic?"

"Sort of. We may stay at Ephemae and not go on to Artemion. Evan and I are very interested in contemporary Turkey, you know and—" He must stop this damned chattering — the more one lied, the feebler the lie became.

Reg looked like a bloody computer, all right, one that was about to spew out an answer. "If," he said, "this might be the sort of picnic at which you could use some help, I'd be very happy—"

"Oh, thank you very much, but — not that sort of thing at all." Hamish rose and made his escape to Hector Seven. This last idiocy had not only compounded but seemed to have completed the effect of his other blunders. He could only hope that Evan had been right as usual, and that Reg was trustworthy.

Hamish inserted the croissants into the yellow canvas bag, shouldered it, opened the door to the corridor and then closed it again. He made use of the toilet; he hardly wanted to have to interrupt the day's proceedings when they were in full swing.

He heard Miss Shaw's voice from the cruise office when

he was still on the stairway. "—won't crowd 280 people onto five buses. You'll damned well find a sixth one if you expect Cobb's to stop at Ephemae again." Hamish saw that her face was self-possessed, almost serene, despite the urgent tones; she gave him a quick smile as he took his landing tag and started down the gangplank. "Of course six of them, one for each bus; no, a French-speaking guide won't do at all."

Two uniformed men nodded Hamish on indifferently from the small customs shed at the pier. It was as Evan had said — anyone with a Cobb's carrying case could go anywhere. He walked into a park where conifers and blossoming red-buds — flowering Judas, they called them here — crowded each other, and Evan appeared beside him from nowhere before he was across it.

"You're early. Marvelous!" He was glowing with achievement. "Come see what I've found for us."

It was an almost new brown Mercedes, one of the big ones. The driver who stood beside it was well over six feet and stoutly built, though not obese; his flesh looked hard and solid. He reminded Hamish of someone, not pleasantly, with his dull, muddy eyes close-set in a beefy face. Hamish stepped toward the car.

"Not yet. We've got to change clothes first, I'm afraid — we're crossing the border in chadri. There's a public lavatory back among the trees." They turned onto an overgrown path leading to a cream-colored circular building.

"Absolutely ridiculous question, but — Men's or Women's? We'll go in as one sort and come out —"

"Women's, I think. No one's about now, but someone might appear."

The odor inside was almost intolerable; Hamish gagged. "No running water, you see," Evan told him. "Can't be helped." The toilets were holes in the floor flanked by styrofoam footrests. "Best strip all the way. These things are hot, and the absence of underwear won't be noticed."

They hung the chadri from hooks on the way and undressed directly into the carrying cases to avoid contact between clothing and floor. Hamish watched Evan from the corner of his eye. Clothed, he had a strong, wiry look despite his slightness; now he appeared merely thin and terrifyingly vulnerable. Hamish thought of a film he had seen recently about an American who spent five terrible years in a Turkish prison, and had his first deep stab of fear for both of them.

They helped each other adjust the chadri, and long blue eyes locked unexpectedly with Hamish's. They were in each other's arms, then, Evan's body pressed tight against his, Evan's head nuzzling into his cheek. Quite as suddenly, they were three feet apart. "For luck," Evan said.

"For luck," Hamish repeated dumbly as they walked through the wood to the waiting Mercedes. His fear was gone.

The driver opened the door for them and grunted unsmiling to Hamish's thanks. Hamish placed the resemblance; it was to the villainous prison commandant in the Turkish film. "Does he speak English?"

"No. I remarked in conversational tones that the back seat was on fire; he didn't turn his head. A bit sinister, isn't he?" Evan read Hamish's concern, "but his was the only car that looked really reliable."

They drove from the quay through winding streets constricted by low, shabby mud houses — slum streets, but the school children swarming along them were neat and rosy-cheeked. "What's his name? How did you arrange with him?"

"Mohamad, of course. I hired and briefed him through a trilingual shoeshine boy who wanted to come with us. He knew too much, though; Mohamad seems conveniently dense."

They had reached a shopping area, its open stalls narrowing the street to a single lane. The driver's method of passage was to press on the horn and sustain a steady speed of about thirty miles per hour. Hamish went rigid, closing his eyes, as shoppers scattered before them like terrified fowl. This cringing before the first imagined danger wouldn't do, Hamish thought, determined to bear himself in a way that would justify Evan's trust. "Their dress is very colorful," he said, pleased that his voice sounded cool and self-possessed. "I don't think the chador is going to catch on here, do you?"

"I can't look. I'm too busy praying for their deliverance from the Mercedes."

The town ended abruptly, and they passed small farms, less prosperous than the ones in Crete, their fields worked by an occasional man with a mule or a tiny tractor but largely by women in pantaloons and bright kerchiefs.

"They *are* a colorful lot," Evan agreed belatedly, in the nonchalant drawl he used to hide excitement or anxiety.

85

Hamish grinned inside his veil — Evan was showing off too.

Two low stucco buildings grew in size on an otherwise flat horizon, one flying the Turkish crescent, the other the black sphinx of Tariq on its field of gold. Mohamad stopped beside the Turkish one and disappeared inside it.

"What is he doing?"

"He's explaining that we are two important women who must see someone important in Tariq — secretly. He's saying that we'll return in a few hours, and he's handing out money in lieu of passports."

The driver came out and nodded to them. Evan sighed. "Halfway now."

Mohamad opened the door to the second building and leaned inward, then turned back toward the car, his arms extended, palms up.

"What does he mean? Won't they talk to him?"

"I don't—" Evan began. "My God, he means there's no one there."

Evan had known that he couldn't plan for every contingency, but this one, which made entry to Tariq so much easier, theatened chaos. According to Peter's sources, every border point was tightly monitored, and this one would twice have been the major barrier to their altered plan — its desertion frightened Evan deeply. Perhaps Palat and the prison had been abandoned as well.

How would the Shiites leave it? The retreating forces of the Emir had left thcir prisoners alive, but they had been few, and the officials who stayed had hoped only to dissociate themselves from earlier murders. This lot, who preached to a majority that mercy to heretics was heresy, would be capable of any kind of savagery.

Evan was glad that Hamish couldn't see his face. He was looking out the window at the largely unfarmed desert. An occasional roughly cultivated patch appeared; on one of them, a single woman in chador pushed a wooden plow. "Jesus, how can she stand it?" Hamish murmured. "Must be ninety degrees out there."

There were no vehicles on the road, and no further signs of habitation for miles. A mud hut thatched with straw appeared then, and another, but they were deserted.

"I suppose a new sex change is in order before we reach the prison."

"I don't know." Hamish wasn't understanding it, Evan thought, and perhaps for now, that was best. He tapped Mohamad on the shoulder, motioned for him to stop and moved into the front seat, unfolding the street map of Palat. They passed age-eroded mud houses with increasing frequency, then a stripped, ravaged bazaar. A skeletal cat raced across their path, its flurry of motion accenting the lifelessness around it.

"It's the poorest, saddest place I've ever seen," Hamish mused. "Do you realize we haven't seen one painted wall, one flower, any attempt at ornamentation whatever?" Evan, directing the driver through progressively narrower and more wretched streets, didn't answer.

Something like a fast-flying insect buzzed behind him, and he looked back to watch cracks spread outward from a small round hole in the window near Hamish's head.

"All right?"

"Rather exciting," Hamish said calmly. "I've never been shot at before."

The Turk, though, wore a fixed look of fright and pressed down on the accelerator, shaking his head when Evan motioned for a turn. Evan took the revolver from its case and gently prodded his knee with it; he made the turn, and the prison was before them.

"Evan, it's wide open!" A rusted metal gate, topped with barbed wire, sagged inward. The Mercedes stopped before it.

A stench of death enveloped them as they opened the car doors. Hamish's eyes, wide and wild, met Evan's through eyeslits; he understood now. Evan took the car keys, inserting them into a seam in the right sleeve of his chador, and replaced the revolver in its case; there seemed to be no further argument in the driver, who looked sick.

A very old building to the left of the gate was the prison's headquarters. The gold and black flag sagged limply from its top, and a blind sandstone sphinx appeared to have died centuries before beneath it. Its heavy door was ajar, two of its three small windows broken, and it was empty of life or furnishings. Evan and Hamish walked through it and out a side door that led into a central courtyard; the stench had warned but not prepared them for what it held.

There seemed to be movement, and, side by side, they tensed against each other, but it came only from the rise of clouds of flies. Colors sorted themselves out, the grey of prison uniforms, black of hair and flies and everywhere the rust of dried blood and torn flesh.

"Wait here," Evan said. "I'll look."

"No, both of us will look."

Simon's was not among the bodies nearest them; these lay singly, face up, only their blood mingling on the tan stones. Those in the center, though, had fallen across and over each other and would need to be moved. They used their hands; to prod and shift with feet seemed a new violation. The bodies were limp, rigor having passed, but not yet bloated; given the heat, Evan would guess they had been dead a day or less despite the smell. The flies clung stubbornly to their meals, and Evan saw Hamish flick one off a wide brown eye and pull long-lashed lids over it and its fellow. The still childish mouth beneath them was rounded in terror.

"That was a good thing to do. I'm glad you did that."

"He looked as if he still saw it."

"Simon's not here."

"There are more on the other side."

"All black-haired and — half-grown like these. Oh, God." There was no time to indulge the nausea churning at Evan's throat. "Let's have a look inside the buildings." He took the prison map from the yellow case. "Six of them, built in a square around this yard. We'll go clockwise."

The cell doors in the first block were open, the cells stripped; water trickled from a faucet above a dented basin. They washed their hands there, unable to get at their sweating faces through the chadri. The second block, identical except for the absence of a wash basin, was empty as well. "Do you think they took him with them?" Hamish asked.

"Possibly." That, by now, seemed to Evan one of the more hopeful alternatives.

The door to the third block, an infirmary according to the map, was closed. Evan drew the Luger, slowly turned a filth-encrusted knob and drew the door outward, pressing himself and Hamish behind it. He heard nothing and peered around. It was then that he saw Simon lying on a cot directly opposite the door.

He had been sleeping, but the slight sound awakened him, and he turned toward them. "Water. Please give us some water." Evan knelt beside him and felt his head; it was terribly hot, and his breathing was ragged and rasping. He pled in a foreign language then, probably again for water. There had been a tap — no, God only knew what form of bacteria bred in it. There was a canteen in the car.

"I'll get water, Hamish. Get him into your chador."

Evan ran to the Mercedes, his head churning with urgency to escape Palat before the Kurds arrived or the Shiites returned, joy at finding life in Simon and anxiety about sustaining it. Would Simon be able to walk, and, if not, how could he be transported undetected onto the ship? Evan opened the passenger door and found himself suspended suddenly a foot above the ground and shaken until his teeth rattled.

He went limp and slid out of the chador, realizing too late that it was what he had been meant to do. He lay on the ground, looking up at the still expressionless Mohamad, who now held the chador, the car keys and all their money.

Or almost all — the violent shaking had sent two bundles of it out onto the cobblestones, and one had broken apart. A desert wind blew paper dinares toward the broken prison gate, and the driver pursued them. Evan used his diversion to scramble to his hands and knees and grasp the sleeve of the garment the Turk dragged behind him. He found the keys and managed to extricate them just as Mohamad felt his pull on the chador.

Evan popped the keys into his mouth between his teeth and his cheek and tried to get to his feet to run from the enemy looming over him, but the Turk got a finger inside the loop of his earring and reached out for the rest of him. Evan threw his weight away from the Turk, who pulled mightily at the same time. The ear gave way, and he was freed — long enough to roll under the Mercedes.

"Hamish, Hamish, bring the gun—" he screamed.

Hamish pulled off the chador and took his slacks from the carrying case. The glittering eyes in the gaunt, bearded face focused on him then. "Bloody Christ, it's you! And the other one was Davie."

"That was Davie. We're taking you home."

"Mikhail as well?" he pleaded.

Hamish, pulling on his slacks, became aware of a figure prone on the next cot, its ruined back giving off an echo of the odor from the courtyard. He touched the undamaged skin at the neck, beneath the blond hair; it was cold. He lifted a bloodless hand, and the entire body, still as a statue's, shifted with it. "He isn't alive, Simon."

"I don't believe you. I almost had him standing — I won't go without him." Simon turned his face away and held his arms under his body so that Hamish couldn't dress him.

"He's quite stiff and cold, honestly, Simon."

"It isn't true," he whimpered, but let himself go limp so that Hamish was able to pull the chador over his head. It was then that he heard the high, distant call. He eased Simon down and ran for the gate.

"Hamish! Ha—" He saw only the driver, lying on the cobblestones and trying to insert his bulk beneath the car. "Gun, Hamish, get gun!" The cries came from under the Mercedes. It was too late to go back for the gun. The monster had a hold on Evan now and was pulling; the last yell had been one of pain.

Hamish took a run at the man on the ground and landed a kick at the V between the huge legs. The driver roared and snapped into a fetal position, rocking back and forth on the stones. That wouldn't last. Hamish pried a cobblestone from the ground and drove it down beside the man's left ear. The monster regarded him balefully, rocking and groaning. He hit again, harder, and the creature subsided onto the dusty street.

Evan scrabbled from under the car, got to his hands and knees and stayed there, only shaking his head until Hamish pulled him upright. He was naked, and the right side of his face, neck and shoulder were awash with blood. "Oh, Jesus. Oh, Jesus." Hamish pulled him close and held him hopelessly, feeling Evan's blood run down his chest. Evan leaned on him for a moment, his breathing fast and shallow, and then pulled himself away.

"It isn't that bad. Ears bleed a lot." He was speaking peculiarly; he reached inside his cheek and pulled out the keys to the Mercedes. "Keep them, please." He knelt beside the monster, feeling inside its shirt.

"Is he breathing?"

"To hell with his breathing," Evan gasped. "I want our money." He withdrew five wads of dinares. "Yes. He's breathing only too well. Take these. I've no place to put them."

"Let me look at you." Hamish grasped Evan's shoulders and saw that the right earlobe had been torn through and was bleeding steadily onto his neck and shoulder. "Take it between your fingers and pinch, just above the tear. Can you hold it that way?"

"Yes." He had gone very quiet and obedient suddenly and held the ear tight between thumb and forefinger. The bleeding slowed. Hamish turned him round, inspecting scrapes and bruises.

"What happened to your back?"

"Something under the car when he tried to pull me out. I thought I was finished, Hamish — would have been finished without you."

Hamish unlocked the boot and drew out a tire iron which he gave to Evan. "Watch your Turk; if he moves, hit him with this. Now get back into the chador while I fetch Simon."

"Bring me the gun. I'd best finish him so he can't raise an alarm."

"What could he alarm here? And there are enough corpses without him."

"Yes. All right." Evan leaned against the car.

"I'll take his shoes, though; Simon has none." They were loafers and slipped off easily; Hamish took the canteen as well.

Simon was standing, looking at the body of his friend, tears streaming down his wasted cheeks. "Mikhail is dead," he told Hamish. "I knew you were coming; I dreamt it. But I thought you'd be on time. Why weren't you on time?" Fevered and irrational as he was, he had understood the need for the chador and was in it. Hamish gave him water through the eyeslit.

He was able to bear some of his own weight and move his legs along as Hamish supported him to the Mercedes. He caught sight of the bloodied Evan through the eyeslit then and moaned, collapsing face down across the back seat before Hamish could push his legs inside.

Evan hardly moved at all, had only sagged further over the bonnet of the car. "I told you," Hamish berated, "you've got to get into that chador."

"No need. You're the one who'll be wearing it. I've got to get into my clothes." He made no move toward the yellow case, though, and regarded Hamish vaguely, still pinching his ear. It had stopped bleeding, but his face was white and beaded with sweat.

"It's got to be you in this. You're not fit to drive, and we have to pass the checkpoint."

"I see. Yes." Evan let Hamish pull the chador over his head, holding his arms out like a child helping to dress itself. His skin felt cold in the afternoon heat — shock. There were two casualties now and only Hamish to cope. He propped them against each other as best he could in the back seat.

"Try and keep Simon sitting up," he told Evan. "He'll breathe more easily."

"He can't," Simon mourned. "Don't you see how hurt he is?"

"He's only stunned; you'll see, he'll be fine soon."

"All right now, only a little muddled. I think the Turk addled my brains." Evan slid his left arm behind and around Simon, holding him upright.

The car started instantly. Hamish tried to make out the map on the seat beside him, then realized that, if he kept bearing downhill toward the sea, he couldn't miss the way. "Keep your heads low for a little," he warned, remembering the single shot. A shadow shifted behind a glassless, curtainless window, and, a block away, something moved a few feet inside a recessed doorway; there were people in Palat, hiding and waiting. They passed the mud shell from which the shot had come and the empty bazaar, and Hamish turned right onto a road which, having two lanes, was unmistakably arterial.

Bits of life showed now like a turtle's nose from its carapace. A rickety farm cart and an ancient Volkswagen passed them going the other way, and Hamish remembered in time to take the right hand lane. They reached open country, and he fumbled inside his hand case until he found the crumpled croissants. He passed them back to Evan.

"How the devil—" The muffled voice was now recognizable as Simon's, and he sounded hungry. Hamish's spirits rose.

"Through the eye slit," Evan answered thinly. Hamish, at ease now with the Mercedes, watched them from the rearview mirror. If they could eat, perhaps they could walk; he began to allow himself hope.

Several horsemen approached then across the seared countryside, and Hamish pushed down on the accelerator. They were waving rifles in the air, and the wind generated by their speed sent the horses' manes and tails and the long

92

scarves wrapped round the riders' heads flowing straight out behind them. He passed the section of road where they would have intersected before they could reach it.

"Jesus! Did you see them?"

"No, what?" It was Simon who answered. "I had the croissant where my eyes ought to have been."

"I thought we'd driven onto the set of 'Lawrence of Arabia.' Horsemen, with guns and things."

"Oh, God, Kurds. I've no idea how they'll feel about all this, and I'm not curious. Can you go any faster?"

Hamish got the Mercedes up to 80 mph, then slowed slightly; the road was quite awful, and it sounded as if something important had been knocked loose at the last pothole. "Evan?"

"He's asleep." Hamish saw the black cloak sagging against the door, and Simon must have read his alarm in the mirror. "He's breathing," he said, gathering up the chador so that it rested against his shoulder, "but he's awfully cold."

Hamish's spirits dove again. If they weren't captured by hostile nomads or arrested by the Turks at the checkpoint, he was still faced with the problem of bearing his wounded onto the Alexandros from the quay, where discovery would be equally disastrous. The small buildings with their two flags grew before him, more sinister and secretive than they had looked before. The border police might shoot if he made a dash for it. Hamish had to hope that Mohamad had paid for a two-way passage.

He slowed the car to jogging speed. The building beneath the sphinx remained empty, but he could see two men inside the Turkish one. They turned their backs deliberately at sight of the car and appeared to busy themselves with something on the opposite wall. He let himself breathe again a hundred yards or so past the checkpoint and slowly allowed the Mercedes to gather speed.

"Simon, dear old chap, we're not in Tariq any longer, we've crossed the border." He had only a long sigh for an answer.

Traffic thickened as they moved from the outskirts of Ephemae to its center, heavier than it had been in the morning. Hamish, no master of aggressive driving, found himself blocked for minutes at a time. The pier came into sight at last and the beautiful, towering Alexandros. Six buses, empty, lumbered past the car. After Miss Shaw had called their names and numbers a few times, the ship would, as she had warned them often enough, simply lift anchor and sail without them.

Evan awakened. "You're driving too close!" he cried. "We've got to change clothes, you and I!" His voice was fuzzy, almost drunken.

"We're not going to do that, we haven't time. You always said we must be flexible, and this is it." He stopped the car, as near to the gangplank as he could park it. "Get out. I've got to see if you can walk together."

"I'm walking alone. You're walking with Simon."

"I don't think you can walk at all." Evan could stand, at least. "All right. Lean on him, Simon, and take a few steps." They moved unsteadily, like two drunks in drag — precisely as they ought to look, it couldn't have been better. Hamish took the map of Turkey from one of the yellow bags, then slung both over Evan's free shoulder and pressed the two landing tags into his hand. He leaped behind the wheel of the still-running Mercedes.

"No," Evan wailed, "you haven't a passport. Hamish, come back!"

He drove out of their sight, then turned round and parked behind a taxi to watch the uneven progress of his friends toward the gangplank.

7

At Sea: Max felt grubby after the long hike up and down the five hills of Artemion. He had worn the wrong shoes, and the outside of his left foot seemed partially worn away, but he was too tired to take the extra steps to Hector Six and change into easier ones. He sank down in the lounge between Sarah and Milly.

The bar boy, who was also their cabin steward, stopped beside him. "Scotch please, Georgi."

"You won't get ice, you know, unless you ask for it," Sarah said, but Georgi was gone. She was savoring her own undiluted whisky, looking as effortlessly well-groomed as she had in the morning — in contrast to Milly who had dust on one cheek and whose hairdo was out of balance.

"I didn't, honestly," Milly was protesting to Reg. "I only take the ones that are loose on the ground and too worn down to be reconstructed." Reg had been teasing her about her potsherd collection, saying it was in violation of international law, and she hadn't tumbled to it.

"There's a complaint from the captain as well," Reg went on, "he claims the Alexandros has begun listing to port since you and Lindsay began your collections."

Milly caught it now and began to laugh. "Seriously, though. It's exciting to hold something in your hand and wonder about the people who held it centuries and centuries ago." Max wished she wouldn't throw herself into things with such abandon; it left her, at the moment, with all the dignity of a grubby ten-year-old.

Miss Shaw's voice filled the lounge. "Will passengers holding landing tags 221 and 256 please report immediately to the cruise office?"

"I'm afraid they'll have short shrift today after Miss Shaw's problems of the morning," Sarah said.

"The woman's a magician," Milly bubbled. "How she managed to arrange the day on such short notice, and so beautifully—"

Max gave her one of his down-Milly-down looks; she understood it and composed her face into blandness. "I suppose I should remove some of this Turkish soil before the party," she said, rising. She had spent much of the afternoon questioning George Hodgkins about the Alexandrian period, Max remembered, and had gotten herself invited to the small birthday celebration the professor had planned for his son.

"Odd." Reg was thoughtful. "Everyone came onto the ship directly from the buses." He drew the passenger list from his pocket and studied it.

"Perhaps they forgot to replace their tags when they boarded," Sarah volunteered.

"Evan." Reg frowned over the list. "Number 256 is Evan."

"Your wandering boys. I think you've appointed yourself protector." Sarah looked irritable and, unusually, quite unamused.

"Old school ties, you know."

"Those boys went to Steppingford? How on earth did you know?"

"I keep up with things there. I knew all the Talbots had—"

"Mr. Hamish Saunders. Mr. Evan Talbot. Report to the cruise desk immediately." The loudspeaker voice would cut diamonds.

"When I recognized Evan, I remembered the other boy. Hamish and Simon Roud divided most of the prizes that year."

"Roud." Max placed the name. "The journalist who's in prison—"

"Good lord, look at that!" Max followed Sarah's astonished gesture toward the window.

"Muslim women, in chador. I was surprised not to see more of them at Ephemae."

"No. Look at the Cobb's cases. And the shoes. And the staggers." The two black-cloaked figures moved uncertainly onto the gangplank, watched by three wide-eyed sailors and a catatonic first mate. "I'd say your prize-winning student and distinguished Talbot were letting down the old school tie a bit, Reg."

Reg didn't wait to hear her out but left them in a rush; they heard his footsteps drumming down the stairs and then watched the sour little farce from the window. The figure Max took to be Hamish, the taller — much taller for some reason in this garb — was also the drunker and wavered uncertainly from Evan's inadequate support toward the outer edge of the gangplank and the water beneath. Reg appeared beside them and helped to support him, and Evan, relieved of part of his weight, tilted and came near going over the guard rail on the other side. Reg caught him, and the three continued their irregular progress, Reg propelling his charges by their elbows.

"I've got to see all of this, I don't believe it," Sarah said. Max followed her from the lounge to the stairwell which looked down upon Heracles deck and the cruise ofice. The robed figures wobbled aboard, and the smaller stopped at the cruise desk to replace, with deliberation, two landing tags. Miss Shaw regarded them with the open-mouthed immobility of an ice maiden. Reg, still supporting elbows, guided them up the stairs, past Max and Sarah, whom none of them seemed to see, and to the corridor that led to their cabin.

Evan stopped. "Good of you, Reg. Thank you very much."

"Nonsense. I'd like to be of some real help."

A low gasp, almost a moan, came from the larger chador. "I— oh, God, Reg, please," the smaller whimpered, and the three disappeared inside Hector Seven.

A few drops of room temperature Scotch still waited in their glasses, and Max and Sarah tossed them off wordlessly. "I think another might be in order."

"Never more so," Sarah murmured, and Max signaled to the steward just as Milly reappeared in her newest dress, vibrating again with enthusiasm.

"Don't wait for me for dinner, dear. We may take the buffet," she told him and was gone before he could answer.

He anticipated regaling her with the chador incident, which confirmed all his instincts about Evan, to whom she had taken an inordinate fancy. Max was a little disappointed in the other boy — he had given an impression of dignity and decency. Hamish had been made drunk, he imagined, and then persuaded to take part in some nasty shore game dreamed up by Evan. It had been a dangerous game. Hamish's pace and posture showed pain as well as drunkenness, Max was sure, and the corridor wall where Evan had leaned briefly was blood-smeared. Surprising they hadn't gotten themselves killed.

"It isn't easy being married to a saint," Sarah signed, tossing off half her second Scotch at a gulp. "His tolerance — oh, he hates that word, says it's patronizing — is a bit much at times. He sees a lot of queers, working in the theater, and maintains that they're often more talented than the rest of us. That's all well and good, but the sort that we dine and travel and work with are people — I mean people first and queers parenthetically. This awful boy—"

"I know what you mean," Max said. "The flamboyance."

"That's the word — one of our jet set types who set out to explore every sensation as publicly as possible."

"Strange. On our side of the world we get quite a different impression of the Talbot family."

"Not strange at all. I suppose one oughtn't repeat it, but—" Sarah leaned toward Max, her eyes sparking mischief. "Oh, no harm, I think — Lady Barbara is dead, after all. It's thought by those who knew the family that this boy is what we might call a catch colt."

Max understood her, but the relish she took from gossip amused him, and he put on a look of interested incomprehension.

"That's paddock language you wouldn't follow. What I mean is that Evan's birth was oddly timed in relation to one of Sir Francis's expeditions, and Barbara's social life was original, not to say creative. At the time, there was talk of a Welsh actor, much younger, named, strangely, Evan Davies. I worked twice with him, and he absolutely glistened onstage, though he was no larger than this Evan — and very like him.

"Max, thank you so much for the drink," she said, tossing off the rest of it and rising. "That was really quite naughty of me. Poor Davies is dead as well now, killed in a car crash years ago."

"Not at all. In fact, you've restored my respect for the legitimate Talbots."

Left alone, he finished his whisky and stood up, feeling the scrape of his shoe against his foot and catching a faint odor of sweat from his own moving body. It was time for a long hot shower. The door to Hector Six, when he tried it, was locked, and Milly had taken the key up to Achilles Deck. Max didn't want to walk that far nor to break in on a party to which he had not been invited. Georgi would have an extra key.

It took him ten minutes, though, to trace the cabin steward, who had been replaced as bar boy, and by the time Max gained entrance to his room and the anticipated shower, there was no more hot water. The spray went from tepid to icy before the dust and sweat of Artemion could be washed away, and he turned it off, deciding to shave over the sink. Milly came in.

"Forget something?" he asked with sarcasm.

"No, *I* didn't, but George certainly — oh, I forgot to leave you the key. I'm sorry, dear." She was bubbling still and not sorry at all. Max was angry at her for accepting an invitation from which he had been excluded, at her thoughtlessness in locking the cabin, at the disordered pattern of the entire afternoon.

"If you think *I'm* absent-minded," she went on, "imagine what it must be like to be married to George Hodgkins. He ordered the cake and ice cream and all, and it was quite pretty, but he forgot to invite Robin. We ended having the party without the guest of honor, who had disappeared somewhere with the oldest Berwick boy."

"Mmf." The cold lather felt stiff on his face. "You missed another little drama while you were dressing. Your 'disciplined, sensitive' artist and his friend—"

"If you mean that business with the chadors, I saw it through the porthole. Max, I don't think that was what it appeared to be—"

"Well, what in hell *do* you think?"

In Hector Seven, the subject of their conversation was washing too. His voice sounded through the thin partition. "No, of course we can't bring the ship's doctor into it." Blurred sounds, presumably from Hamish, came from the bedroom. "I suppose you're right," Evan answered. "We'll have to use Max."

Use? A tingling began in Max's wrists and continued upward until his temples were pounding. "I don't really know what was happening," Milly said mulishly, "and neither do you."

"Oh, yes I do." He turned off the water and pitched his voice low and clear to carry. "A nasty little pervert was playing a nasty game of dress up. I think he found more trouble than he bargained for."

The silence that fell behind the partition was as complete and full as an answer. Max had been heard.

Milly opened her mouth, appraised him and closed it. "I'm going down to Heracles Deck and buy some postcards," she told him. He was alone then when the rapping began. He put an arm into the shirt Milly had set out for him and inserted the other as he opened the door.

"We need your help, Max. Rather urgently." Reg's face was set and serious.

"Look." He buttoned the shirt without haste. "I know those boys have had trouble, but there's a ship's doctor. I simply don't want to be involved in this distasteful little business."

"The business in Hector Seven is neither small nor distasteful. As a personal favor, Max—" Begging did not come easily to Reg, who reddened visibly. Max drew the Black Bag from under his bunk, relenting wordlessly, and followed him to the adjoining cabin.

Evan, dressed normally, opened the door. He was paper white, and his ear was torn raggedly.

"You *have* had trouble. Sit down, and we'll see to that."

"It can wait. Please." He was pointing at the bunk nearest the door. Max saw chestnut hair.

"That's not Hamish."

Dinner began with only the four women at the table. Milly and Sarah were all smiles, talking over the events of the day and enjoying one another's company. It would be pleasant, Lindsay thought, to have a friend with whom to share the color and stimulation of the cruise.

A day before, Dirk would seem to have answered nicely — as a reformed peddler of gossip, he was not merely acceptable but attractive. As an unregenerate one, though, he would be best avoided. As for her cabin-mate, Lindsay wished her back in Florida.

As the ruined Palace of Minos had done yesterday, the remains of Artemion had set Sharon off on God's plans to destroy the cities of sin, but this time she saw Lindsay's unresponsive abstraction and, for the first time, put religion aside for several hours. The rest of the morning and early afternoon had been lovely, the two young women tramping over the ancient hills, questioning their guide, collecting potsherds and history. Sharon was not a quick learner, but she had been cheerful and curious, actually good company.

After Artemion, the two went up to Achilles Deck to eat Italian ice. The ice was delicious, and they laid their potsherd collections out upon the table, savoring them as well. Without warning, Sharon's face transformed itself into a tragic mask.

"I can't bear it." The words seemed to have been torn from her.

"Sharon, what is it?" Lindsay's eyes followed the staring brown ones down from the deck toward the gangplank and the two figures in chadri. Reg appeared then and began to guide them onto the ship.

"How can he touch them? Do you understand what's happened?"

"Not really."

"Deviates dress that way — like women — and then solicit men as if they were prostitutes. They go to hotel rooms or bathrooms and — and then they do the unspeakable things that they do."

"Just how do you know that, Sharon?" Lindsay asked and then wished that she hadn't spoken at all.

"Oh, I know. When I was working with Gwen in Florida, a pervert sent us the most hideous thing I have every seen: a picture of two nude men doing — what they do. I have never been able to get it out of my mind; Gwen and I both still see it when we close our eyes."

Lindsay wanted to wash, as if she had stumbled into one of the boggy patches in that pretentiously pure mind and been dirtied by it. The woman was actually weeping now, her head thrown back, tears running down the tilted cheeks; she cried beautifully, like a painted saint.

"When I think how such a sight must hurt Christ Jesus — as if nails were being driven again into his body — I could kill."

The gun! Lindsay's embarrassed disgust turned to horror — and such fear for Evan that she almost told what she knew: that the chadri were not drag but disguise and that the larger man, who was inches taller than Reg, was most certainly not Hamish.

"I didn't mean that," Sharon hastened to explain. "I don't hate *them*, you know, only their sin. It's their sin I could kill."

Lindsay was not reassured, but the temptation to tell Sharon anything passed with her first guess at what Evan might be up to and her quick certainty that it was a serious business.

"Seating seems to be flexible tonight. May I?" Dirk Wilder appeared, leaning over the empty chair beside Lindsay, just as the starters were being cleared away. She had managed to avoid him all day since Evan's revelation, hiding behind Sharon whom she knew he disliked, but now she decided that the company even of a tabloid reporter would be better than that of her cabin-mate.

She let him shepherd her to the lounge after dinner. The band hadn't yet formed. "A stroll on deck?" he suggested tentatively. Lindsay had brought a sweater this time and agreed.

"I was afraid you wouldn't come with me," he told her as they looked out across the water.

"Why?"

"I suppose Talbot told you about me — that I still deal in gossip."

"Your means of livelihood aren't my concern." She heard her own voice, cool and patronizing, and wanted to slap herself.

"What he didn't tell you — doesn't know — is that it's only one more time. There's an opening on a magazine, rather a good one, and it's mine if I can come up with something impressive within the next few days."

"I do wish you luck." That had sounded better.

"How much do you know about Talbot?"

Was she being pumped or did she detect a note of jealousy? "Only that he dances awfully well."

"Do you know who he is?" She nodded. "And that this faggot performance is completely fraudulent? You wouldn't know what the little drama in the chadors this afternoon was in aid of?"

"I couldn't imagine. Completely mystified."

"Well, I'll simply have to wait. He's promised to let me in on it later. Lindsay—" The moon shone on the clear skin and good bones of his face, and Lindsay had a ridiculous impulse to touch his cheek. "Oh, I have no right to say this."

"Please say away now that you've begun."

"You do know that he's involved with someone again — very seriously this time?"

So it had been jealousy. "He made that clear the first time we talked."

"Ah, truce on Talbot, then. Will you dance with me, Lindsay?"

"How does this sound? 'We have the shipment you wanted from Tariq and will deliver it April 6th at Piraeus. Signed, David and Hamish.' Do you think they'll understand it?" Simon was concerned about getting word to his family without revealing his presence on the ship.

The young journalist had a magnificent constitution and would probably have recovered without Max's attention or the antibiotics from the Black Bag. It would have been a slow business, though, and Max took considerable satisfaction from the clear eyes and steady hands with which Simon studied and then devoured the late snack they had brought from the buffet — less than five hours after the first penicillin shot.

"They'll understand," Evan answered. "Let's insert 'in good condition,' though. 'Shipment' might sound a bit sinister without it. Reg, would you please send it for us? I'm not quite ready to face Miss Shaw."

"Delighted," Reg said, yawning. "Then I think I'll be off to bed. Max?"

"Simon should have another shot at eleven. Then we can all sleep." Reg left them. "Evan, is the ear giving you trouble? I have some medication for pain."

"No, thank you very much, I think I shall sleep through anything."

The ear had begun to bleed again during Max's first examination of Simon, and Evan had disappeared, returning with it already stitched.

"No reason I couldn't go to the ship's doctor," he had told a solicitous Reg. "He thinks I'm a nasty piece of work, but no matter."

"God, Evan," Reg had protested, "the boy is barely out of the egg. You ought to have waited for Max."

"I've imposed upon Max enough, I think."

Max had been sorry then, for the bathroom outburst, as Evan had no doubt meant him to be. He consoled himself with the truth that Evan had worked hard at seeming precisely what Max had called him.

Simon dozed off, and the uncomfortable silence between Max and Evan — ought Max to apologize or to pretend nothing had happened? — stretched the waiting minutes. Then, as Max prepared the eleven-o'clock injection, Reg reappeared at the door. He looked smug.

"Some interesting news. I sent the cable, then was able to reach Colonel Cobb on the ship-to-shore — he's an old friend from the war days." Max granted Reg a right to smugness; Cobb was not only brilliant in his present field but was said to have been one of the brightest stars of British Intelligence during World War II.

"By happy coincidence, he told me, the government employees in Athens have scheduled a strike for April 5th — the museums, the Acropolis and all will be closed. Since Athens is more or less the *pièce de résistance* of the cruise, we've been rerouted; we're sailing straight to Piraeus."

Something was wrong with Evan; his body stiffened, his eyes rolled back as if, Max thought, he was going into a seizure. "What is it, Evan?"

"Hamish." It was a cry of almost animal anguish. "He was to meet us at Antalya."

And so Max felt vindicated; as he had thought from the first, the pretense had been the actuality carried to its extreme. "Simon needs medical attention," he said harshly, "and not from a vacationing internist's Black Bag. This is a stroke of luck we couldn't have expected and should be appreciated. Your misplaced friend is not noticeably retarded and can find the ship."

Reg sat down beside Evan, a comforting arm around his shoulders. "Has Hamish a map?"

"Yes." Evan recovered himself. "Oh, I know this is best for Simon. But Hamish is — not a traveler. He's never left England before save for a few visits to his family in Scotland. I brought him into this, and I was to have been where he is; I got a second passport to use in Turkey, learnt the roads. But he drove off—"

"How is the car?" Reg asked.

"Good, too good. I ought to have killed that bastard driver, I knew it then. He'll be back in Turkey now and have

104

reported it missing. The Turks will find out what we did and they'll hunt down the car—"

"You and I will go down to the cruise desk now, Evan," Reg soothed. "We'll use the ship-to-shore again, and we'll see that someone is waiting for Hamish at Antalya. He may reach Piraeus before we do."

At Sea — April 2: The alarm clock had been knocked to the floor during the night's heavy seas and rolled beneath Evan's bunk. It lay just out of his reach now, ringing out the time for Simon's morning antibiotic. Evan scrambled after it, hating the broken silence but grateful for the end of night. That had been quite awful, his waking fears for Hamish punctuated by ugly dreams.

In the one he remembered, his father had found him *in flagrante delicto* with someone and then — it had been the American doctor, of course, and his use of the old, nightmare words, the ones Francis had used when Evan was twelve and had been caught with Geordie from the stable.

"Simon." The shoulder that had felt like a stove top yesterday was no warmer than Evan's hand, and the flush had left Simon's cheeks. "You've got to have another of these horse pills." The things were nearly an inch long and luridly colored.

"First a visit to the loo if you don't mind." Evan supported him there and waited while he urinated.

"Better?"

"Oh, much. Finest sleep ever." He got back to bed without help and Evan dispensed the capsule. "One awful dream, though. Mikhail. I dreamt I'd got him from the prison, but I'd hurt him some way, and he was screaming as he did when they beat him. One hates remembering him so."

"You won't after a bit." Evan dredged up a memory of which he had never spoken. "After Mum was drowned, I dreamt of her for weeks as she was when we found her. It stopped, though, and now she's herself in my dreams."

"He wasn't a screamer, you know. After the first blows, no one could hold them back."

"Could he have been saved, Simon, if we'd come earlier?"

"No. And you'd have been sitting there with me, Hamish still cooling his heels in the barracks. There was a premium on Englishmen just then. As for Mikhail, there was terrible kidney damage. He'd been pissing blood for days, like a little ghost of himself — physically. They never got to the real Mikhail, he was unbreakable. He reminded me of you."

The compliment in its context moved Evan more deeply than any he had ever received. He had never understood the reasons for Simon's evident regard for him — Simon the athlete, the scholar, the golden lad at school and home — but it had been an important part of Evan's life for years, and the thought of losing it was hardly endurable. The hint that he had given Lindsay, though, was growing and pushing inside him, crying out for birth as a full, direct declaration. If it was to be done, this was the time, the only time for it.

"Simon."

"Mm?"

"I'm going to tell you something about me, something you may not like so much. Simon, I'm not like Mikhail — nor like you, I'm like Hamish. Do you understand?"

"Not precisely." He was going to be careful, Evan thought. "What do you mean?"

He had gone too far now to turn back. "I think," he said slowly and distinctly, feeling his sweating skin turn to ice, "I think I am a homosexual."

Simon sighed, almost irritably. "What about it?" He was not being careful, he was hardly even listening, impatient as if he wanted to talk about something of real importance. He was ill, he had been through terrible times, and it was rotten of Evan to trouble him with this now, but — hear me, Simon, please hear me, something pleaded from inside him.

"I don't want to be awkward, to embarrass you, but what you think about it is important to me."

"Davie, I *don't* think about it, never have. It was simply the way things were with you and Hamish and nothing to do with me at all."

"With me and Hamish. Did you think we were lovers? At school?"

"Yes, of course."

"We were not. We have never been lovers."

"Jesus, I *thought* you were, I — now I *am* embarrassed."

"Oh, please, no need. Why, though, why did you think that? Do I look bent, act bent?"

"I don't like your choice of words, and I don't think I can answer you. You're Davie, and you've been a fact of my life

106

since we were twelve and thirteen. I can't see you objectively."

"Did the others think we were lovers?"

"Yes."

"School joke?"

"In *my* hearing? Hardly."

"So. So. We learn something new each day. Thanks, Simon. I'm not sleepy any more, think I'll have a wash." Evan gained the privacy of the bathroom and vomited.

It was finished; what he had feared for years had happened and long ago. He had fought his battle, been wounded and wounded Hamish, for nothing. The world — and Francis with it, no doubt, had seen into his soul, and the past ten years had been like one of his paintings — a lie he had told himself.

Evan felt unclean even after his shower. It was like him, he thought, that what he was seen to be troubled him more than what he was.

"Would you like me to shave you?" he asked Simon.

"That would be super — to get the last trace of that filthy country off me."

Evan brought his shaving things into the bedroom and set to work. "I've wasted my life, you know," Simon said suddenly, and Evan tried not to laugh. "Oh, that sounds stupidly melodramatic when one isn't thirty yet and has a wife like Chris and a new baby and all. I've wasted a devil of a lot of time, though."

"No one else would say that of you; you've done marvelously at your work."

"Work I shan't do again. I learnt Arabic, you know, understand several dialects, learnt Persian, learnt — oh, hell, savages, all of them. Don't want ever to have to look at them again."

"You're still in shock from losing your friend and all the rest of it — perhaps you'll feel differently—"

"Not that alone. Did you see what was in the prison yard?"

"Yes." Evan had hoped it had gone unobserved or unrecorded by Simon's fevered brain. "Do you want to talk about that? Now?"

"I have to. I'm going to write it first thing when I'm home; it's got to be told. Early in February, before I was arrested, the mullahs closed the secular high schools in Persarum, and some of the students protested. The Shiites had over a hundred of them rounded up and sent to Palat where they could be kept quietly. They were releasing them by twos and threes — after 're-education.' There was a hell of a lot of screaming.

"Then, early that last morning as the guards and the commandant were stripping the place of everything portable, two of the holy ones appeared. They and the guards marched all those who were left out into the yard; some of them were so young their voices hadn't broken, and they cried. The mullahs ordered the guards to machine-gun the lot, and then all of them clubbed the few who were still moving. Animals. No, worse." His face twisted, and Evan thought he was going to cry, but he stiffened himself and went on.

"I never imagined I could think this way, Davie, never." His eyes, fixed on Evan's, were too bright, fevered again. "But I should like to kill them, as many as I could. To bomb and bomb again."

"Bombs don't discriminate, Simon. Surely some of them are civilized, decent." The boy whose eyes Hamish had closed and looked like a murdered angel.

"I met one once who was, though I learnt it too late. I watched the others stone him to death."

Small wonder that he had been unable to take an interest in Evan's soul searching. Evan wiped a last dab of soap from his ear. "There. You're quite yourself again."

Someone rapped on the door. Seven o'clock — it would be Max Ross coming to look at Simon.

With the Alexandros steaming toward Greece, Simon's presence on board need no longer be kept secret. Max, however, found himself in no hurry to break the news to Milly and got through their late, solitary breakfast with no reference either to the journalist or his rescuers. She returned to Hector Six, though, after a mid-morning appointment with the ship's hairdresser, pale and shaken.

"Max, I've just heard something dreadful. Mrs. Godolphin speaks Greek, you know, and she heard one of the sailors say that Hamish had been killed yesterday in Palat, helping a friend to escape from prison."

Max had to set her straight, of course.

"So that's why!" she cried, delighted. "That's why the Evan and the earring and all of it. The magnificent little posturer!"

"He still wants to be called Evan," Max said, ruffled by intuition triumphant, "and, unless I'm very much mistaken, he remains as queer as a three-dollar bill."

"I hate that expression. And what the hell difference does it make?"

"Man's mystic purpose is procreation." Max, having had no religious training whatever, despised mysticism, but his use of the word usually subdued Milly who feared being thought insensitive to his Jewish heritage. "It's unnatural—"

"Oh, heterosexuality is unnatural if one happens to be homo. As for procreation, any animal can do that and discard the results. I'm going out to the lounge for coffee." And to spread the news, Max thought. "Want to come?"

He didn't. His awareness that she was totally in the right added to his irritability and to the unreasoning dislike he had taken to the youngest Talbot.

The new itinerary was arranged at last: Athens tomorrow, Delos and Mykonos, the unscheduled stops which they would substitute for Antalya and Perge, now too many nautical miles away, on Wednesday; Ephesus, then, with the possible side-trip to Priene; Canakkale and Troy; Istanbul; Dikili and Pergamum; Rhodes. Barring some new catastrophe, the cruise would then follow its original pattern.

Miss Shaw set down the telephone receiver and leaned back, as near to exhaustion as she could remember being. "Fetch me a cuppa, will you please, Sybil?" She watched the fair-haired, very proper young cruise girl suppress a shudder at the "cuppa" — Miss Shaw had been born near Bow Bells and enjoyed letting Sybil's sort know it. "Don't spare the sugar."

Her satisfaction dimmed as she studied the map before her. What with the strike in Athens, the museum hours in Istanbul, the petrol shortage at Canakkale, the difficulty hiring launches to Delos, buses on Rhodes and English-speaking guides for Pergamum, the Alexandros would be zig-zagging about like a ship demented.

It was too early for another full day at sea as well, the voyage having reached that point where the honeymoon was over but the marriage between passengers, ship and staff not complete. In the lounge a few minutes earlier, the British buzzing had been unrestrained, the newly acquired vocal moderation of the Americans quite lost.

"They must have gone mad," she heard from one passenger, just after the change in destination was announced. "Look at that map." Most of the wall at the aft end of the lounge was ornamented with a contour map of the Mediterranean and its countries, green and gold land embracing blue sea. It was written there for all to see that Piraeus ought not, logically, to be their next port.

"This day is lost altogether; we'll surely miss one of the stops they've promised."

"I suppose they intend to make the day up by keeping the ship at breakneck speed. Everything moveable fell from our desk last night."

"Mine as well. My alarm clock smashed."

"I lost a whole God-damned bottle of bourbon."

The mini-rebellion had as yet brought no direct complaint to Miss Shaw, but it disturbed her. Sometimes, rarely, the marriage didn't take at all — too many minor disappointments (major ones, such as disastrous weather, seemed to draw a ship's company closer together) or too many sour apples on the passenger list. More often, when this mood struck one of the cruises, some little miracle like the appearance of a school of dolphins or last year's rescue of the Turkish fishermen would occur, and then all would be well.

The "cuppa" arrived, sweet and refreshing, and Miss Shaw set to work on the drastically revised bulletin. She finished duplicating it just after lunch had been called, sent the cruise girls to distribute it in the lounge and dining room and took her place alone at a table in order to devote an hour to study.

Today she only pretended to immerse herself in the writings of Herodotus, keeping a sharp ear out for the voices around her. They were raised now in a spirit very different from that of the morning, and it was evident that one of the little miracles had come along and just at the right time.

"Did you know that Simon Roud is on board?"

"I heard that; does anyone know how he is?"

"Ill, they say, but not dangerously."

"Who is Simon Roud?" A moment's shocked silence from the other seven at that table, then full, enthusiastic briefing.

"How the devil did they get him out? I heard Colonel Cobb was in intelligence during the war, but—"

"He wasn't involved. It was that gay couple — you know, the two English boys who are always together."

"The ones that came on board yesterday in burnooses or whatever you call them? Ho, I see now — that was how they got him out of Tariq and past the harbor police."

"The chap with the earring is Francis Talbot's youngest son, the one with the rakish reputation. It's straight out of *The Scarlet Pimpernel.*"

"They say Talbot was wounded during the rescue — shot."

"Not shot, but the poor fellow had his ear torn off during the escape."

"And the other boy, the handsome one, gave Roud his landing tag and is stranded somewhere in Turkey."

"You can't judge a book by its cover. What a coup!"

Satisfied, Miss Shaw returned to Herodotus.

Dr. Cameron would be lecturing at fourteen hours. "Evan, why don't you go?" Reg suggested. "I can listen here with Simon over the speakers, and you can get out and stretch your legs."

"Oh, thanks very much, Reg." Evan didn't care about the lecture, but he hadn't had a cigarette in hours. The small cabin had become stuffy around mid-morning from his non-stop smoking, and Simon had begun to cough again. Knowing he shouldn't light another had kept Evan edgy and he lit one as soon as he closed the door to Hector Seven.

Lindsay had been waiting just in sight of the corridor and ran to him from the lounge. Friendship grew quickly on ship-board; he felt he had known and admired this girl half his life, and her face was wreathed in welcome.

"Evan, let me look at you. They said you'd been shot."

"Wrong. Hamish was shot at but not shot. I'm very well indeed."

"You don't look well — awfully dragged out."

"It isn't done yet. Hamish is still in Turkey—"

Wilder appeared at her side, and the comfort that Evan had taken from Lindsay evaporated. "You won't forget, Talbot? Four o'clock in the upstairs lounge."

"I won't forget." Wilder had stood outside Hector Seven half the morning until he had Evan's promise.

"I wish you'd reconsider and let me send the story out this evening."

"Not, as I told you, until Hamish is back on the ship."

"Why? Everyone on the Alexandros knows about it now; you promised me an exclusive, and I'll be beaten."

Must everything be spelled out for the man? "The Muslim extremists are going to call this a crime against Allah — and loudly. The Turks are under pressure from those people, and one can't predict how they'll react."

Wilder sulkily agreed once more and returned to the lounge where Cameron was about to speak. Disappointingly, Lindsay went with him.

Going upstairs to the deck, Evan passed a Canadian couple known to him only by sight; the man stopped to shake his hand.

"Remarkable achievement, remarkable." The woman smiled shyly. Three middle-aged British women beamed at him from deck chairs. Nothing like this had happened to Evan since third form when he had fished first-form Peter from a thaw-swollen river.

The deck was emptying, passengers hurrying below to hear the lecture. Sharon brushed past him ignoring his nod and fixing him with a look stranger than usual. Why? He was exonerated, if falsely, as a homosexual — oh, of course: her Christianity was of the Shiite sort, and now he had offended that.

The Hodgkins boy sat at an easel near the bow painting a seascape. "An artist," Evan said to him.

Robin looked up at him and flushed with pleasure. "Not really, only messing about with paints. I've heard that you actually are one." The flush deepened; Robin wasn't sure he had said the right thing.

"I try. That's very good indeed, you know." It *was* promising, combining strength with a precision that pleased Evan. "You might have something happening — oh — near there." He indicated a spot lower left on the canvas.

"I see. It's getting top-heavy. Did you bring your painting things, Mr. Talbot?"

"Only a sketching pad. I sketch impressions, then paint later. I hope to begin something Wednesday on Delos." If Hamish would be with him.

"Does it bother you to have people watch?" Evan shook his head. "Might I then?"

"I'd be flattered; perhaps we can picnic together."

Miss Shaw's voice rang through the loudspeakers directly

112

over their heads. "Will Mr. Talbot please report to the cruise office at his convenience?" The tones were bell-like, almost flowery. It couldn't be bad news.

Miss Shaw was transformed, her small, intelligent brown eyes sparkling with pleasure. "We have Mr. Saunders," she said. "He'll be flown to Athens in the morning."

8

At Sea, Piraeus — April 3: Abul was whimpering in his sleep — or was it — no, Abul was dead, Mikhail as well. And Simon was on a ship sailing towards home. He found a light switch, flicked it and saw that the sounds were coming from the next bunk. Davie didn't appear in pain, but his sleeping face was terribly puzzled as Simon had seen it at school when Davie had been told to read something and his eyes had played tricks.

Simon watched him for a moment, thinking. Davie must have faced the odds that he might give up his freedom, even his life, for Simon's. Yet Simon had chosen not to hear the cry for help he recognized now in yesterday's conversation. That had seemed so strange, almost extraneous, and contradicted Simon's long settled impressions so strongly that, though he had not once known Davie to lie, he had hardly believed him. He believed now and was stabbed by the sick guilt that had filled him only days before for his coldness to Abul.

"Davie."

"Mmm." The creases left his forehead, but his eyes remained closed.

"I can't sleep."

Davie opened his eyes and looked at the alarm clock. "It's almost time for your horse pill anyway."

"We shan't have much time to talk."

"True. What would you like to talk about?"

"About you, for a change."

Davie turned onto his stomach, supporting his chin in his

hands and regarding Simon warily. "There's no more fascinating subject."

"Particularly about your overwhelming modesty. No. You asked a question yesterday, and my head was so mucked up I couldn't answer—"

"Please not to worry — pure trivia and my head wasn't at its best either."

"Shut up. You asked me yesterday if you looked — I think you said bent, and I fumbled around stupidly. God, Davie, you don't. I used to envy your success with girls — it seemed you had only to smile on them—"

"I think it's be-kind-to-faggots day. Next you'll be asking me to lunch." Evan got up and began laying out his clothes — he was shutting Simon out.

"Don't be cute, Davie. Listen to me. I thought as I did only when I saw you with Hamish. You were like a well-married couple, each of you seeming to know what the other was feeling — and to care very much. I knew something came between you the last year at school, and I hated it — felt you had both lost something extraordinary. What happened?"

"Nothing. I understood suddenly what *might* happen — and stopped it."

"Why?"

"Family."

"Hamish's?" Simon asked mendaciously.

"Hardly. You know Mrs. Saunders — to change Hamish in the least would strike her as sacrilege. I think she likes me as well. My father. I had disappointed him in every possible way but that one. It seemed more than he should need to endure."

" 'Let me count the ways.' "

"School. You were there, you know I barely got through. And Cambridge. I was the first Talbot in generations not to have gone up—"

"That's ridiculous. You didn't choose to have your eyes behave as they did — and they show you things the rest of us don't see."

"Now it's be-kind-to-dyslexics day. I shall grow fat on lunches."

"You'll grow fat on self-pity." Simon's inattentive audience disappeared into the bathroom. "Davie, *hear* me."

The telephone jangled, and Davie returned to answer it.

"Yes, Miss Shaw. That was extremely thoughtful of you. I can't tell you how much we appreciate—" He set down the receiver. "We've dropped anchor, Simon, and Miss Shaw thought you might want to disembark early. She says it could take you hours to escape the interested passengers.

"I wanted to apologize, you know, about the chadri and all, but she rang off before I could even thank her properly. 'Nonsense,' she said, 'pleasure.' "

"I should like to finish what I began before we go ashore."

"There are more urgent topics for discussion. What the devil will we dress you in? The chador? Just for old time's sake?"

"I'm staying in this bunk until you hear me out."

"Yes, Simon." He sat down facing Simon, his expression withdrawn, distant, but Simon plodded on.

"Sir Francis's life would seem to have been a series of triumphs, with accompanying adulation and two sons that follow him about like spaniels trying their best to emulate him. I don't think that the decision of a third son to follow a different path would break his spirit. You're cheating yourself horribly, of course, but that's your own choice. What's rotten is that you're hurting Hamish as well. I don't think he will ever love anyone as he's loved you."

Davie's eyes widened. "Mm. I heard you, Simon." His smile was remote. "Please, we've got to dress you now." As they left Hector Seven, Simon tried to embrace him as he had often done before — Simon's was a family that showed its affection — but Davie shied self-consciously away and out into the corridor.

Simon loved this man, probably more than his only brother, and he saw that he had failed him.

Assessing Simon as if through the eyes of his family, Evan saw how thin he looked, the shirt and slacks donated by Max Ross right as to length but sagging in places. He had lost, too, what Evan and Hamish called the Roudian glow and wore a tired, downcast expression. Hoping to avoid new drains on his energy, Evan hurried him out of the cabin and off the ship before the other passengers were stirring.

Cobb's — or more likely Miss Shaw single-handedly — had worked magic again, and the tall Rolls Royce with the important license number waited alone just past the customs shed, no cameras, no reporters about, only Simon's parents and Christina, holding what looked like a package with tiny, moveable extremities. There was no crying, not even much talking.

Simon and Christina held each other as if they were melding while his parents stood in queue waiting their turns. Evan ended holding the baby, who realized his fears by wetting him properly, sending a warm, odorless stream down his clean shirt and slacks. They all saw him then, and he was kissed as well as wet on. Dr. Roud shook his head. "It can't be said," he said anyway. "It's beyond thanks."

They hadn't known that Hamish was found, and learning it seemed to make their small communion perfect. It was for this that Evan had risked Hamish and himself, and he could hardly wait to escape it. He turned from them with the briefest of cheery farewells, but Dr. Roud caught up with him before he reached the gangplank, insisting that he be allowed to assume the expenses of Simon's deliverance.

Evan shook his hand and promised. The money with which he had planned to bribe the commandant — more than half that he had borrowed — was presumably still with Hamish. He would accept the Roud's money, though, because he sensed that the burden of gratitude could be too great, and, despite his present discomfort with them, he valued their affection.

He breakfasted alone in Hector Seven on a roll as tasteless as his victory and bitter coffee. He drank it that way, though his tray held hot milk and sugar, because it suited his mood. Why? His shyness with the Rouds came, no doubt, from the new self he saw reflected in their eyes. It was an old image to them but strange and disturbing to Evan. It was like a case of mistaken identity in a silly film, solved after long years — only this time the outside world had been right, the illusion in the mind of the subject.

Something else had been off — something lacking? He had watched a British family, reunited, victorious for now over death and danger, like the happy part of a World War II drama — rather a good one, its characters full of warmth without effusion, devotion without mawkishness. Actually, nothing at all had been lacking, and perhaps that was the problem.

He imagined his own restoration to another British family under similar circumstances. His mother, if she were alive, might have been there, emoting girlishly and trying too hard to cover her boredom with anything pertaining to parenthood.

Picture Francis, though, leaving an expedition in embryo, in process or in summation — he always had something in one of those stages — as Dr. Roud had left the frenzied electoral campaign on which his future balanced.

Evan supposed he was arming himself for the action he knew now he must take to stop his stomach from devouring itself, to free himself from the bonds that kept his work trivial. It was petty of him, though, to fault Francis. His father had been almost finished raising one family when Evan was born. And there had been a time—

He let the scene run through his head like a film clip, the one that had begun so many of his childhood fantasies. It must have been in autumn, just after his sixth birthday; trees had been changing color. His new pony had balked at a small hedge and sent Evan over it head-first. He hadn't been badly hurt, but there had been a lot of blood, and his father had got to him first, lifting him and holding him tightly and tenderly to his chest, carrying him to his bed in the house.

He hadn't cried at all, and everyone had made a great fuss over him, not knowing that he had never been happier. Evan had hoped for years for a similar incident and had even tried to arrange one, taking deliberate spills. His father had never embraced him again.

Reg came in. "We missed you at breakfast. Are you feeling all right?"

"Fine, thanks very much, only a bit let down with Simon gone and all of it over."

"You're coming to the Acropolis."

"I thought I'd wait here, actually."

"I spoke to Miss Shaw just now." Reg wore a Father Christmas look. "Hamish should arrive at the Parthenon within an hour after the rest of us. Colonel Cobb wants to see to it that he doesn't miss a thing and is sending him from the airport by limousine."

"Ah." Evan smiled. "Awfully good of them — and of you to tell me."

Alone again, he combed his hair. "Hello, Evan," he said to his mirror image, and it smiled back at him, transfigured. The muddled impressions of the past hours, the past days, the past ten years, snapped into place in his head, and he looked with joy at the picture they formed. He was awfully hungry. Sometimes they served tea and biscuits in the lounge.

"Promise you won't go without me, Lindsay. The Acropolis is so crowded, and I get all claustrophic." Lindsay wished she could pretend not to have heard; she had left Dirk last night with the understanding that they would spend the day together.

Sharon turned on the shower and disappeared inside it. She had tried to tune in BBC news, which was unintelligible as it had been since they left the Adriatic, and forgotten it. Lindsay, annoyed by static, reached out to snap it off.

"Roud," she heard between sputters ". . . Tariq . . . David Talbot . . . murdered schoolchildren . . ." The static prevailed then, and Lindsay turned it off, her spirits gone utterly flat. A spark of hope flared briefly — perhaps the press had learned it from the Rouds — then went out; Simon's family wouldn't yet know of the massacre and would be too concerned for Hamish's safety to break the story now.

Despite his promise to Evan, Dirk hadn't waited a day — in fact, not an hour. It had been during the lecture just afterward that he had left the lounge at the signal of the young Greek radio operator. "Setting things up for tomorrow," he had told Lindsay over cocktails. They had danced then until almost midnight, and the story, cabled to a newspaper at that hour, could hardly have reached BBC by morning. She thought about him, dancing last night, looking down into her face with his direct boy's eyes wide and trusting, his need for her worn as openly as his clothes.

"Another of Lindsay's lame ducks," she had heard from her family with infuriating frequency. But they knew her. Lame ducks needed someone to lean upon, and Lindsay needed to be needed. She liked Evan so much, and had let both of them believe she was not attracted to him because of his feelings toward Hamish — not true. Lindsay knew that her regard for Evan would stay platonic simply because he could stand upright without her support.

All right. A change in her inclinations was unlikely. Perhaps next time she could find herself a physical cripple, even a mental one, anything to break this succession of moral weaklings. Withdrawal, not confrontation, would be her best exit from this situation. Only a part of her wanted an exit, but that was the cautious part to which she was learning to attend, the part that would keep her from being drained to the quiet, maidenish core that she sometimes feared was the heart of her.

Dirk preferred, he said, to ride in the last bus; they were to meet near the end of the disembarkation queue. "Sharon." She was out of the shower and nearly dressed. "Let's hurry. I should like just once to ride the first bus; perhaps they see more."

Athens: Evan had first climbed this hill when he was eleven with Will, the tutor they had got for him, by then without much hope. They had walked up the long green and gold path to the Acropolis, and then the tall, brave, broken propellae smashed out at them. Past the ruined columns and up the old, old hill, and there it was, not cold and stiff and grey as in the text books but sunny beige and a bit embarrassed about what time and wars had done to it.

For days he had anticipated taking this walk with Hamish, watching his face as he discovered what the books could barely hint at. Instead, the Rosses were beside him, Milly glowing. "Max," she said, "it's so much more than I expected. For the first time I feel what Dr. Cameron spoke of — the numinosity."

"Good God, Milly, must you romanticize everything? If the local numina survived rape by the Turks, bombardment by the Venetians and aren't stashed away in the British Museum, they surely have the sense to avoid a mob like this."

Her face fell, as she dropped back, pretending to examine a Doric pillar. Evan stopped beside her. "You're right, you know, and I feel it too," he said. "It was built to be admired, and the crowds — listen to that babble of tongues, must be guides holding forth in twenty languages. I think the crowds help keep it alive."

"Thanks, Evan." She grinned at him, resilient.

He had no right to interfere and knew what drove him: his hurt and anger on his own account. That was hardly justified, since he had teased the man into despising him, but it came out anyway. "Milly."

"Yes."

"You ought to hit back, you know."

"I've tried that over the years, and it isn't safe. Max can hit harder." Evan's horror must have been apparent. "Oh, verbally, of course. The bruises are only to my ego, but that's a cowardly one. I hate quarrels."

Despite the tension of his vigil for Hamish, Milly's confidences interested Evan and didn't surprise him. Her gaffe at table the second night had, in retrospect, been rather flattering, and Evan had made an effort to soothe her obvious distress about it. From different continents, different generations, they shared a kind of bond, not sexual, not filial, not maternal. Perhaps it was only mutual acceptance, the absence in each of any will to change the other, but they found themselves increasingly comfortable together.

By common consent, they veered off from the Parthenon toward the Erectheon, where the crowds were less, since it was, as usual, undergoing some sort of exterior repair, and the view of the entrance path was unobstructed.

"Max is honorable and amusing and effective and — well, I suppose most of the time I'm in love with him, though those feelings are a little thin at the moment. He's also a spoiled child."

"I shouldn't have thought that. He seems very much in control."

"Oh, not in the sense of having been either abused or overindulged; he's got the assurance and self-discipline of a well-reared king." She stopped herself. "I'm sorry, Evan, I don't know what got me going like this. Now you too can speak of those Americans who burden you with their life history on first acquaintance."

"Oh, Milly, not at all, please go on. Max reminds me of someone, you see, and I can't help but be interested."

"Well, a park and a museum in San Francisco are named for his family; they damned near founded the place. Max is the only heir, not to a great deal of money but to the glory. His parents regarded him as a little god, and he grew up thinking he could control the universe.

"He's quite bright and learned differently — only he still must control everything in his immediate vicinity, particularly me and the boys. I can cope, particularly since I've decided to teach again next year, but the effect on James and Alex is disheartening. They're such good boys, wanting so much to please, and one can see James at least forming slowly into a very pale carbon of Max."

Evan, startled, grasped a piece of galvanized scaffolding propping a caryatid. One could use much the same words to describe his brothers — possibly a father's indifference was not without its rewards.

Milly looked past him suddenly, down toward the Propellai. "Evan, look — just past that Japanese group. He looks a little lost — perhaps you should make yourself known."

He was there, shabby and beautiful as the hill he stood upon, and Evan's eyes homed in on him, past and through the multi-colored, multi-lingual crowds. Evan began to run but collided with a small brown woman with a red dot painted on her forehead and slowed, twisting his way through several nations.

They met at the west end of the Parthenon. Evan remembered Hamish's horror at his clowning on the deck and pressed his nails into his palms to keep from touching him. He compensated by babbling, though, words pouring out without sense or volition.

"You did so well. You can do it, you see, you coped perfectly. Oh, Christ, you're really here."

He hadn't done a damned thing except drive to Antalya on an adequate road with almost no traffic, and then abandon the car. He had let them see a little of the money — a very little, after the experience with the Turkish driver — at the small hotel, and they had asked no questions. He had walked down to the quay around noon the following day and been immediately enfolded in the protective embrace of Cobb's, and after they found one, all thinking could be safely suspended. He wished Evan wouldn't make such a fuss over him, especially with several dozen of their fellow passengers watching, waving and smiling welcome. It made Hamish feel fraudulent.

And now that he looked at Evan, there was something awry; it spoiled Hamish's pleasure in the Parthenon as if that had gone suddenly out of proportion. His friend's eyes, in the plucky, clever face, were too bright, pricking at Hamish's composure. After all the years, there was no mistaking it: a new project, no doubt involving Hamish, was coming to life in Evan's head.

Hamish watched him in the bus on the traffic-choked way to the National Museum: Evan chattered about Simon, about Lindsay, Milly, who was so very nice after all, the achievements of Reg and Miss Shaw, his eyes sapphires in the sun. Something was brewing.

Hamish forgot it all at the museum. The fat, flattened golden death mask of Agamemnon leaped at him from the first display, then treasures superbly crafted by hands that were dust in Homer's time. Wonder upon wonder unfolded, spoiled only once.

"You!" Evan cried before Praxiteles' Hermes, in hearing distance of half the ship's company. "You're as like as twins."

"No. Shut up," Hamish growled. The statue, exquisite a moment before, now seemed glaringly naked.

The Cobb's group began to disperse, some going outside for cold drinks in the museum garden, others lingering over favorite displays. Hamish and Evan drifted upstairs into a small room which they had to themselves save for a large, serious German family whom they had seen devouring each exhibit with methodical dedication. The subjects here, by artists and craftsmen throughout the ancient world, were exclusively children.

"Something terribly touching about a two-thousand-year-old potty," he said to Evan.

"I say, look here." Small boys chased across an even older Cretan frieze, each playing with something different to the next — and one held a toy that was part of his neighbor's anatomy. "They didn't think that was peculiar." Evan looked surprised.

Of course they didn't; the two children wore expressions as endearingly innocent as their fellows who were playing with hoops, kittens and puppies. Evan understood so little about homosexuality; Hamish began to choose words to explain that not only the ancient Greeks but most Oriental cultures had thought it a natural alternative — or accompaniment — to marriage. He both yearned toward and shrank from talking of it to Evan and ended saying nothing.

On the Alexandros, the Greek dinner was unexpectedly comfortable and familiar — probably in contrast to the Turkish ones that Hamish had picked at the past two nights. He and Evan had gone from the focus of one sort of attention to another; people from all over the dining room waved and smiled. Evan loved it; he shone like a sun, dispensing warmth and wit in all directions but one. He responded to an overture from Max with the chilly stare and raised eyebrows which he had used very occasionally to wither at Steppingford. The man had treated Simon and must, Hamish thought, have patched Evan's ear — he deserved more from them.

White envelopes waited on their desk in Hector Seven: invitations to dine with the captain on Tuesday.

"You see? From pariah to celebrity in two days—"

The intensity of Evan's strange mood increased by the moment, as did Hamish's distrust of it. Hamish sat at their desk and began with outward deliberation to work on the journal he had begun in Venice. Evan, elbows on knees, chin in hands, watched from his bunk. "Please don't write now. Look at me."

Hamish hadn't known what he was writing anyway; he closed the notebook and turned towards Evan.

"I know now. I know who I am, what I want. Would you like to hear when I knew?"

"Yes." But Hamish would have preferred to hear nothing at all from Evan just now — alarm signals were going off all through him.

"When you left us at Ephemae, when you drove away so that we should be safe. When I was afraid I'd never see you again."

"I don't understand—"

"Perhaps this will help you to understand." He stood, took Hamish's face between his hands and kissed him gently upon the lips. It was a gesture of pure love, and Hamish had dreamt of it from those lips for nearly half his life. He felt only fear.

Evan sank back on the bunk, eyes narrowed, forehead clenched in thought. "Sorry. I'm sorry. What an ass I am — expecting everything to stand still for a decade or so while I examine my inner being. There's someone else. Ought to be. Please forget all this, and I shall aim for relatively civilized behavior until the cruise is done. I want you to enjoy it."

"There's no one else — never has been — that I could love either completely or for very long." Hamish ought not to have said that, ought to have left the idea intact in Evan's head — so much simpler than what he must do now. "What's happening to you, though, is that you're having a new sort of adventure, a shipboard romance—"

"Sixteen years — rather a long voyage."

"Friends for sixteen years, not lovers. You can't possibly

know how it is. You've been playing at it on the cruise, knowing that you can slip back to normalcy as soon as we're ashore. And normalcy is there, waiting for you. All those girls—"

"Yes, *all* those girls. And why so many, why not settle down with one? Because for me that kind of sex is like taking a drink of water when one is hungry — it distracts, but it can't satisfy. So one drinks a great deal."

"But you *can* drink, Evan. You can beget children, you can lead the sort of life everyone else lives. Do you understand, all through you, that this means no children, ever? That it means having others look at you not just with amusement or dislike, but with pity? My choice is limited: this or a lie I can't sustain. Yours is open, and you simply don't know—"

"I'll show you what I know." Evan's eyes had gone flat as dusty tile, and he wore a hard, rather coarse look that Hamish had not seen. "Come here."

Physical excitement was rising in Hamish, still controllable, he thought. He found himself standing, though, and taking the single step across the narrow space.

It had been all wrong, and Hamish knew he was completely to blame. His conservatism, his fear of change — if heaven were offered him, he would no doubt refuse it because of its difference to the world he knew. Evan had performed like an efficient whore, giving, refusing to accept. He sprang from the bed suddenly, fully clothed, his face quiet and empty. "Tired now, I think. Would you prefer to stay here and I take the other bunk? Or do you want your own?"

"Your ear is bleeding again. I've hurt it."

"Not to worry. I *am* tired, though. Please, Hamish, which bed?"

"Oh, take that one." Evan was very pale, and a droplet of blood fell from the torn ear onto his shoulder as he undressed. He lay on Hamish's bunk outside the covers, his face turned to the wall. "This isn't new to you," Hamish mused.

"Hardly. Nor has been new since I was twelve and the stable boy and I had each other in the shrubbery. There've been others — many." Jealousy might come later; now, knowing himself innocent of seduction, Hamish felt anxiety lift and a great tenderness surge into the void. He rose and lifted Evan enough to draw back the bedding and cover him, then squeezed himself into the narrow bed. He had smashed the certainty that had been brought him, and the ugly words in the dull voice flowed from the wound he had made and must now try to heal.

"Please go away. I want to sleep." Evan went rigid, tight to the wall.

"You know that I love you, that I've never been so happy. I thought I knew what was best for you, but now I think I was wrong." Hamish buried his face in soft, clean hair, nuzzling the nape of Evan's neck, and Evan relaxed to his touch with the half trust of a hurt child in the arms of a stranger.

Hamish stroked his head and shoulders until the last reserves thawed and Evan pressed close — this friend, this lover, this high-born street boy was offering to humble his body to Hamish's. Nothing like it had happened in Hamish's wildest, most indulgent fantasies, and pride and gratitude swelled in him, but Evan's bones under his hands felt so light, almost fragile.

"I'm afraid," he said, "afraid I'll hurt you."

"You won't. Please."

9

Delos, April 4: Hamish was inordinately fond of lions; he stroked the blind, weathered face of a stone one lining the agora on Delos. It saddened Evan, looking as if it had lived but was now dead and rotting.

"Why, why can't they put it back together?" Robin Hodgkins mourned, touching a huge fragment of the colossal statue of Apollo that had looked out over the harbor two millenia before. The boy was with them as planned, though Evan had wondered earlier whether he would be.

Hamish and Evan had awakened early and lain together in the growing light, talking, making plans, making love. Evan would sell the cottage, and they would buy a flat, probably in Hampstead. Hamish thought that location too expensive, but Evan had prevailed, dangling the nearness of Kenwood and Hampstead's position on London Transport's Northern Line, which, by much use, had endeared itself to Hamish.

They dressed, went up to the deck and watched the sun separate itself from a brilliant sea. Daylight had come, and with it, Hamish could see, Evan was getting some qualms.

"Something is chewing at you — and seems to have got its teeth in."

"No—" Evan smiled with careful carelessness, but Hamish faced him unmoving with that direct, serious look that demanded answer. "I was thinking of Francis. An announcement is in order, I suppose, and I was hunting words. Hamish, what do we call ourselves? I'd like us to be a matched pair, so to speak, but I don't care awfully much for a five-syllable label."

"Auden liked bugger. That's short enough and simple."

Evan was offended. "*I* don't like it at all. Self-deprecation has never been my strong suit."

"No. There's that American word — gay." Hamish was fighting a smile.

"We'd be attacked by every amateur semanticist in London. I've seen those letters to the *Times*."

"Isherwood opts for queer."

"That implies peculiar. I don't feel peculiar at all, actually rather average," Evan said with false modesty, beginning to enjoy his role as comic's foil.

"Bent?"

"That sounds as if one has been twisted out of shape; I've been straightened into my right one."

"All right. Try faggot, then." Hamish had said that differently — it must be the one he used in his head. It would have to be five syllables then, for the world and Francis, but between them Evan could accept this one.

"Yes. That will do nicely. 'Faggot, take my faggot's hand.'" As he lifted Hamish's to his cheek and pressed it there, both of them saw a man's face appear at the glass partition of a doorway — and shy away.

"Oh, Christ, I'm sorry. I know how you hate public display."

"To hell with it," Hamish grinned at him, ruffling his hair. "We *thought* we were alone."

They hadn't spoken of it afterwards, but Evan thought the face was that of George Hodgkins.

Robin now found a mosaic among the ruins and called them to look at it. Dionysus in tile rode a spotted panther, vital and vibrant in contrast to the lions. "I say, it's as good as new!" Hamish was as excited as the boy, both scurrying in and out of buildings deserted for centuries but still largely intact.

Evan saw a fist-sized piece of terra cotta on barren ground a few feet from the path; it looked like an amphora top, and he picked it up to add to Hamish's collection. A small brown snake had been coiled round it and slithered drily over his hand and off into the grass — he yelped and jumped back to the path.

"What was that?"

"Snake—" His hand felt defiled where the thing had slid over it.

"It must have been one of those little lizards."

"No, a real snake," Robin said, "horrid little brown chap, I saw him. What have you there?"

"Nothing." The snake had given the amphora top an evil feel, and Evan threw it back into the dry grass.

Hamish and Robin bounded up the single steep hill toward the pinnacle of the island, avid for new discoveries, but Evan hung back. For all the sun on golden rock and piercingly blue water, the smiling tourists in their bright summer clothes, the winding path dotted with wild flowers and yellow Cobb's satchels, Delos had a feel of death almost as real to him as that of the prison yard at Palat. Perhaps it was the snake, perhaps a surfeit of monuments to those long dead — no, it was more.

Hamish and Robin stopped to examine a vivid, cheeky lizard, and Evan caught up with them. "Something awful happened here," he said to Hamish.

"Yes. It's amazing how much you remember—" Hamish looked surprised and pleased — probably at what he thought the result of his tutoring of long ago. Evan hardly remembered having heard of Delos before the cruise, much less its tragedy, but chose not to dim Hamish's satisfaction.

"What happened?" Robin demanded.

"I think it was 87 or 88 BC that a king of Parthia — later to be part of Persia — began to wage a holy war against Rome—"

"A *holy* war?" Robin asked. "Islam wouldn't begin for centuries. What were they?"

"The popular religion was one of those witch-burning ones, full of mysticism and righteousness. Rome recognized their god, but that wasn't enough. Theirs had to be the only way, and those outside it were regarded as inherently evil.

"Delos then was a prosperous trading port but without military defenses, and the Parthian king — one of a series named Mithridates — sent in an army. They put every man and boy to the sword and dragged the women off as slaves; Delos was never resettled."

The chatter and laughter of passing tourists became suddenly the screams of women and girls, and Evan saw the rocks below him awash with blood — all in the name of a god. Perversely, he found his mind shaping a prayer to his own for the repose of the Delians.

The sea to the east came into sight, a half dozen other Cycladic islands floating upon it, and Hamish pressed ahead to the hill's highest projection — he looked very Byronic standing there, Evan thought, his black hair ruffled by the wind.

"That's an awfully nice prospect — with Hamish in it." Robin wanted Evan to get to his drawing as promised. He took out his sketching pad and began to block things — he would not include Hamish, though he wanted a figure there. He wasn't ready to draw Hamish nor sure that he would ever be ready, and the picture he planned had an ominous quality, one he surely didn't want round his friend.

"Don't you want an easel?" Robin asked.

"I shall later, of course — only trying to sketch shapes now. We shan't be here long enough for more."

"And then?" Robin was spreading their lunches upon a flat, clean rock: hard-cooked eggs, chicken, fruit, cheese, rolls, biscuits.

"You'll see. I'll show it to you at various stages." This part was one of his strengths; it was afterward, when he was "finishing," that he seemed to refine away any power from his work. And one simply couldn't see until it had sat for weeks what had been lost and where.

"Oh, I see what you're up to; you've added that island, and — it's going to be a bit sinister, isn't it, with then imposed over now?" A perceptive kid — Evan began to appreciate the satisfaction that Hamish found in. teaching.

George Hodgkins appeared beside them, grinning like a nervous teddy bear. "Robin, you must have forgotten. We promised to picnic with the Rosses down the hill."

"Daddy, I *told* you—"

But not with whom. The poor devil was so transparent that his misery was the worst of it. Robin didn't understand yet what was going on, but he would soon, and Evan wanted not to be near when that happened.

"You won't miss a thing. I'm about to fold my sketches and steal away to the edibles. Thanks for setting them out, and don't forget yours." Evan helped to repack Robin's lunch, avoiding the glance of a blushing George, who ended taking Evan's orange as well; he would realize that later, and it would add to his consternation. The two set off down the path.

"What in hell was that about?" Hamish sat on the rock beside him.

"Nothing much. Have an egg." Evan proffered one, hoping to avoid discussion; he was embarrassed for Hodgkins whom he had liked.

"It was too damned much." Hamish's cheeks were wine-colored. "You ought to have cut him dead."

"Gaining what? And at what cost to Robin? Anyway, I was sorry for him."

"I don't understand you. You smile on Hodgkins, knowing he thought you'd corrupt his damned kid, and yet treat Max as you do—"

"Altogether different people. George acted out of anxiety and muddle; Max enjoys hurting." He wished he hadn't said that; he had no intention of revealing the events or non-events that had shaped his relationship with the American.

"I haven't observed that."

"Listen to him." There was, anyway, something else. "With Milly. He batters her verbally."

Hamish chewed on that along with the chicken. "Possibly. Doesn't make me like Hodgkins, though, and the man's a fool. That boy knows more about sex than his father."

"Too right." Robin had at least a touch of the worldliness so noticeably absent in George. "And he likes girls. He was watching that archeology student, Maggie, climb the footpath this morning. She was wearing very short shorts, and I thought his eyes would pop out of his head."

Mykonos: The opulent bustle at the harbor of Mykonos was a refreshing contrast to the ghosts of Delos. Lindsay would have the afternoon to herself here, since Sharon planned to meet the friend who was traveling parallel to them.

"I'm anxious to have you two meet," she told Lindsay. "I know you'll like him."

"Surely you'd like some time to yourselves; I'd planned to shop—"

"Just have tea with us — here, this cafe with the striped awning, at three-thirty. I won't hear no."

She might not hear it, but it was being said all through Lindsay, who planned to be at a distant corner of the island at the hour named. She had a glimpse of Dirk a street or so away and turned in the opposite direction, studying merchandise, shopkeepers and shoppers on the long, shiningly clean street that faced the harbor. There were lovely things to buy, but her gift allowance would be spent in Istanbul which her parents had never visited.

Lindsay would need to take some sort of action about Sharon. The stab of fear she had felt on Achilles Deck had been brief and probably an over-reaction. Sharon must have recognized then her lack of sympathy with religious extremism — there had been no further reference to Gwen Noyes or homosexuality. She had begun, in fact, to indulge in girl-talk with Lindsay — men and clothes — not of the most fascinating variety but reassuring in its normalcy.

The problem was that she clung to Lindsay like a limpet, having left her side only once yesterday in Athens to ring the young man she would meet today, and Lindsay thirsted for privacy. She would be free tomorrow, having bought a ticket for an alternative tour of Priene, knowing that Sharon wanted to see Ephesus and follow the tracks of Paul whose writings were dear to her. But all the other days which had seemed to promise delight threatened now to be soured by the omnipresence of her cabin-mate.

Lindsay had yet to learn why Sharon had chosen this cruise. With its professors, its comfortable but hardly elegant food and living accommodations, little time free for shopping and no stops at resort areas, it appealed to a very specific sort of tourist: the scholarly with an interest in classical thought and history. Sharon, with her bent for dogmatic mysticism, could not have expected to find many soul mates among this crowd.

She had chattered through half Professor Ewing's lecture about Delos this morning, and Lindsay had missed hearing some of it. She would, she supposed, have to be rude to avoid other days spoiled by Sharon. Lindsay was very bad at rudeness, taking far too long to work herself up to it when it was necessary and even longer to exorcise the little shame-filled vibrations that seized her afterward.

Not appearing for the command tea would be a beginning. Lindsay tired of skimming shop windows and their irrelevant contents and decided to explore the island. She turned into a narrow street whose white cobblestones, walls and buildings dazzled in the afternoon sun. A large windmill above the town attracted her, but she caught sight of Dirk and the ship's doctor nearing it and changed course to follow a high-walled, winding pathway uphill and away from the town.

It opened out eventually onto a green plateau where two dozen sheep and goats were grazing. Wild irises bloomed everywhere before her and, turning, she had an exquisite view of white town on blue harbor, the Alexandros tidy in the distance. For the first time in weeks physical well-being filled her, and the annoyance she had felt seemed silly.

The pathway, blocked only by a latticed gate, continued across the meadow to a fern-banked grotto set in an emerald hillside. Lindsay opened the gate to follow it, but a cacophony of angry barking broke out from a hut near the grotto. Dogs defending their sheep from her intrusion, no doubt — she stepped back behind the gate and peered through it. The dogs were tied, straining against their ropes and facing away from Lindsay towards the hillside.

Later, when she would try to reconstruct the scene, it would take on a sinister quality, the enchanting ferny cavern containing the seeds of pain and fear and death to come. Now she was only surprised to see two figures, one red-haired and carrying a yellow Cobb's case, appear at the mouth of the grotto: Sharon and friend. They looked towards the dogs, then vanished again inside.

The meaning of Sharon's appearance here struck Lindsay after her first few steps towards the town, and she almost laughed aloud. Sharon was as tired of their tandem touring as she, and her invitation to Lindsay to meet her friend had been made to ensure that she didn't. Lindsay was to have been sitting at the sidewalk cafe, half an hour's walk from the meadow, at this moment. Had she feared Lindsay might try to poach the friend for herself? He had looked darkly handsome in the distance, but Lindsay would not have sacrificed the afternoon's privacy for a rendezvous with Prince Charles.

Privacy was abruptly shattered around the path's next turning.

"At last! I thought perhaps you'd fallen overboard." It was Dirk, shining like the whitewashed walls. To push aside all that vibrant affection was going to be like kicking a puppy who had run up to be loved. "Lindsay, Lindsay, where have you been? I waited hours for you last night. I missed the last bus yesterday to the Acropolis, hoping you'd come; the taxis were on strike, and I didn't get there at all. You must have gone. Your cabin was empty."

"I'd promised Sharon; we were on the first bus."

"Sharon! That's a dreadful girl, and one can see that you don't like her awfully either. I'm afraid I've done something to make you angry at me."

"You know best if you have." That hadn't come out at all as planned; Lindsay had decided on remoteness and civility, and her voice had contained neither.

Dirk's eyes widened, the thinking process going on behind them as evident as the workings of a glass timepiece. He was wondering how much she knew and how much he need admit. "You're thinking I jumped the gun on the Roud story."

That acknowledged nothing, merely sent the ball back to Lindsay's court. She began to return it — "Did you?" and then took pity. "The radio had a spell of clarity yesterday morning — during a BBC news broadcast."

"Oh, God." The puppy, forced to look at the mess it had made. "It all turned out beautifully anyway; Hamish is back, covered with glory." A wag of the tail, rather brave, actually.

"Did you know he'd been found when you sent the story?"

"I — no, I didn't know. I was sure he was safe, though, or I shouldn't have done it, honestly. Lindsay, it got me the place I spoke about — I talked to them yesterday from Athens. Quite a step up from those tabloids of which you disapprove."

"Oh, I *am* glad. What magazine is it?"

The innocent eyes stayed on hers. *"Private Eye."*

Lindsay began quite helplessly to laugh. Dirk must have been sent here to try some element in her. She had seen the magazine, and its prurience differed from that of the worst tabloids only in its overlay of smarmy schoolboy wit. She recovered herself. "I'm sorry about the Acropolis. Did you get to the National Museum?"

"Yes." He studied her. "You don't like *Private Eye*. I ought to have known. I shouldn't like it either, except that I've got to eat and sleep somewhere until I can get into what I really want to do. I write serious things, you know, but I haven't been very successful yet." Oh, God, another of those. "One only needs one sale, you know, one entry." The round brown eyes pleaded for her to take him seriously.

She was being an absolute bitch and had no right whatever to sit in judgment of this — boy. And her playing at judge placed more importance than there was on their relationship. Lindsay could carry on a shipboard flirtation, fleeting and probably fun if she could stop taking herself so seriously. After the heavy going of the winter, it might be precisely the right thing.

"Peace," she said and held out her hand. Dirk took it, not as it had been offered in casual friendliness but to hold as they turned down the walled path that led to the town.

Milly found two embroidered shirts for the boys and an odd, colorful necklace for her brother. Her shopping allowance was half gone, and she planned purchases in Istanbul and Rhodes, so to avoid temptation she sat down at a sidewalk cafe between Max and Sharon, who had inexplicably attached herself to them.

Ah, the inexplicable explained: Milly saw Lindsay and Dirk in close communion at a table outside the next cafe. Max would be pleased, having pointed out to Milly Dirk's general superiority to Evan, who shared Lindsay as a dancing partner. Milly too was glad to see some social reshuffling; Lindsay struck one as a private little person and appeared half-smothered by Sharon.

Sarah, package-laden, sank into a chair beside Max while Reg pulled another up beside Milly. He carried five or six newspapers, all yesterday's but the first they had seen in a week, and distributed them around the table, keeping for himself a French language paper published in Cairo. Milly, sipping cold fruit juice, immersed herself in the *New York Times.*

"Good God, listen to this!" Reg exclaimed. "The Muslim version of Simon's rescue, loosely translated. Our Evan, accompanied by twenty counter-revolutionary agents, broke into the prison at Palat, killed two heroic guards and the Russian prisoner, and made off with Simon. Pursuing forces claim to have captured and executed several of the agents, and they suggest that others may be abroad in the area."

"But the place was deserted—"

"What magnificent imaginations they must have, all Lewis Carroll," Sarah said. "It's almost amusing."

"Not so amusing if one is wearing Evan's hat," Reg said

thoughtfully. "They label him thief and murderer and, damn it, the paper places him on this cruise. No mention of Hamish, fortunately. Good luck we're stopping at no Shiite ports."

Milly was frightened. "There's a large Shiite population in Turkey."

"Reg, this concoction almost tops that," Max interrupted from behind his *London Telegraph*. "It's datelined Ephemae where Kurdish tribesmen reported discovery of the bodies of twenty-nine youths and children in the prison at Palat. Now a statement from a mullah in Persarum: the 'young martyrs' were murdered by the Kurds themselves and will be avenged by the heroic soldiers of the revolution. Ungh. Well, Simon's story will set most of the world straight."

"Simon Roud?" Sharon asked. "What does he know about it?"

"He saw it," Reg answered, "and saw two mullahs order it just before they evacuated Palat. The victims were school-children."

"It's so terribly sad," Sharon said, including them all in her gentle, mournful smile, "how much indignation is aroused by the execution of a few criminals, when we heard almost nothing about the thousands murdered by the Emir."

"Criminals—" Sarah began, and then stopped herself. They had a tacit agreement to ignore Sharon's proselytizing. Sarah assumed the sweet expression that Milly had learned to recognize as dangerous and directed crinkly green eyes at Sharon.

"What's that you've been reading, my dear?" Sharon, all innocence — Milly was almost sorry for her — brandished a paperback. "Ah, Gwen Noyes. I've heard of her — remarkable woman."

"Yes." Sharon looked not only surprised and pleased, but a light seemed to have been turned on inside her. "She's a saint, really. I've worked beside her."

"Have you heard of her, Reg?" Pollyanna would have detected menace in the sweetness and light exuding now from Sarah, but Sharon remained bright-eyed and expectant. "It seems that almost ten percent of the population is susceptible to this dreadful perversion, and, if the times or the culture encourage it, even greater numbers can be affected."

"What perversion is that, my dear?" Reg asked. They

136

must, Milly thought, have rehearsed it.

"A compulsion to prune or hack everyone into conformity with their own religiosity. It must be dreadfully embarrassing for the poor families. Imagine having to listen to one's moppet tell all and sundry that God will punish them for their evil ways."

The faint pity that had touched Milly ended quickly; the girl thrust her lips forward like a snake's, her eyes hot with hate.

"I understand." Max had unfortunately snickered, and her glance raked them all. "You call the teachings of Christ Jesus perverse."

"Oh, hardly that, my dear," Sarah said blandly. "I call myself a Christian, though a lax one, I suppose, and Reg attends a service each Sunday. But, try as I will, I can't remember any comment whatever from Jesus about homosexuality."

"I suggest you study your Bible." The saccharine tone had returned, but it was strained, and Sharon's toothsome smile was nearer a snarl. "It is said directly that man who lies with man is to be put to death, and his blood will be upon him. God's law does not change."

"It bends a lot, though," Reg said. "That's from Leviticus, which calls for the same penalty for a man who lies with a menstruating woman. Deuteronomy prescribes stoning to death for a disobedient child, parents who try to protect him and women who cannot prove virginity on the wedding nights. So far as I know, no Jewish nor Christian cult has acted accordingly for many centuries."

"It wasn't the ancients alone. Paul himself said that 'such are worthy of death.' "

"Paul of Tarsus." Max had set down his newspaper to join the sport of bigot-baiting. Milly wished they would all stop it. Reason would never shift Sharon, and Max might now say something that would offend Reg, who was devoutly Church of England. "A man with a way with words but — some fairly severe sexual hangups. 'Better to marry than to burn,' he said, implying that it was not much better. He referred to the bodies of women as 'vessels of putrescence.' He would seem to have regarded the activity in which the Noyes woman must have indulged at least twice — she has more than one child, hasn't she? — as an abomination in any form."

"The devil and scripture," Sharon said softly and she headed back to the ship.

Shoppers carrying yellow cases began to separate themselves from the crowds and to straggle down the quay toward the Alexandros. Max gathered his packages, pushed his chair back from the table and collided with Evan, who had been passing behind them.

"Oh, sorry, stupid of me," Evan murmured and hurried off to the quay. It had not been his place to apologize, and Milly had seen white lines of tension form around his mouth. It wasn't, as she had thought, merely that they hadn't taken to each other; Max had hurt him in some way.

"What's happened between you and Evan?" she asked Max as they dressed for dinner in Hector Six.

"Not a happening, only a condition. It's just there. I won't tell you it's caused by my fictitious religious bent if you won't tell me it's an unconscious attraction to them."

"That never entered my mind — I've watched you watch girls for too many years." No, Max's homophobia had its roots in deeper soil, Milly knew: his obsessive anxiety for the boys, particularly Alex who resembled Milly's only and egregiously gay brother, Tom. She had watched it form over the years in nervous silence, having no answer for Max. She had read that the direction a child's sexuality would take was determined before he was five, and possibly it was true, but at sixteen, Alex remained a cipher. He was gentler than other boys and more appreciative of beauty just as Tom had been, but he had none of the mannerisms early apparent in his uncle. As for sex, he continued to regard any form of it with the bored distrust of a ten-year-old.

"You were comfortable enough with Tom years ago. You two were great friends."

"Tom's different. I like Tom." So much, she thought, that he had avoided having the boys hear him since they could toddle. "Possibly these feelings increase with age, I don't know, don't care, really. Show me what you bought for the kids."

"After dinner. Reg doesn't have those feelings, and he's very hetero indeed."

"Reg is bucking for sainthood, I'm not. Look, I have to sit down to three meals a day with people who make me uncomfortable; I don't want to spend our few minutes of privacy being made uncomfortable by discussing them. All right?"

It was Greek night in the dining room, the fare more peculiar than usual. "Christ, Evan, what is it?"

"Put it on my plate." Hamish did, quickly; the single bite had slid down his throat as if alive.

"Octopus," Max said.

"Oh, my God." It threatened to escape the way it had come. Hamish secured it by downing a full glass of retsina.

"Bread." Evan pushed the basket at him. "Eat some bread."

Milly arrived late and a little fussed. "Bad news. Miss Shaw says they've had to cancel the Priene tour. They needed twenty, and only eleven signed for it."

Pity. Hamish had anticipated withdrawing his name from the list, if possible with Hodgkins, whose tour it was, looking on.

"They can't do that; they promised it — in the brochure!" The red-haired woman, Sharon, ought to have been a trage-dienne; her eyes were round with horror — as if she had heard the ship was sinking and the lifeboats gone.

"Oh, but I'm afraid they can," Reg said. "The same brochure says that Priene is an alternative to Ephesus and contingent upon the number of passengers booked."

"Sharon, you're not signed for Priene," Milly said. "I just saw the list."

"I forgot to book," she answered in the numbed tones of one who has just discovered a fatal, irreversible error.

"I wonder if there are others." Milly looked hopeful.

"We'll go if you need us to reach your twenty," Sarah offered.

"No, not fair," Milly answered. "I know Reg is interested in Ephesus — oh, George!"

Hodgkins was passing their table, late and distraught as usual, and stopped at Milly's call. "Sharon forgot to book for Priene and wants to go. Perhaps if we make an effort tonight, we can reach our twenty."

Hodgkins brightened. "Oh, super, super! I shall ask at our table, and you try, Milly — " His eyes fell on Evan, and confusion returned. "I'm so awfully sorry, Evan — or David — or — about the orange, I mean."

"I never eat them, actually." Evan bestowed a gracious smile upon the old bumbler, and Hamish seethed.

The hurt to his friend had throbbed in him all day like a

wound. Evan had been so open, no guard at all, giving himself to the boy like the best kind of teacher, and then Hodgkins with his filthy mind had spoiled it all. "Best subtract one from your list before you add," he told the professor. "I shan't be going."

"But I thought you were so keen on Hellenistic—"

"My keenness evaporated. At Delos."

Hamish saw Robin, too late, a bit behind his father, looking round at the three of them as if trying to compute a sum quickly. He found his answer, flushed scarlet and stalked away.

"That was totally unnecessary," Evan told him later in Hector Seven. "You embarrassed the boy."

Hamish was sorry to have spoken before Robin but he was not about to apologize. "Well, he ought to learn. You as well. If we keep taking that kind of thing from them, there's no end to it —"

"That's the sort of paranoid thinking that would appall my father."

"Your father." The most dangerous of their enemies, Hamish thought, and then it snapped out. "Are you quite certain that is Talbot?"

Evan's eyes went wide, his cheeks pale, and he turned from Hamish to disappear into the bathroom. Hamish stripped and crept into his own bed.

Why in God's name had he said such a thing? That was easy enough to answer: he wanted it to be true, wanted to remove the threat Talbot posed to their life together.

Evan came from the bathroom now, naked. "Good night, Hamish," he said gently but spread himself clean across his bunk, denying access to it. After the years without hope and their wonderful fulfilment, was this the sort of lover Hamish would be? Bruised by remorse, he set off toward sleep, letting tears scald his sunburnt cheeks.

10

Kusadasi; Priene — April 5: Evan wished he were back on the Alexandros; they had got one over their twenty anyway and wouldn't have needed him. He sat instead at the back of a half-filled bus beside the American with the odd accent. The man was well over six feet and solidly muscular but skittish, as if Evan were some kind of wild animal whose next move couldn't be predicted. Another homophobe like Ross, no doubt — Evan had had no idea that there were so many of them.

Milly, who usually sat in the seat just across from them, might have eased things. But, drunk with will power, she had decided to stop smoking and sat well forward on the bus, a few rows behind Lindsay and Sharon. John — was that his name? — and Evan could barely understand each other, and their few timid conversational openers had been so sprinkled with "whats" and "beg pardons" that they were not worth pursuing.

The situation was less uncomfortable than his arrival into it. George and Robin Hodgkins had preceded Evan onto the bus, George taking the front seat, opposite Sharon's, from which he would lecture. He motioned Robin to the place beside him, but Robin ignored the gesture and went to the back where he sat in the spot usually occupied by Hamish.

"Sit with me, Evan, would you please?"

Evan's decision had needed to be quick and had probably been wrong. He had pretended not to hear and passed Robin, ending up beside the American whose wife had taken the other excursion to Ephesus. Evan had meant to remove himself as an irritant between the father and son whose companionship was usually so appealing, but he had hurt the boy. The back of Robin's neck was pink with mortification, and he stared fixedly out the window at an empty bus labeled for Ephesus.

A young Turk who would be their local guide climbed inside the bus just before nine, sitting in the empty seat beside George, and they drove into the countryside toward the ordered jumble of stones and shards that had been a prosperous market village two thousand years earlier. George got his microphone going at last.

"Priene. We are about to see the outlines of an Hellenistic community, not a large or important one, but typical in its plan...."

Hamish would have come if Evan had insisted, but he could see that Hamish felt an about-face now would put him in a ridiculous light and had not pressed him.

Evan had lain awake for a long time after their quarrel, thinking at first of the hint at his bastardy. He had received others, the first when he was still at prep school, and for years the mirror had offered the broadest hint of all. He had broached it finally to his older brother. Andrew, always kind but preoccupied, had given Evan his full attention and a long, convincing lecture about the behavior of recessive genes, and the mirror had lost its horror.

Until the reading of his mother's will: whether from caprice, guilt or some knowledge of Francis' plans, she had made Evan's share of her estate as large as Andrew's and Monty's together, though during her life she had treated the three with even-handed disinterest. None of them had spoken of it nor in any way looked askance, but Evan had felt set further outside the magic circle occupied by other Talbots.

He had thought he understood the reasons for Hamish's outburst, but then minutes went by, seeming hours, with no overtures from him. Perhaps he was having second thoughts. Then real hours passed, Evan projecting a future without Hamish. Despite his physical needs, he knew no other man with whom he would want to share his life. His years as a homosexual would stretch before him, punctuated as they had been before by brief affairs, barren of any near and lasting relationship. Marriage? He could imagine a lifetime of dancing and housekeeping and talking with someone like Lindsay, but the thought of sex with her was as ugly as that of bedding a little sister.

He had drifted off after a while and then disturbed himself with his own whimper. "Cold. I'm cold."

"I'll give you my blanket." Hamish was wide awake.

Still sleep-fogged, Evan had murmured, "Don't bloody want your blanket," and had wakened himself completely. He had sounded like a child on the edge of tears. Hamish was in his bed beside him before he could finish the thought, and the spectres of lonely years or a dishonest marriage had dissolved in his warmth.

Since Evan was here, he ought really to be listening to George so that he could tell Hamish about it. George had circled back to Alexander the Great. ". . . peaceful, ordered existence that was unknown on the continent before the arrival of this extraordinary man. His genius for government actually outstripped his more widely acclaimed military gifts.

"An interesting aside: some of you may not know that Alexander, like so many other great men, was most probably homosexual."

Ho, rather nice! They hadn't taught *that* at Steppingford. Evan realized suddenly why George had said it and that it hadn't worked. Robin still stared out the window to his right, not a glance for his father. Evan ought to do something about that; planning what it would be, he missed the rest of George's lecture.

The driver stopped at a flower-spotted meadow beside the footpath that led to the site, and passengers lined up along the aisles for drinks and picnic lunches from the cartons beside him. Evan decided to plant himself firmly beside George and to invite Robin to join them, but it was too late. The professor was taken in tow by three British matrons before he reached the door, and Lindsay grasped Evan's arm urgently as he stepped from the bus.

"Let's take our lunches round the other side, Evan — quick, before they see us." Wilder and Sharon were engaged in argument beside the soft drinks.

Lindsay and Evan found privacy at the cost of comfort between a granite boulder and the sharply rising hill on which stood Priene. Evan set their lunches out on paper towels, and they hunched down in the narrow space. "Has Wilder been troubling you?" A ready, protective anger swelled in him.

"Not at all; it's Sharon. I'm beginning to feel like a prisoner, just had to get away for a bit."

"Odd girl. You've lost your egg." It had rolled into a crack beneath the boulder. "Have mine, won't you?"

"Thank you, no — there's far too much here to eat." She nibbled at cheese and water biscuits. "Odder than you know; she keeps a gun."

"My God! Lindsay, that won't do at all. I insist that you let me speak to Miss Shaw — she's forgiven me for the chador, and we're in the way of becoming friends — about finding you another cabin. There are several not in use on Achilles Deck."

Lindsay peeled her orange, thinking. "That might be best, though I believe they're more expensive. And perhaps you could speak to Miss Shaw about the gun. I'm concerned about Sharon's — well, her stability. She wanted above all things to see Ephesus, tried to talk me round to going there with her, and then you saw the performance last night when she heard this tour was cancelled."

"We'll do it this afternoon; you shan't spend another night with that woman."

"I'm probably being overly dramatic, but — oh, enough of Sharon. I'm tired of chicken as well. Would you like to have mine?" He would, and he ate it. "We sat with the young guide, an awfully nice boy. He's going to lecture about contemporary Turkey on the return trip. He's a medical student."

Yellow satchels could be seen on the footpath above them. They gathered their picnic debris and began the long climb to the site. Robin, ahead of them, had attached himself at last to the archeology students and was being talked to by the long-admired Maggie.

Priene had been laid out all at once, it seemed, very foursquare, and one could see where everything had been. Evan imagined a market day there, farmers displaying their produce, bleating goats tethered nearby, housewives testing this and pinching that, their children squatting at games in the smooth-tiled streets. It became almost real enough to draw, but he had left the sketching pad on shipboard.

Wilder apppeared beside them. "Oh, here you are, Lindsay — something I *must* show you." He dragged her off toward the ruined theater, and Evan saw Sharon bearing down on the two of them from the temple.

He spotted a prettily fashioned potsherd, pocketed it for

Hamish and, in rising, collided with Dr. Cameron. "Very exciting, all this. One would think archeologists would be standing in line to develop it," Evan chattered away, hoping to cover his embarrassment at being caught with the potsherd; probably Cameron regarded that sort of thing as childish.

The man looked down at Evan from his height, surprised as if one of the cur dogs that followed the group had spoken to him. "There are many more interesting sites waiting development in Turkey." He turned, bent over and picked up a shard of his own.

Evan had certainly lost his persona grata status today. He decided to climb up Priene's acropolis, but that was further than it looked, and he hadn't gone halfway before people were calling him to come back to the bus. He was down again before the last stragglers — Milly and Max — had left the ruins.

"Did you enjoy it?" Milly asked with proprietorial anxiety; she had revived the excursion almost single-handedly last night.

"Oh, *very* much. Look, I've something for your collection." He gave her, on impulse, the pottery fragment he had meant for Hamish and searched unsuccessfully for another on their walk down the footpath.

"I say, that's a different bus driver." The first had been greying and rather square; this one was slight, inches shorter than Evan, with an aquiline, boyishly handsome face.

"Ours not to reason who, ours but to load and queue," Milly quipped. "Perhaps Miss Shaw got wind of the other passing on blind curves and had him liquidated."

"There's a car back there and someone in it," Max said. "Probably it's the first driver, and this one's relieving him."

Evan was last on board, and, when he turned in his seat, the man from the car had joined them. The American beside him looked edgier than before. "Something is funny," he said.

The second man was clearly not their driver. He was very thin, and something was terribly wrong with his face; his mouth appeared to stretch almost to his ears, but irregularly, most of the lips composed of livid scar tissue. The two men faced the group from beside the steering wheel, the scarred one holding something. He lifted it now. It was a machine gun.

The boyish one spoke. "My name is Haneef, and I am

your new driver, my friend Sayed here your bodyguard. We are going to drive this bus with you in it a short distance. Most of you will be safe if you stay very, very still. There will be no talking." He started the engine, maneuvered the bus expertly from the cul-de-sac in which it had been parked and drove in a direction opposite to the one from which they had come.

The first mind-stopping thrill of fear passed, and Evan assessed their situation. Such things usually ended peacefully with surrender or exchange, but these chaps seemed the worst sort — mad ones. The driver's eyes had glittered like a cat's at night, and the other, Sayed, scowled evilly, directing his gun at each of them with little jerks. There had been Entebbe, of course — but also the Israeli athletes, the Spanish diplomats in Guatemala City, the 73 Cubans blown up by anti-Castro terrorists. The amulet — of being oneself and singularly alive — that one wore against disaster was a paper shield.

Cat-eyed Haneef drove them five miles over increasingly rough terrain and finally down an unpaved road where they were screened by a grove of trees. "We are going to wait here for a time." The vowels were American with a pretty, almost bird-like undertone of something else. "Sayed likes to practice his marksmanship; I suggest that none of you give him reason."

No one did; they sat rigid with increasing discomfort — the bus was in full sunlight, windows were closed. Evan saw sweat roll down Robin's neck; his own shirt was soaking. Their captors were in no better state. Haneef spoke to the scarred chap at length in a tongue that seemed all consonants. Sayed nodded or shook his head, never speaking, never taking the gun nor his eyes from his captives.

"We are going to leave you for a few minutes," Haneef told them. "No one is to change his place nor move at all. We will be watching from only a few feet away, and your windows are not bullet-proof."

"May we smoke?" young Maggie asked pertly. Haneef, beside her in an instant, slapped her face.

"No talking or smoking; I thought I'd been quite clear about the first. Sayed will deal with the next rule-breaker." The machine gun was brandished on cue. Haneef left them first, moving to the shade of the grove, and stood watching, directing a pistol at the bus while Sayed ran to join him. The shift was accomplished in seconds.

"Considerate chaps," Dr. Cameron remarked casually. "They might have parked us all in the shade."

"Only think of last month in Yorkshire," a British matron said firmly, "and it will pass."

This was going to be the tone — no hysterics.

"Robin, are you all right back there?"

"Oh, fine, Daddy, very well."

"Lindsay?"

"Fine, Evan." This time Wilder had managed to take the seat beside her, and Evan couldn't see her at all past the red head of Sharon who sat alone four rows in front of him.

John spoke slowly and distinctly beside Evan. "It might be we ought to make some plans. Is anyone thinking about how we can take these bastards?"

"I'd think very slow and easy if I were you," Max said. "They look to me like a couple of grenades with loose pins."

"Agreed," Evan said softly. "Please don't move your head so much; the machine gun is trained at our window."

"Sorry." John straightened and was quiet, but something was happening with Robin. He had been sliding imperceptibly down in his seat until by now his head must be invisible from outside.

"What's wrong, Robin?" Evan whispered.

"Nothing. Please be still." Perhaps he was planning to crawl along the floor and join his father at the front.

"You mustn't change seats; stay where you are, and when they get back, pretend you've been sleeping."

That hadn't been what he was up to at all. Robin's seat blocked a second, unused door to the bus, and he was down behind it; Evan heard him working away at the handle. "No, please, old chap, don't do it. You've nowhere to go."

"Only a few miles to that village outside Priene. I can raise an alarm—"

The door opened, and Evan heard the light impact of Robin's feet on the dust outside. Robin's tidiness defeated him. He tried to ease the door back to a closed position, and it snapped shut with a metallic click. Both men in the grove started at the sound and fanned out, Sayed loping with long strides toward the front of the bus, the other running lightly to the back.

Robin scuttled, head low, towards the maquis that would shield him but found himself in focus of the machine gun as

147

Sayed rounded the front. "Freeze, Robin!" George shrieked. Instead, possibly remembering Evan's refuge at Palat, Robin dove under the bus and out of sight. He was trapped, and their captors knew it; they circled the bus slowly.

The young guide, Ahmad, stood up and opened the front door. "Come this way," he called down to Robin, "back onto the bus." A pistol shot pierced the windscreen and hit squarely at the back of Ahmad's neck where it joined the skull. Someone screamed once and stopped. Ahmad toppled slowly like a felled tree out the door and lay motionless in the red-brown dirt.

They would kill the boy as well. They would give him minutes, perhaps, to feel the hopelessness of his position, and then one of them would lie on the ground and aim his gun — Evan saw again a face from the prison yard, the child whose eyes Hamish had closed. He wouldn't look at that again, wouldn't let it happen.

Evan ducked down and crawled to the side door which Robin had worked free. He opened it and, lying on the floor, pushed his head and shoulders over its threshold so he could see beneath the bus. "Here," he whispered, "hurry." The boy scrambled towards him, but two pairs of feet by the front of the bus began running in the same direction. Evan reached under and hooked Robin's arms in his, hauling him into shelter just as the second pistol shot sounded.

He flung Robin into the seat beside the American and stood blocking the doorway as Haneef reached it. The pistol was leveled at his face, and Evan closed his eyes as if their lids might shield him.

"Don't shoot," someone called, "that's Talbot."

Nothing happened, and Evan let his eyes open. The face before him had changed and now wore a lively, charming smile. "Mr. Talbot, ah. It would be better if you moved back so that I could come in." Evan, confused, stayed where he was. "The boy will be safe — if he behaves properly. We don't war against children."

Evan stepped back uncertainly, keeping his body between Haneef and Robin. Haneef swung himself through the doorway and pressed his gun against Evan's chest, steering him into the aisle and backward toward the front of the bus. They passed Robin without casting a glance at him.

Haneef reached into a pocket and drew out a package of matches which he let fall on the floor between them.

"I seemed to have dropped something, Mr. Talbot, and my hands are occupied. Would you be so kind as to pick it up for me?"

Evan reached out with his left hand, then withdrew it, substituting the right one. Haneef's boot flashed out just as Evan touched the matches, its heel grinding slowly into the fingers at the knuckles. Evan flung his head back, and his eyes caught those of Max Ross, beside whose place this was happening to him; he choked off the scream that had welled in his throat. It would evidently never stop; one could hear bones snapping like party favors. The specific agony, which he couldn't have borne much longer, turned to an enormous aching that seemed to contain him. He hardly felt himself subside to his knees, then over, until he was lying jack-knifed at the feet of his tormentor.

The boot heel was removed, and Haneef smiled down upon him. "I'm afraid I was awkward, Mr. Talbot; you may stand now." Perhaps he might, if he could get his knees under him, but they weren't responding to the commands from his brain. Max knelt beside him on the floor and tried to help him up. "Your assistance is kind but unnecessary," Haneef chirped, and Evan caught sight of the pistol again. It was pointing at, touching, the back of Milly's neck.

"Go back, Max," he breathed, and Max saw it too and left him, giving his shoulder one hard, helpless grasp as he went. Evan got himself up, using the seat across from Max's as support. The hand of the woman occupying it touched and pressed his, and he was pushed backward and away from them until he collided with the steering wheel.

Haneef was beside him with the shining look of a host at a successful party. "I'm sure all of you know Mr. Talbot," he said. "Twice a thief. Islam has a way of dealing with theft." Evan, between spasms of pain, was able to look at the others. Before him, Lindsay's face was set and ashen; Wilder sat beside her pop-eyed. The big American at the back had buried his face in his hands; Cameron was bloodless. He felt their collective, horrified support, and it strengthened him. There was no screaming yet, though one could see that building in the girl, Maggie; Evan had to stop it.

"The game they are playing is called Terror," he said, his voice reassuringly clear and even to his own ears. "If we show it, they win. Let's show them instead—"

Something exploded on and inside Evan's head. There had been no gunshot, and he wasn't dead. He refused to lie down for them and began to rise from someone's lap where he had fallen. It was Lindsay's. "Stop," she whispered to him, "stay still, dear. You've done it, there'll be no panic — unless you succeed in getting yourself killed altogether." She held him down firmly by the shoulders, and he let his head, in which heavy seas roared, relax into the crook of her arm.

"They killed him. The filthy bastards went and killed him." There was no fright in the Mississippi drawl, only rising fury. Fear, the sharpest yet, joined the dismay Max felt for Evan — this idiot could trigger a massacre.

"No," Cameron quieted. "I can see his head. He was trying to get up."

The pretty one with the mad eyes walked down the aisle and stood over John Trimble, smiling his sweet smile. The man from Mississippi glowered back. "Please," Max called, low and soft, "I'm a doctor. Please let me see to that man in the front." Max had little hope that he would be allowed to do that — or to examine the Turkish boy outside who was surely dead — but he wanted urgently to end the confrontation between John and the terrorist.

Haneef didn't answer, but he left John to stand beside Max and prod him with the muzzle of his pistol, the one with which he had struck down Evan and shot Ahmad. Max strained to keep his head still despite the nervous contractions of his neck muscles. Haneef moved back to the front with the step of a carefree child.

"There will be no more talking, I think. Sayed and I wish to meditate."

Max and Milly pressed hands. George Hodgkins' desperate glances over his shoulder toward Robin had been ended by a prod from the pistol. Evan stirred again, and Lindsay murmured something to him, like a mother soothing a sick child; the terrorists ignored them.

One of the English women was going into an asthma attack, her coughing and desperate attempts to suppress it resounding in the absolute silence. The sound of a motor grew behind them, and Max saw a green Volkswagen pass his window, bouncing over the uneven ground; it stopped a few feet away.

Haneef jumped from the bus to meet a much taller, slightly older man from the car, but the scarred fellow stayed, saluting each of them with the muzzle of his gun. The new one bent down and out of Max's sight at the door, evidently to examine the young Turk who lay before it. He rose, looking saddened and displeased, speaking vehemently to a sheepish Haneef. Haneef bent down and reappeared, dragging the body of their guide off to the scrub brush.

The tall man saw Evan before he was inside the bus and went to him first, bending on one knee to study him. "So this is Mr. Talbot. Beautiful." He spoke in unaccented American. "How in hell did he get in this state?"

No one answered, and he stood looking from face to face at his captives. "This is over now, for the rest of you; you will return to your ship. I'm sure it's been very unpleasant, very frightening, and I'm sorry that it was necessary. Mr. Talbot will come with us."

This one looked almost sane. Max ventured. "Your people won't gain much from a dead hostage. I'm a doctor, and I would like to treat—"

"Doctor — ah?"

"Ross. That man received a severe blow to his head."

The new enemy leaned over Evan once more, feeling his head and chest. "This man isn't dying, Dr. Ross. His breathing is quite normal."

"You are going to have to get him an antibiotic; that hand is certain to become infected."

"Please." George Hodgkins stood up suddenly and looked valiantly up at the taller terrorist. "I know that you want to take someone who is well-known, and I understand your reasoning. I happen to have an international reputation as an archeologist, and my taking would not go unnoticed. It seems that you might do better to take me — someone all in one piece, so to speak."

The sane one looked back at George mildly. "I'm afraid, professor, that your prominence is not the stuff of which headlines are made. Not only is Talbot the son of a famous man, but his own recent crime against Islam justifies his taking and any steps that may later become necessary." He turned again to Max.

"Dr. Ross, you are a physician, you've shown concern for Talbot, and I'll tell you how you can best help him. A ransom demand will be delivered, to you personally, at one of the sites your group will visit. You may surround yourself with the entire British and American secret service if you choose. We insist only that you not stray from the other tourists so that our contact can see and reach you." He pulled Evan to his feet, and Sayed led him from the bus.

"Take care, Evan," Lindsay called. He turned a blind, misdirected smile toward her and walked without support or protest to the Volkswagen.

Their captor took the keys from the bus's ignition. "I leave you a way back to your ship but a start for us too." He threw them out as far as he could into the maquis and ran for the Volkswagen.

They rushed from the sweltering bus, all nineteen, some to hunt for the keys, others merely to suck in the air so long denied them. Cameron stumbled over the body of the young guide and asked Max to help him carry it back to the bus. They laid him out on the back seat where Cameron would sit on the return journey to keep him from sliding to the floor.

Dirk Wilder found the keys and turned them over to the man from Mississippi who knew how to drive the bus. He drove slowly back onto the road and then gathered speed, not slackening as they approached Priene.

"John," Cameron said, "we've got to stop and look for the bus driver."

It was Lindsay who found him, behind a granite boulder abutting the hill. He was conscious but in great pain from the tight bonds around his wrists and ankles. They bore him onto the bus where Milly and others took turns massaging circulation back to his swollen hands and feet.

She returned to sit beside Max after a while. "Evan couldn't see," she said.

"No, that often happens, even with minor head injuries."

Just in front, Robin Hodgkins let his head droop onto his father's shoulder.

Something was awry again at the cruise desk; Miss Shaw failed to return Hamish's smile as he replaced his landing tag and she was the nearest he had ever seen to being disconcerted. Hamish didn't stop, presuming it was about the launch to Kusadasi which had damned near tipped its passengers into the sea — definitely not standard Cobb's service.

The Priene group had been scheduled back half an hour earlier, but Evan was not in Hector Seven. Hamish went upstairs to the deck and had almost rounded it before realizing that he had not seen any passenger who had gone to Priene. Miss Shaw's consternation, the way the Turkish bus drivers rushed about—

He returned to the cruise desk to ask Miss Shaw what it was about, but he heard her first, speaking into a telephone, and turned his back pretending to study the postcards displayed opposite her office.

"I've told them to search the ravines — of course, you're quite right. It's flat most of the way to Priene. One feels so helpless. Oh, hold on, please do — I think I see them on the quay."

Hamish turned and looked out. The bus was there, the small launch captained by a wizened octogenarian and crewed by his small great-grandson awaiting its passengers. Its appearance didn't relieve Hamish's anxiety altogether, perhaps because of his own queasy passage in the same launch. And the tiny, distant figures leaving the bus weren't behaving properly; they looked straight ahead, huddled together with none of the random movements of head and arms that one has in a holiday group.

The sea had quieted a little in the past hour, but the launch threatened to founder in each trough as it approached the Alexandros. It missed the gangplank completely at the first try and took ten minutes rounding the ship to line itself up again. The connection was made at last, and the Alexandros' first mate helped a passenger onto Heracles Deck. It was the elderly woman whose luggage Evan and Hamish had rescued in Venice, her face gone grey as her hair. She saw Hamish and pressed his elbow.

"Chin up, young man," she said. "It's going to be all right, has to be." One of the cruise girls hustled her away before Hamish could reply, and now all of the launch passengers came into view; Evan wasn't among them.

Robin was next, helped by his father and Dr. Cameron. Robin's mouth quivered at sight of Hamish. "I'm to blame," he began.

"Nonsense," Cameron said. "You were very brave and with better luck would have saved us all." Lindsay then, followed by Wilder and Sharon — Lindsay's dress front was spotted and smeared with blood.

"You've been hurt," Hamish cried.

"No. No, I —"

Hamish knew then whose blood it was, and Lindsay saw that he knew and reached out to him. "He's alive, but—" She clung to him, comforting and being comforted.

"Miss Wilson, we have the authorities on the ship-to-shore, and you're needed in the captain's quarters." It was Miss Shaw, pale and grim, backed by the captain. Hamish released Lindsay and caught her again as she tripped blindly over the first step to Hector Deck. Wilder tried to support her from the other side but she shrugged him away.

"Hamish, wait for me in the lounge; I'll be there as soon as I can—" Gently, the captain hurried her up the stairs.

"I know she blames me, thinks it wouldn't have happened if they hadn't known about Roud," Hamish heard Wilder tell Sharon as they pressed past him. "She'll never forgive me—"

Hamish must be in some Kafkaesque dream in which people tried to deliver an urgent message in an unintelligible language. Max Ross took his arm and led him back from the stairway.

"I don't think Evan is badly hurt, Hamish, but I have to tell you that he's been kidnapped."

11

At Sea — April 6: Max arrived first at the breakfast table and sat alone for a few minutes picking at food he didn't want. Reg appeared.

"Where is everyone?" The room was half empty and very quiet. Max shrugged. "How is Milly bearing up?"

"Not awfully well; I almost wish she'd go back to martinis. I think she blames herself more than the terrorists."

"Because she revived the Priene excursion? That's ridiculous; they'd have found another way."

"No, because of her blunder the second night at table when she let slip that Evan and David Talbot were one and the same."

"Max, the newspapers had had that for two days. Remind her of that piece of mythology from the Cairo one."

"I did, and I've been thinking about that. How did it get out so quickly? You'd think that Simon would have withheld it until Evan was back in England."

"That Dirk someone, Lindsay's friend, is — a tabloid reporter." Reg pronounced the words as if he were picking up something nasty. "The radio operator told Miss Shaw that he'd sent out a story for him on April second."

"I see. Even so, Reg, this operation has to have been in the works longer than that."

"No question but it was." Reg eyed him assessingly. "The intended victim was someone else." Though he had not been on the bus, Max remembered that Reg had been closeted on the ship-to-shore longer than anyone else, speaking to his old

155

associate, Colonel Cobb. Perhaps the secret service ties still existed.

"The tennis player, Frank Culver," Max said.

"Yes," Reg looked pleased as if he had said something unusually bright. "His mother is Jewish, and he's made some pro-Israeli sounds that could have made him target." Reg fell silent, dipping his croissant into an egg yolk.

"I imagine this kind of thing takes a lot of planning. Someone must have been appalled when Culver didn't appear on the cruise."

"Quite. Pass the bacon, would you, Max?"

"Then to find someone of Talbot's prominence on board and learn he'd pulled off a coup they could call a crime against Islam — Reg! They have to have had a contact here — on the Alexandros!"

"We think so." Reg continued to eat calmly and a great deal while Max sipped his coffee, and thought.

"You don't suppose—" He glanced at Sharon's empty chair.

"No, we don't. The contact is not a casual one but someone with power to make decisions. At least two major changes of plan have to have been made from the ship. Evan wasn't booked for Priene originally. He and Hamish signed for it in Athens."

"Hamish too? Thank God he changed his mind; there'd have been more blood shed on that bus. As for the girl, Reg, Milly finds her rather sinister — after our set-to on Mykonos, she's asked me to confine our exchanges to 'please pass the butter.'"

"I think Sharon's merely gaga, and I was sorry for my share in the Mykonos business; those things never help. At any rate, Max, these Shiites are puffed up with male chauvinism, and one can't imagine them taking orders from a woman."

"Mm." The British monosyllable was contagious and Max, who held determinedly to his American accent, caught himself using it to express all shades of agreement and its opposite. "The people with whom you spoke — do they give Evan any chance at all?"

Reg considered him seriously. "I'd got an impression that you disliked Evan."

"I'm afraid you were right, and I have nothing to plead but

the grossest kind of prejudgment. I saw that for what it was yesterday. I don't think I've ever respected a man more than Evan at — " He stopped, oddly unwilling to describe the surge of pride he had felt at Evan's shining gallantry, as if sharing it might make it less.

"I'm glad," Reg said. "Your good opinion of Evan makes it easier for me to ask something of you." Max had never seen Reg smoke, but he drew a package of Sarah's cigarettes from his pocket now, lit one and inhaled it deeply. "First in two years. This tastes marvelous.

"Max, we think it's possible that another contact will be made between the terrorist on this ship and the ones holding Evan. If we could find and watch him, he might lead us to them. I thought the three of us might put our heads together."

"To think I could do anything at all would be comforting. Three — Sarah?"

"Actually not. Sarah tends to be a bit — ah — gregarious and totally lacking in paranoia. Delightful qualities in one's wife but not so fine for this sort of business. I'm thinking of Hamish."

"Of course. For all that peaceful, sleepy look of his, his handling of the driver at Palat showed what I'd call flair."

They found Lindsay with Hamish when he admitted them to Hector Seven, and it was evident that she had been saying something important and unfinished; she was waiting for Max and Reg to leave as Reg was waiting for her. Silence followed their rapid-fire pleasantries and settled over the cabin. Max broke it.

"I'm sure we've all been discussing the same thing. I'd be interested to hear your conclusions."

Silence resumed, Reg and the girl sizing each other like strangers. Remembering Lindsay's sense and courage on the bus, Max plunged. "Look, I think Reg is concerned that nothing we discuss should leave this cabin. His reasons are good."

Lindsay flushed. "If you're concerned that I might tell anything whatever to Dirk Wilder, you needn't be."

The two-way appraisal looked as if it might go on for hours; Hamish stepped into it. "I think Lindsay is onto something, and she's anxious that it be kept quiet as well. One of the kidnappers is on this ship."

Reg leaned forward from his seat on Hamish's bunk. "And

Lindsay has a guess at who it might be?"

"More than a guess, nearer a certainty," she answered reluctantly. "Reg, what use would you make of a certainty?"

"There's a possibility that the terrorist here may try to contact the others once more, and a close watch on him might just lead us to Evan."

"Ah." The appraisal was ended, at both sources. "I knew you'd been in touch with the authorities, Reg, and was afraid you might have her arrested immediately — and lose our only hope of locating Evan."

"Her?"

"Sharon."

"Why do you say that, Lindsay?" Reg looked disappointed. "Because of her addled religiosity?"

"Not at all." Lindsay's eyes were huge, her cheeks pink with intensity — she was straining now to convince. "Because I saw her meet with a man on Mykonos who resembled the third terrorist, and she had made elaborate arrangements to keep their meeting private. Because she carries a pistol. Because she was so disturbed at the cancellation of the Priene tour that she reversed her own plans. Because, though she claimed to dislike him, she was distressed at Frank Culver's failure to appear. And because she has a pathological personal hatred for Evan."

"Mm." Reg lit another cigarette and inhaled it thoughtfully. "Did she know that you saw her at Mykonos?"

"No. She apologized for not meeting me, saying that her friend had been very late. I only said I hadn't waited long."

"That's good, that's very good. But how would she, an apparently protected American girl, have met such a person?"

"Sharon is not so protected as she looks. She's been traveling on her own for several years as a representative for her church, which has connections with some right-wing political group and seemingly limitless funds. She carries money in bundles."

"That might explain their willingness to take orders—" Reg began.

"Lindsay," Hamish interrupted, "you hadn't told me about the gun. I don't like that at all, and if you insist on staying in the cabin with her, I'm going to dispose of the thing. Where does she keep it?"

"We can't do that—"

"Lindsay's right," Reg said. "If the gun disappears, she's

158

certain to get the wind up. You've made a convincing case, young lady, but I wish I could be absolutely certain. If we're watching the wrong person or if more than one is involved, we'll lose our chance."

"More than one," Max said. "I've been thinking about that possibility. Reg, would Miss Shaw give you access to the passports? The stamps on them and their dates would tell us if another passenger's travels coincided with Sharon's."

"You can consider that done, Max — and Miss Shaw's discretion is boundless. But if the girl isn't involved at all—"

"She's involved, Reg," Max said with some satisfaction. "I've remembered something as we've been talking. At the time my attention was so riveted on Evan that it didn't register. The one called Haneef had his pistol to Evan's face, and someone called, 'Don't shoot, that's Talbot.' Did you hear it, Lindsay?"

"No, but I don't think I'd have heard a call to Armageddon just then. I suppose one's senses freeze at moments like that."

"It was definitely a woman's voice, I can almost hear it. Now: Maggie was almost afraid to breathe after she'd been slapped and was looking straight ahead; she couldn't have seen Evan at all. The other women were Lindsay, Milly, Mrs. Padgett-Brown, who's well past eighty, and those three Hokinson types that are always together. If it was one of them, these people have achieved a new dimension in the art of disguise."

Reg lit his third cigarette of the morning and shook his head in confusion. "But if the terrorists didn't know Evan by sight, it would have been crucial for Sharon to be on that bus; yet you've told me that she'd first planned to go to Ephesus."

"The third terrorist knew Evan and went straight to him, Reg. Look," Max said, "I have no doubt at all that Sharon is a conspirator, perhaps even the engineer of this thing, but I don't understand why all of you believe she'll contact the others. Put yourself in her place: her job is done; why run further risk? Or in their places: Sharon must be considered a valuable asset in her role as Judas goat — American, attractive, apparently beyond suspicion. This thing has the earmarks of something that will be repeated, and they'd hardly chance losing her."

"But I'm thinking about Sharon herself," Lindsay said. "She has a frenetic quality; one can't imagine her calmly leaving well enough alone."

Hamish, haggard and taut, looked at the wall above Max's head. "I have to think it," he said. "I don't believe these people will ask only for money, and I don't believe they'll be given what they ask. We seem to be Evan's only hope."

Reg and Hamish spent the next minutes before disembarkation working out arrangements to back up Lindsay should Sharon slip away from her on shore. Max's vigil for the ransom note would begin in less than an hour at Canakkale.

Hall of the Grand Master: Two men stood looking down at him; no, it was one. The figures merged together, blurred despite the bright light outlining them from behind.

"Good, you can see me now." The slight nod hurt Evan's head and was regretted; he ought to have let them think him still blind. "I'm Altaf. I wasn't part of what happened on the bus, and I'm very sorry for it — the death of the guide as well as your injuries, Mr. Talbot."

Evan said nothing, trying to pull the ragged edges of his mind into focus as the figure before him became clearer. Altaf was older than Sayed and Haneef, probably, like Evan, in his late twenties. The face, framed by curling dark hair, was strong-featured, thoughtful, almost benevolent, the dress casual and European — an open-necked blue sports shirt over tan stay-press slacks.

"We are going to be together here for a few days." The accent was standard American. "I hope we can manage it without hating each other too much."

"And after the few days?"

"We hope to return you to your family. Now, if I might look at your hand—" Evan had covered it defensively with the other, which he lifted now. The change in pressure set it throbbing again, and he looked down at his stomach where it rested. The fingers were a bloodied purplish jumble swollen to twice normal size.

Altaf reached out to touch it, then drew back. "I'm afraid there are broken bones which should be set. I don't know how soon I can produce a doctor here. Are you in much pain?"

"A bit." Odd how social habit persisted under the most bizarre conditions.

"Aspirin, perhaps—"

Evan was allergic to it and would then have nausea to deal

with too. "I should prefer a cigarette, actually, and a drink of water."

"One moment." Altaf flashed a white-toothed smile and was gone. Evan studied his quarters. Spacious, lofty and light, the room was not at all eastern in feeling but seemed to be part of a decaying palazzo. Plaster cherubs, trumpets and vine wreaths moldered on the high, water-stained ceiling. The corners were cluttered with debris — rags, bottles, empty tins, a discarded broom — as if it served as a rubbish heap for adjoining living quarters. The metal bed and bare mattress on which Evan lay must have been trashed as well; the odor of mice and mildew pervaded its protruding ticking.

One long, narrow window stretched almost across the wall facing the bed; it was chest-high and glassless, open to what felt like a sea breeze. Evan would investigate it but without great hope. Looking out from the bed, he could see only the tops of large trees; it would be a long drop, and the tree tops were far out of reach. The only other exit was the doorless doorway through which Altaf had gone; Evan had heard him running down a number of steps.

He returned with an enamel pitcher of water and a paper cup, both useless as weapons, and a camping stool which he unfolded and sat on. Evan drank, thirstily.

"The cigarettes are yours, from your jacket." Altaf set them down beside him, along with a book of matches. "I'm afraid I can't let you keep the matches." He waited to have them used and returned. Evan waited too, silently and stubbornly.

"You've changed your mind? You don't want the cigarette?"

"There's a trick for lighting a match with one hand, but I don't know it." He would exercise the fingers and get the hand back into working order when no one was about.

Altaf lit the cigarette and gave it to him. "I'm sorry, that was thoughtless." Evan began to sit up to smoke it, but the sudden pain in his head was obscured by that from the disturbed hand. He fell back to see the rotting cherubs fly round and round the ceiling above him. Use the hand, hell — he was immobilized by it.

"I'm going to fix a sling for you so that won't be jarred when you move." Altaf took the cigarette and disappeared again, returning with a large patterned silk handkerchief.

"Hold it still with your left hand." He eased Evan into a sitting position.

"Awfully sorry, but I'm going to be sick." Altaf got the plastic bucket they had left him under Evan's chin in time, and he spewed the water he had drunk into it, continuing to retch after it was gone.

"This is too bad; this is really too bad," Altaf said solicitously. "There was no damned reason for it." After the retching subsided, he arranged the scarf to support Evan's hand. "Do you still want to smoke?"

"Please." Altaf lit him another and for an ashtray gave him an empty tin from the pile of trash that Evan had assessed for possible weapons — hopeless. He couldn't crawl that far.

The smoke in his lungs made him dizzy at first and then soothed. Altaf would evidently stay until he had finished the cigarette; he must have noticed the flammables in the room too. "Are you asking for money? I'd like to know what I'm thought to be worth."

"We're asking for a couple of million — not for ourselves, of course — and freedom for several patriots."

"What organization do you represent? Are there a great many of you?"

"We have no official ties as yet; that should come after the second or third operation when we've proven our worth and can set policy ourselves rather than hear it dictated. There are — a number of us."

Evan felt suddenly certain the number was no more than four. "I see. By 'operation' you mean this sort of thing?"

"Yes. It's a new kind of plan, one that I think will catch on — safer and more flexible than taking large groups hostage and, given the peculiar characteristics of the Western mind, probably more effective.

"I want to show you something." Altaf tamped out the cigarette, down almost to its filter, and picked up a newspaper from the floor beside the camping stool. It was a three-day-old copy of the *London Telegraph*. SIMON ROUD HOME SAFE was its lead headline, and Altaf read the news item beneath it aloud. That must have been gleaned from Wilder's first report to one of the tabloids and was largely fiction, implying that he, David Talbot, had wrested Simon from the grasp of hordes of armed Tariqis. Given Evan's present position, he was relieved to hear no mention of Hamish.

162

"Then, let me see –" Altaf skimmed the front page. "A popular musician totaled his car and someone else's on the highway. Nasty cuts and bruises all around. Mrs. Thatcher has unpleasant words for Mr. Callaghan, Mr. Callaghan for Mrs. Thatcher." He turned pages, studying the paper as if it were new to him; it obviously was not.

"Back here is the trivia. In Chile a score or so bodies have been found in a common grave – a clue to the disappearance of hundreds suspected of opposition to General Pinochet. A Nicaraguan refugee has brought out documented proof of Anastasio Somoza's murder of thousands of young people. An African chief, popular with the West, like Pinochet and Somoza, is accused of having over one hundred schoolchildren beaten to death.

"These items didn't reach the tabloids at all; those were exclusively devoted to your heroic rescue of Roud. I wonder if you see what I'm getting at – about the western mind."

Evan was in no state to think about the Western mind or anything at all but the agony that radiated from his hand through his whole body. The room was uncomfortably cold, but his hair and the dirty, uncased pillow beneath it were soaked with his sweat. Altaf looked from the paper to Evan's face and sprang up from the camping stool. "Oh, but I'm as bad as Haneef – you're in misery. I'll see what I can find." Evan heard his footsteps on the stairs.

He had never felt any pain like it. It didn't come in waves as before but was simply there, no relief at all. He got on his left side somehow, facing the wall, drew his knees up nearly to his chin and rocked to it.

Altaf was beside him again. "I insist that you take this." He held out a spoonful of brown, powdery paste, and Evan caught a sweet, tobacco-like whiff from it – hashish. Remembering his first and only experience with that, he turned away sharply, jarred his hand and came near to drowning in a sea of pain. When he could see again and swallow, he took as much as Altaf gave him, washing it down with water. "I'll try to find a doctor before I leave you."

The hashish took effect just as Evan had given up hope for it; it was quite nice. He watched his body float away to a place without sensation, but his mind stayed clear. He used it to will Altaf back, and he came, bearing tinned beans on chipped but good china, tarnished silver cutlery and a pot of coffee.

"Better?"

"Oh, much. Actually hungry, I think." Evan was able to swing his legs over the edge of the bed and sit; the hand protested, but distantly. "What was that stuff?" he asked, thinking of Muslim strictures against intoxicants.

Altaf pulled a small table between them and busied himself dividing the beans. "I'm not sure."

"Not something one picks up at the local chemist, I imagine — not legally, at least. Pleasant effect but very peculiar."

Altaf, wearing a prim look, obviously preferred not to discuss it. "You're going to have to put up with some amateurish cooking over the next few days. Haneef and Sayed only do canned beans and spaghetti. Neither was born to the kitchen."

Even so, the beans tasted good, and Evan devoured them, then sat back waiting for the strong coffee to cool. "I understand why you showed me the newspaper," he told Altaf. "You find our preoccupation with individuals inane in a time when masses of people are being slaughtered or abused. Forest for the trees kind of thing is what you're saying."

"Particularly if the tree is of the right sort ethnically."

"Oh, hold now. I've seen half a front page devoted to the plight of a single Pakistani baby flown to UK for exotic surgery. Since you seem to have made a study of British psychology, I'm surprised you didn't take a child in my place—" That had not been politic and Evan stopped himself.

"We are not common kidnappers." Altaf was not in the least offended, though; he looked serene and animated at the same time, like a debater sure of his ground. "And our war will be waged humanely — only one life in jeopardy, not a random plane or busload, and more sound and fury at least in the Western press than if it were half a Third World country.

"We are going to take individuals whose names are known — not political figures who might be on guard, but celebrities: actors, athletes, musicians — at our convenience as to person, place and time. We'll exchange the freedom of each for people or things useful to the revolution."

"For whom are you asking now?"

"Two in Israeli prisons, one in Greece, one in America—"

"That would be Sirhan Sirhan, I suppose." Altaf nodded. "I'm surprised you didn't ask for Adolph Eichmann as well."

"The Jews executed him; I thought everyone knew that."

Evan studied him; the man was dead serious. No good making jokes, then, for Altaf.

"You, David, are distinguished by being the first. I hope you don't mind my calling you David—"

"Given all the other liberties you've taken, that one seems hardly worth mentioning." The first, Evan thought. So much for his future, then, if their plans unfolded: dismissal of these impossible demands would be followed by his execution. The atmosphere of terror established, ransom for future prisoners would be scaled down to a reasonable level.

"Your engineering of Roud's escape makes it singularly appropriate."

"I didn't engineer anything. The prison was deserted, and he'd been left there to die."

"What really happened is never as important as what's thought to have happened. Anyway, your activities in Palat were merely a lucky coincidence — you had been chosen before."

"When Frank Culver failed to appear."

"That's right."

"That woman, Sharon Campbell, does your choosing, doesn't she?"

Altaf gave him a considering look, stood and folded his camp stool. "This has been enjoyable. I'd been led to believe you were a member of the jet set with fluff where your brains ought to be."

"It's hard to understand what goals you and she could share."

Altaf ignored that pleasantly. "We'll talk again, though not for a couple of days. I have an errand."

"The ransom note?"

"Yes. If you need anything at all, another cigarette, coffee, whatever we have, just ask Haneef or Sayed for it."

Evan's discomfort must have been evident. "They are under orders not to lay hands on you again — and to see to your comfort."

"Can they hear me? I thought Sayed had no English."

"One of them will stay close enough to hear, and Sayed understands, though he doesn't speak." Altaf moved the table away from the bed and out of Evan's reach, started toward the door and then turned back suddenly.

"We have no goals in common with the American woman, and I can't leave you thinking that we do. Her fixations are useful to us at this time — and the money from her strange church. There is nothing else."

Canakkale: Lindsay wore a white blouse and blue cardigan, not the red and grey checked pullover that had been agreed upon as a signal of separate or unusual plans on Sharon's part. Max was relieved. He couldn't stray from the group until the ransom note was delivered, Reg must wait in Canakkale for a call he had arranged to England, and Hamish would be left alone as backup for Lindsay.

Sharon stood a few feet from Max now on Heracles Deck, from which the disembarkation line was oozing slowly down the gangplank and into the launches that would put them ashore. He wondered how he could ever have thought her beautiful. She was being endearing, now, threatening almost to devour Lindsay with the smile someone must have told her was animated. The woman was, at least by association, a murderer, and her presence beside civilized little Lindsay sent a slight, sudden *frisson* of physical fear through Max. And not merely for Lindsay. He himself was involved in a business for which he was totally unqualified, and even Reg, for all his calm competence, had been out of this kind of work for years.

They were armed now, or at least Reg was. Hamish had produced Evan's Luger a few minutes before. "I haven't the least idea how to use this, so perhaps you ought to have it, Reg." Reg had checked it over with reassuring expertise and was presumably carrying it.

This launch was larger and more seaworthy than the one at Kusadasi. Milly and Max sat on a wooden bench near its center, Lindsay and Sharon across from them. Wilder, looking like Oliver Twist at the nadir of his fortunes, took the place beside Lindsay, spoke to her and was given some civil but distant answer. He subsided into a defeated silence that lasted until they stepped ashore at Canakkale.

Evan had slept again despite the torment his hand was giving him. He awakened, dizzy and nauseated, to see Sayed on the camping stool in the doorway, the machine gun to which he seemed permanently attached lying across his lap. "Sayed." He didn't move his head. "Please, I'm going to be sick."

The breakfast beans went into the bucket, and Sayed and the gun disappeared, returning quickly with a damp cloth and towels. He washed Evan's face and offered him, with gestures, a drink from the pitcher across the room. Haneef appeared before he could get it and sent Sayed downstairs.

"Can you write, Mr. Talbot?" The cat-eyed boy smiled ingratiatingly at Evan.

"Not well," he lied, "probably not even legibly with my left hand."

"Oh, that's all right. It will still be your mark. Would you sign your name here, please?" Haneef placed a book beside his sound hand, a bit of folded paper on it, and thrust a pen at Evan. He picked up the paper instead and shook the folds from it. The words he was to sign his name to were typewritten.

"I, David Talbot, conspired in the escape from prison of the convicted criminal Simon Roud under direct orders from the Pajitsinan." This was a left-wing student group, active in the revolution, which had been, according to Simon, nearly exterminated by the mullahs. "These orders were to free Roud at any cost. In carrying them out, I murdered a prison guard and the Russian prisoner, Mikhail Tiomkin."

"That's not true." Altaf couldn't be involved in this idiocy. If Evan signed and lived, he would disavow it; if not, his death would be proof enough of duress. "I won't sign that."

"Allah knows our intentions, Mr. Talbot, and it is true in His eyes. I think you will sign it." He took the paper and pen away, though, setting them on the table beneath the window which held Evan's cigarettes and the water pitcher.

"It must be boring lying here with nothing to read, no music to hear, and Sayed doesn't talk." Haneef was full of smiles and sparkling, like a young, playful animal anticipating a romp. "We are going to bring you entertainment. There will be a trial, and they are always fun."

Haneef left him to chew on that, which he did; the trial would, of course, be Evan's. They wouldn't kill him so soon, the ransom note undelivered. A body must be produced to complete an exercise in terror, and, if Evan were found to have died days in advance of their deadline, his kidnappers would lose credibility. Why then a trial?

Footsteps on the stairway outside echoed in the great room, and Haneef reappeared accompanied by a fat man in a black business suit who carried something resembling Max's black bag. He had a square, blunt-featured face with a mustache made up of two perfect rectangles and small considering eyes which never touched Evan's but moved rapidly over the room until they came to rest on the ruined hand. The boy thief at Palat! Evan knew what was going to happen as suddenly as if he had been slapped.

"You told me there was to be a trial," he said to Haneef.

"We had that just now downstairs," Haneef sparkled at him. "No good bringing you into it, since Jemal speaks no English. I was your lawyer."

The newcomer slid his hand under Evan's and lifted it with surprising gentleness. Even so, Evan came near fainting and felt cold sweat running down his temples. Jemal looked at his face now, uttered a long stream of consonants and turned to Haneef for translation.

"He says that this hand is in such bad condition that it doesn't seem enough. Since you have been convicted of violent theft, perhaps he'll take the other one." Evan felt his mouth opening and closing silently. "That's for the crime at Palat; I didn't tell him about your theft of the boy on the bus or he might want both hands. As your advocate, I'll see what I can do for you." Haneef made a little speech to Jemal, gesturing like an actor.

They would probably do it without anesthetic. Evan lived in an instant the long, careful slicing down to the bones, the sawing through those, the clipping of veins and arteries. Both hands or one, it was not to be borne. He measured the distance to the window with his eyes and gathered his body for the spring he would attempt when one or both looked away from him. Sayed's gun would only free him sooner.

The man in black turned from Evan, bending over the black bag and fumbling inside it, Haneef watching him.

The spring Evan had planned got him to his feet, but his knees collapsed under him and he fell, banging the hand against Haneef's leg. Pain from it traveled up his arm, through his shoulder, engulfing his body and paralyzing his will. He lay perfectly quiet on the moldering mattress where someone had placed him and watched Haneef's "judge" prepare a hypodermic injection. It was the last sight he had of the man.

12

Troy: It was so small — village-sized, really — yet this city had once been the capital of a kingdom whose fall had captured the imagination of the Western world. A huge horse had been constructed of thatch at its entrance, and this struck the Cobb's group, still edgy and volatile from yesterday's ordeal, as incomparably hilarious. Milly was made to stop and take pictures of Maggie and Richard, the archeology students, clowning round its feet. There were purple smudges under the girl's eyes, and her laughter was strained.

A high wind rose shortly after the buses unloaded, and the Alexandros' company gathered in the shelter of a third-level wall to hear Dr. Cameron read — first in Greek and then in English — Hector's farewell to Andromache. The deep voice vibrated tenderly, compellingly, and Max shivered, in thrall to it. Before Cameron finished, an unfamiliar group poured through the gates, and Max, hearing several languages, turned his attention to it. A random busload of tourists of mixed age, nationality, dress and undress, it was precisely the kind of crowd in which his courier might bury himself.

He began to edge toward it and away from the Cobb's group, then remembered his instructions, hoisted his yellow carrying case into prominent view over his shoulder and moved back. Cameron was done, and Max had missed the last heroic lines in his assessment of the dozen or so new tourists who had eased themselves into the Cobb's lot to catch what they could of a free lecture.

Milly called to him from atop a small hill. "Come up here, Max. You can look down on the plain where they fought." She was wan but determinedly cheerful, an attitude she had striven for since leaving the ship. "This has to have been the battlefield. Imagine it — Achilles, Patroclus, Hector — all that insane courage and love and heartbreak and death." Her enthusiasm pleased Max this time, and he squeezed her hand.

A round-cheeked, tidy pair of children, evidently brother and sister, climbed toward them holding hands and waving two bouquets of wild flowers. They extended them to Milly. "For you."

She looked worried and didn't take them. "Oh, dear, Max, I've no Turkish money at all. Do you?"

"No, no money," the boy said seriously. "We pick for you. To give." She took them then, and the children flashed bright smiles, whirled and were gone so quickly that thanks had to be shouted. Milly was enchanted, Max thoughtful. That was how it would be done, how he would do it: an obliging child. Max could be pointed out, instructions given and the courier long gone before the note was delivered.

They began to walk around the site, which had been stripped to its bones — no potsherds for Milly or the other collectors. Hamish appeared beside Max, and they dropped back to avoid being overheard.

"I've bloody lost them — both!" The calm that Hamish had clamped upon himself was slipping; his eyes were wide and beginning to roll.

"Where did you last see them?"

"Just over that bridge. I stopped to speak to some children, and when I looked up they were gone. Oh, God, Max, if any harm has come to Lindsay—"

"I'm sure none has — or will."

"I raced out to the shop, thinking they might be buying postcards."'

"We'll go all the way around again." They had fallen back toward the end of the Cobb's group and now stepped up their pace. Max saw a deep, trenched walkway running at right angles to the path, its entrance half-screened by shrubbery. "Did you check that?"

"I didn't see it—"

The two came out of it then, Lindsay wearing her anti-quarian glow. "Dead end," she told them cheerily, "but great fun to know you're treading the stones trod by Priam's ancestors. It's first level."

Max investigated it briefly with Hamish; it was incredibly barren and held no ghosts for him. "Don't worry so much when they're together," he told Hamish. "I've noticed she lets Lindsay take the lead in their touring and seems to be trying to please her. She needs Lindsay; if she were questioned, I can imagine her saying, 'But I was with my friend almost every minute of the cruise.' " They were buying postcards when Max and Hamish reached the entrance kiosk.

"I'm going to sit with Sarah on the way back," Milly told Max quietly. "She's a little shaken; I think she's afraid that Reg is taking up where he left off years ago. The man he's calling from Canakkale is evidently secret service." Max went back to the smoking section before remembering that there was no need for it and sat down alone.

"Can I sit here?" It was John Trimble, the man from Mississippi, and Max made a welcoming gesture. "Thanks. Mary Lou's with Janet, and if I have to spend five more minutes with that son-of-a-bitch Cartier, I just might kill him."

Cartier was a small, insipid man who complained about things; he was bursar to a prep school in Ottawa, and Max found it hard to picture his challenging someone of John's size and disposition. "Why?"

"He said a filthy thing about young Talbot and his friend — as if their sex life was any of his God damned business. Those boys' nail parings are worth more than he is."

"Perhaps he senses that, and that's why he says such things," Max soothed. "I'm glad we had no one like him on the Priene bus; he's the kind to have panicked."

"Yeah, that bunch was really something when you look back on it. Talbot set the tone, of course. Without him, the boy would have been killed, and then God only knows what his father and everybody else would have done."

Their conversation on the drive over wooded hills and down to the sea occupied only part of Max's mind. John was sketchily educated and a little in awe of his wife's university degree — the cruise was one of his proud indulgences to her —

and didn't mind telling anyone that he had begun his working life driving a beer truck. His was not the kind of background from which Max would expect tolerance, much less his evident admiration, for a pair of gays.

Max let his thinking tilt so that he was looking at a different facet of himself. Perhaps it wasn't Reg's attitude that was bizarre — or John's or Milly's or Simon's — Max had once shared it. He remembered his anger at the ridicule heaped upon two boys who had roomed down the hall from him during his first year at Stanford. He had tried to fight it but soon learned that their tormentors were unreachable — generally the same people who were anti-Semitic, the dull-witted or the insecure who were fearful that some stigma of their own might come to light.

And Max became an expert on anti-Semitism early in his first year away from home. He had thought his appearance very Jewish indeed, in fact his only ethnic legacy from non-religious parents, and had worn his aquilinity, stronger than theirs, like a banner. Even so, partially because of his perfectly proper and unaltered surname, he was seldom recognized.

"You're putting me on, Ross — you *can't* be a Jew."

By being large, athletic and sure of himself, he had violated their stereotype — as Evan and Hamish had, no doubt, outraged Cartier's by their performance at Palat. Whatever the boys' deeds, the little man would find a way to diminish them in order to preserve the cocoon of bigotry that protected his timorous ego. As Max had done. When, in God's name, had he begun to align himself with the Cartiers of the world?

Memory of a half dozen petty cruelties against Evan returned to him sourly, and he let his mind complete its tilt, exposing what had been lying underneath. To let any homosexual close enough to him to be understood and accepted might have taught Max something he wasn't ready to learn: the nature of his own anxiety. Jaunty, blond Evan, with his resemblance in color and carriage to Alex, had been perceived as a particular danger.

He forced consciousness to study what unconsciousness had kept hidden and realized that, were his second, his golden son, to announce himself gay in a year or two, he would not be very surprised. A little saddened — "Life's hard enough without being queer or Catholic," an Englishman who was

172

both observed — but not surprised. His feelings for Alex would not be affected at all. Max had a sudden vision of himself carrying a placard down Market Street on Gay Pride Day and began to laugh aloud — fortunately just after some folksy witticism from the man from Mississippi.

There was no fear, no pain and no memory of either at first, only thirst. Evan had vomited all the fluid he had taken in the morning, and Haneef had denied him anything to drink through the afternoon. He could force no sound at all from his constricted throat and flailed about in an effort to get someone's attention. It was then that he discovered his left hand, whole and still attached to its wrist. He became aware of throbbing in the broken one and opened his eyes to look at it. Most of it was still there, bandaged white, two fingers and the thumb extended stiffly resting across his chest. The pain came from the vacant space where the two outside fingers had been.

He produced finally a sort of croak, and Sayed was beside him. "Water." Sayed poured it from the pitcher into the cup and brought it to him, propping Evan's head in the crook of his arm and pressing the cup to his lips. Evan managed two or three swallows before Haneef appeared, took the cup and sent Sayed away. "Please," Evan begged, his voice clear again, "terribly thirsty."

"Oh, I *am* glad. That means you are ready to sign your name for me."

Memory returned and with it the meaning of the presence of both of Evan's hands. "That man — he was a doctor."

"That's right." Haneef beamed upon him as if together they had pulled off a magnificent coup.

"What was he saying when you translated for him?"

"That he would try to save your thumb and forefinger but he was afraid the other three would have to go. He did better than he expected."

Evan banked the coals of his fury; later, when he was stronger, he could stoke them into flame. Now the embers were almost comforting, giving an illusion of meaning to his position. "Quite an actor, aren't you?"

"Not too bad. It was what I studied in America, you know — theater."

"Perhaps you'll go back to it some day." An empty wine bottle sat in the far corner of the room; Evan imagined breaking it and scoring, shredding the pretty boy's face that looked into his.

"Oh, no. I've found my vocation. Soldiering gives me more pleasure. Look." He drew a clear plastic container filled with yellow and orange capsules from his shirt pocket. "It's time for your antibiotic now. You may have it and all the water you can drink after you write your name."

Some mulish, vainglorious fiber in Evan still held out against doing that. "Let me see that paper again." He took it from Haneef and pretended to study it. The dressings were beginning to seep, and he lifted his right hand quickly, with surprisingly little pain, then brought it down to rest on the unsigned confession. The resulting blood smears would make it singularly unconvincing were he brought round to signing it later.

Haneef drew it away. "That's all right; it's still legible. Now?" He proffered the pen.

"Don't you think Altaf will be annoyed at my premature death? If that happens before your deadline, it's going to put all of you in a rather amateurish light."

"You'll sign it before we reach that stage. I know about such things."

"In the absence of water and the antibiotic, do you suppose you might give me a cigarette?"

"Of course. That's within rules." He took one from the pack on the table beneath the window and tossed it to Evan, then set a book of matches down beside it; he was not going to light it. They stared at each other for almost a minute, and then Evan took the matchbook in his left hand and hurled it into Haneef's face. It hit the corner of an eye which Haneef wiped with one hand, laughing his graceful actor's laugh and regarding Evan with the delighted expression of one watching an animal or a small child perform a charming trick. "Here. Your award for marksmanship." Haneef lit a cigarette and put it in the hand that was whole; Evan smoked.

At Sea: "Please dress, Max." He had poured himself a Scotch from the dwindling cabin supply and sat watching the Turkish shoreline move past them. "I told Sarah we'd meet them in the lounge at six, and it's five to six now."

Milly studied him as he shed his dusty shirt and slacks. "Worrying at yourself like this won't make it happen any

174

faster, dear. And Troy was too open, not enough people for a contact to hide among."

"I'm not worrying — I'm very good at waiting."

"Something has you ruffled, I can tell; your eyes go all funny, lighter and the pupils very small."

"Sheer fatigue this time — and speaking of funny eyes —"

Milly was, unaccustomedly, applying mascara of the kind Sarah wore. Taken eye by eye the result was pleasing, but the application had been unequal, and the two eyes appeared to belong on different faces.

"Oh, the hell with it." She washed it off as Max showered.

"I've been thinking," he said as he dressed. "How would you like to leave London three or four days earlier?"

"For home? To all the mail and the bills and the laundry? Not much."

"Not for home. I thought we might stop in Boston and spend some time with Tom." Saying it, seeing Milly's surprised delight, Max found that he meant it, that he had missed the company of his brother-in-law, with his outrageous froufrou and his genuine gaiety and wit.

Reg rapped at the door. "Milly, Sarah's becoming a solitary drinker in the lounge; perhaps you could save her from herself." She put on her social face and left them, a little hurt, Max knew, at her exclusion from what she must recognize as serious business. Max had been tempted repeatedly to bring her into their planning, prevented only by Reg's direct stricture to the contrary. Max poured him a drink.

"Cheers. Well, as you people would say, I've some good news and some bad. They've put a man named Jones onto it — younger chap, I've never met him. He's said to be one of our top experts on terrorism.

"He promised to begin a traceback on Sharon Campbell immediately, her associates in London and Beirut, if they can be found. Then too, he'll hunt information on Middle Eastern nationals admitted to Crete and Mykonos on the days the girl met with the terrorist. He doesn't expect much there — too many tourists — though there's always the possibility of an observant immigration officer.

"I gave him the names of the only passengers whose passports show that their tracks might have crossed those of the girl — Professor Hodgkins and Robin were in Pakistan last year when she was — and a score or so with passports too new

175

to show recent travel. None of them look promising at all, and Jones too seems certain that she's working alone on the ship."

"That's all to the good. Do they plan to put one of their people aboard the Alexandros?"

"That's the bad news, I'm afraid." Reg snubbed out the cigarette and lit another. "They agree to wait until Venice to take the girl into custody, in case the ship is under watch, but Jones doesn't think another contact will be made. He agrees with you that this kidnapping may be the first of many and that Sharon would be too valuable to be risked unnecessarily. To be frank, I felt he had little hope for Evan." Reg looked suddenly old and uncertain, his blue eyes dim.

"But I no longer agree with *him* — I watched that girl today, and Lindsay's right. I don't think she'll be able to keep her fingers from the pie." Max freshened their drinks. "Reg, don't tell Hamish what Jones said. The Sharon-watch, however it turns out, gives the poor kid something to think about, other than what maybe happening to Evan."

Hall of the Grand Master — April 7: The hierarchy among his captors was distinct but ineffective. Altaf had forbidden them to hurt Evan, but Haneef thought it within bounds to watch him die of infection. That was severe now, the hand swollen almost to bursting its bandages, and Evan was light-headed with fever.

Sayed obeyed Haneef's prohibitions in a similar spirit. He had given Evan no water but had brought a cup of strong, syrupy coffee up the stairs, ostensibly for himself, and was now sharing it with Evan.

Sayed was silent not from choice but was a mute, probably something to do with that terrible facial scarring, and communicated with Haneef by writing in a small notebook carried in his shirt pocket. The grotesquerie of his mouth made it impossible to read his facial expressions. He had looked quite fierce carrying the steaming coffee, and Evan had cringed away, expecting it to be thrown upon him. Instead, Sayed had helped him gently to sit up and had put the cup in his hand. The coffee was hot and burned Evan's mouth but relieved the rasping thirst.

Sayed lit a cigarette and gave it to him; gratitude swelled in Evan. "Thank you, you're very good. What is your country, Sayed?"

The notebook came into play. "Tariq." His script was sane and legible.

"Haneef's as well?" A nod of the head. "Altaf's?" Another nod.

Sayed wrote, "Where do you live in England?"

"In London, near Hampstead Heath." Perhaps he would. Perhaps he'd survive this business and return to live the life that he and Hamish had planned to share. He thought of the years he had wasted, and something in his chest swelled uncomfortably, crowding up and into his throat.

"I have visited London," the scarred boy wrote. "It is a very great city. There is a book about it here, in English too. Would you like to read it?"

"Oh, please."

Sayed brought a worn paperback copy of Dickens' *Our Mutual Friend* from downstairs. "It is sad," he wrote, "but very good."

He sat down on the camping stool beside the door then, propping his own book against the machine gun in his lap and leaving Evan to mull over the insane coincidence that had put in his hand a book from which Hamish had read him years before. Evan opened it and began to read about Lizzie and Gaffer and the hated river — Hamish had been thirteen, his voice changing, and he would carry on for a paragraph or two in the low, hoarse tones and now and then ascend to a squeak. The fullness in Evan's chest and throat invaded his eyes, and he closed them.

He must have dozed off; he awakened shivering uncontrollably, being frowned down at by Sayed. He gave Evan a bit of hashish in a spoon, and Evan was about to wash it down, using the china cup now refilled with milk, when Haneef arrived.

"Sayed, I'm surprised," he chirruped. "We must obey the spirit of the rules as well as their letter." He reached out to snatch the cup from Evan's hand.

Evan clutched it to him. "Yes, rules," he said. "The other rule is 'Don't touch,' remember? If you lay hands on me, Altaf will be angry." He took advantage of Haneef's hesitation to gulp down the milk, handing the boy the empty cup.

Haneef took it to the window and dropped it, with deliberation, over the sill; the interval between its disappearance and the clink of china upon stone indicated a very long drop. "Now, nothing whatever is to pass Mr. Talbot's lips until he signs his name for us. Is that clear?"

Sayed, immersed in his book, never moved. Later, when Haneef was gone, he showed Evan the notebook once more. "Altaf will return tonight or early tomorrow," he had writtten. "Then you will drink and have your medicine."

Istanbul: Max was almost enjoying tourism again. He could only stay with the group and wait for the ransom note, and nothing stated that he couldn't take pleasure in the scenery as he waited. He watched himself with a certain cynicism but not much surprise — only two days had blurred Evan's image. Were they to hear in a week or two that he had been killed, probably only Hamish would feel the kind of grief that would have wrenched many of them had it happened at Priene; the frail human condition.

Helplessness was a worse dilutant than time. Max thought himself capable of risking his own life to see Evan delivered safe and whole, but his chances of doing that seemed increasingly far-fetched. This day in Istanbul had seemed to them most likely for Sharon to contact the others. The only Muslim port remaining was Dikili, not a large community nor one so rich in hiding places for the terrorists and their hostage. But Lindsay had left the ship wearing a print frock and white cardigan, not the alarm-giving pullover.

Today Sharon had clung to Lindsay as tenaciously as usual through the Blue Mosque and Santa Sophia, now from room to room in the Topkapi Palace.

The Ottoman emperors who had accumulated this dragon's hoard had been infatuated with glitter, unable to leave anything free of it. Max had seen exquisitely crafted jade bowls and vases imported from Japan and China, here crusted over with gilt and ill-matched jewels. The swords and scimitars on display were so weighted with ornament that they would have been useless in battle.

Max was glad that they had gone first to the Blue Mosque, whose airy beauty had moved him. Its structural delicacy, Nateq, their local guide, and the hordes of prepossessing urchins who had sold postcards at each stop had made a dent in the distaste he felt hardening in him for all things Muslim.

Hamish joined Max in the next room, which featured a full-sized bed of solid gold. "That's enough," Max said. "One more monument to greed is going to give me visual indigestion." They walked out into the palace courtyard where the guide sat smoking, Lindsay and Sharon beside him. Across the yard, near the entrance to the seraglio, Reg, whose turn it was to back up Lindsay, sat working on the journal he kept of the tour.

"Cigarette break?" Nateq proffered his open pack to Max and Hamish.

"Thanks, no," Max answered. "I don't smoke. Just too much Topkapi."

"Yes. Execrable, isn't it? I can't bring myself to go inside any more — though, as you've probably noticed, I enjoy talking my tourists to death everywhere else."

"Don't think that your tourists don't appreciate it," Max told him. "Your little histories brought the other places to life."

"Perhaps you shouldn't miss an item in the last room here," Nateq said. "It's so tasteless, it's memorable."

Lindsay rose. "I'm curious," she said. "It can't be worse than what they did to that lovely jade."

They followed her into the easternmost room. Max saw the label first: The Hand and Arm of John the Baptist. The exhibit above it was cased in gold encrusted with rubies, pearls, emeralds, topazes, diamonds and amethysts, and an opening in the shining sheath had been left just over the hand. A desiccated claw showed through it as if to convince doubters that here indeed was a portion of a long-dead human body.

Hamish looked, gasped and gagged; Max shepherded him back to the courtyard. "I should like that cigarette after all," Hamish said carefully to the guide, sitting down beside him. He found a book of the matches he had carried for Evan and busied himself lighting it. Max had never seen him smoke; it was an act behind which he could hide his face and its expression. Lindsay and Max turned away to give him time to compose himself.

"It *is* awful," Sharon said, planting herself in front of Hamish, commanding his attention. "Worse, there are bits and pieces of John the Baptist all over Europe, most of them decked out the same way. He was a hostage for a long time," she said conversationally, "to a Jew king."

The appalling bitch! Max took Hamish's arm, colder than the wood of the bench where it rested, and pulled him almost roughly to his feet. "Come on. I want to get to the bazaar."

They sat alone and in silence for a few minutes in a back seat of the first bus, Hamish puffing frequently and shallowly on the unaccustomed cigarette. It was so short now that it would soon burn his fingers. Max took it from him and snuffed it out.

"Thank you very much, Max. Ought you to be away from the group like this?"

"They've closed the admission gates, and there's no one left inside but our lot and that Swiss family with all the children. I thought we needed a change of scene."

"Too right. I've tried to keep from tearing my hair or otherwise making a fool of myself, but that last — and I don't know why—"

"You've done extremely well. I'm not sure I could handle myself as you have if Milly were kidnapped — " Oh, God, that had been unfortunate; no one had acknowledged openly that Hamish's and Evan's was other than an ordinary friendship, and this boy was sensitive.

Hamish saw his confusion. "You must be a very kind doctor, Max," he said gently. The bus begain to fill before Max could answer.

They were driven with peril and panache to a crowded shopping area. Max was commandeered as he stepped out the door by an urchin who sold Turkish delights. Milly liked the things, and he paid three dollars for a box; he turned away from the salesman and felt a tug at his sleeve.

"You ought to have paid two dollars, you know," the child told him. "Except in these shops," he gestured around their immediate vicinity, "the government ones, you must bargain. Two-thirds is right, usually, sometimes only half the asking price."

"Thank you—"

"Ali. My name is Ali."

Hamish returned from wherever he had been and focused on the boy. "How old are you, Ali?"

"Twelve last month." He looked younger.

"Do you go to school?"

"One needn't, after twelve."

"How many languages?" Hamish, the teacher, spoke to the child as he would to a man and had his full attention.

"Not so many. French, English, a little Italian, some

180

German—" A second Cobb's bus pulled up and began to disgorge passengers. "Excuse me," Ali said. "It is better to be the first one they see. Don't stay here, go down through that archway. That's the real bazaar." He gestured toward the declining sun and was gone.

"An impressive array of abilities in one small head," Hamish said to Max. "One's first reaction is to want to clap him in school, but perhaps he wouldn't have learned so much."

Reg arrived on the second bus and caught up with them just as they passed under the archway. He had put away his journal and looked harassed. "Might I join you? The four women are together immersing themselves in all this."

A tubular passageway lined by small shops stretched further than they could see, its center spotted with makeshift stands displaying foods, clothing and novelties, and the aisles were clogged with smiling, multilingual peddlers who pulled at their sleeves. The interior of a beehive must be something like it — no, this was utterly, humanly random, dizzying in its variety and confusion, and Max found it absolutely charming. It was not a place for love or death, merely one crammed with the business of buying and selling.

Three gamins approached them, offering Turkish delights, and Ali was there to fend them off. "I told them you had bought." He grinned at them dazzlingly.

"I haven't bought," Reg said. "How much?"

"A friend?" Ali inquired, and Max nodded. "Two dollars or one pound sterling."

A large group from an American cruise ship that had followed them since Crete, its passengers distinguishable by their green hand luggage, crowded in under the archway, and Ali was off again.

Reg was not himself. "Sarah and Milly are loving it," he murmured, "but I've got bloody claustrophobia." They watched their wives leave Lindsay and Sharon to enter a leather goods shop on their right. The Cobb's group was being pressed close together by new floods of tourists, and tall Sharon, with her flaming hair, could be kept in view.

The ubiquitous Ali returned and pressed an envelope into Max's hand. "A message," he said and slid back into the crowd.

"Ali, wait. From whom?"

"Your friend," the boy shouted, separated from them now by two or three layers of shoppers and peddlers, "yellow traveling case like yours."

Max unsealed the envelope as they were jostled along in the stream of human traffic. He glanced briefly at the typewritten message inside and pocketed it. "This is it. Reg, you'll need to stay and back up Lindsay. Hamish, possibly you can find the boy and see what can be got from him. I'm going to a hotel I saw two or three blocks away and begin telephoning. Jones first?"

"Jones first," Reg agreed. "He'll know where to contact Sir Francis." Max turned and began to force his way back against and through the clot of bustling bodies.

He wanted to stay awake so that he could change what was happening in his head. The hashish had worked differently this time, not nicely, and Evan kept sliding in and out of the same pretty, pastel nightmare. He was trapped in a painting, of it, though not fixed upon it. Coming up from the distance, it was a lovely landscape with a stream, softly rounded green hills, trees and houses. When one drew nearer, though, one saw figures in varying stages of torment — one chap being sawn in two, another half-flayed, others being impaled or pulled apart or set fire to — all silently screaming. Bosch. The painter could only be Hieronymus Bosch.

Dead center, a serene figure sat unaware on a camp stool; it was Francis.

Evan was only half awake and very hot; perhaps he could make something happen, and that would clear his head. "Haneef, a glass of water, please." He had replaced Sayed and would come to tease Evan — that was better than the dream.

He came now, smiling, almost dancing, a china cup in one hand and the paper and pen in the other. "It's very cool, you know. Wonderful water here. You can have all you want after you sign your name."

"I don't want to sign my name." The game was ridiculous, but it was one Evan could win.

"I know what's wrong." Haneef wore the expression of a crafty child. "You can't write your name with your left hand."

"Oh, but I can."

"Show me." His eyes burned into Evan's like a lover's. "You'll have a cigarette as well and some of Sayed's good spaghetti." He pushed the pen and paper close, and Evan saw for the first time terrible scars on the undersides of both slender wrists, as if Haneef had tried repeatedly to slash them with something not sharp enough.

It was, after all, worse than the dream. No, Haneef was part of the dream. Evan closed his eyes and heard the mad boy walk away. The strange pressure he had felt earlier in his chest and throat climaxed in a flood of silent tears. He peered through them to see Haneef looking out the window — he hadn't seen — and turned his wet face to the wall.

No one had seen Evan cry for twenty years; that had been an old game he had been able to win. He had become accustomed to losing most of the battles and all of the wars at his Dorset prep school. His mother had taken him there when he was six, and they had given him a test. It was rather fun, full of puzzles and numbers, things he understood; they told him that he had done especially well on it and were very kind to him afterward.

He had learned his letters quickly — but not the sequence or meaning of their arrangements. After the first weeks, they had become impatient with him, and after the first months the beatings began. His mother brought herself to complain once, Nanny having shown her the scabbed weals on his buttocks.

"It's the only way to deal with a child who *chooses* to be a functional illiterate, Lady Barbara — let me show you the IQ scores." His mother had left him then, in the airy modern office with the businesslike, modern headmistress who didn't like him, and he hadn't seen her again for months.

He had believed what they said still on his eighth birthday and, tired of losses and determined to win, had set out that day to become the best reader in Dorset. His extended, his complete effort brought so little change that, two days after the birthday he was given the most painful beating of his life. Its unfairness was so patent that he refused to cry, and that turned things. He could and would in the future choose mulishly to read victory in the scrambled letters that spelled defeat simply by ignoring what was done to him.

"The mind is its own place," Hamish had read him from Milton. Perhaps Evan could make a heaven of *this* hell. He created a stream in his head and bathed in it, cooling his body, though he couldn't get the clear water into his mouth.

Istanbul; At Sea: Hamish had bought two boxes of the dreadful candy, but he had handled the thing wrongly some way, and Ali's small, sharp chin came near to meeting his long, sharp nose in disdain.

"No. Too many people. I can't remember."

"You remembered the yellow case. It's frightfully important, Ali."

"You English have an expression for what you want me to do. I think it's carrying tales." Good God, the child thought he was spying on Max. "I have work now."

Hamish held his shoulder lightly but firmly. "The letter you delivered was a ransom demand. From kidnappers. We are trying to find them to save our friend."

"Kidnappers!" Ali's grey eyes rounded. "Oh! Cobb's! The English nobleman! It's in all the newspapers. Oh, I am so stupid." He shook his head. "A woman, pretty, and I thought, you know, a girlfriend."

"Tell me about her."

"American." He studied Hamish. "More young than you, I think." Sharon? "Black hair, long white dress, not very clean, sandals. This tall." He indicated a point just above Hamish's shoulder.

"There is no one like that on our ship. Had you seen her before?"

"Never. Oh, I am angry. No money, you know, only the pretty smile. I will remember, and I will call the police if I see her again."

Ali would not see her again, and there was nothing more to be learnt from him. The girl would have been one of the American hippie types who drifted through the city and had probably done her small job in exchange for the yellow carrying case. Evan's had not been taken and was now in Hector Seven, but Sharon's had not been in evidence since Mykonos.

The boy, displeased with himself, refused the money Hamish offered and disappeared into the maelstrom of the bazaar.

Hamish waited a long time in Hector Seven, holding his body stiff and his mind empty, expecting Max or Reg to appear with news of the ransom note. He heard the ship lift anchor, then the dinner chimes; they wouldn't come until later now, and the next half hour would be Hamish's alone.

He let go, hurling himself onto the bunk he had shared three nights before with Evan, and wept there. He grasped his pillow for comfort and began helplessly reliving the two nights when the friend who had sheltered him in the world had been Hamish's to shelter in their bed.

Then the horrors came, and he saw Evan's light, straight body bloodied and broken by the savages who had taken him. He shut his eyes tight, but the specter crept under their lids. Hamish rose and washed his face hard with cold water, pressing against the eyesockets until they hurt. That ended the tears, but he was still racked by dry sobs — he had to stop it, and now; someone was rapping at the door. He forced himself to breathe deeply and evenly.

"Hamish?" It was Max.

"Come in, Max." The words hurt his throat and emerged rusted and abrasive. "May I fix you a whisky?"

"I'd like one if you'll join me." Max sat down on the bunk where Hamish had lain while Hamish fixed their drinks. A long swallow of Scotch loosened the knot in his throat, and he was able to look at Max, who appeared serious — and angry.

"Hamish, what kind of man is Francis Talbot?"

"I'm not the one to ask, really — I dislike him. I should say, though, that he's thought to be the essence of honor and nobility, even something of a genius in his own way."

"Why do you dislike him?"

"For his treatment of Evan."

"Was he abusive?"

"Nothing so attentive. Oh, Evan had his teeth straightened at the proper time and was given a generous allowance. But the man has always seemed totally unaware of his existence. The sad thing is that Evan is devoted to him."

"I see." Max scowled into his Scotch. "Evan said once that I resembled his father. I hope I'll be given the chance to earn his better opinion."

"You've spoken to Sir Francis — just now."

"Yes. Most of the note was what we expected and not remotely negotiable. They want five terrorists freed, including Sirhan Sirhan, but they set no deadline for that. They ask too, as reparation for Evan's 'crime against the Muslim world,' that the British government pay two million pounds over to Tariq's Revolutionary Council. If it isn't received within ten days, they threaten to kill Evan.

"Jones contacted both Owen and Callaghan immediately; the government is pledged not to bargain with terrorists, but, given the circumstances, they won't stand in the way of Talbot delivering the ransom personally. In fact, they suggest that he should at least make noises indicating he's trying to raise the money and hint that they might help him, secretly — to play for time. Jones says that the longer a hostage is held, the more difficult it becomes for his captors to kill him.

"The problem is that Talbot refuses altogether to deal with them, says he will not submit to blackmail."

13

Hall of the Grand Master — April 8: He was dying, not painfully, and his father was holding him in his arms for now, against the night. He had fallen from his pony — no, he had done something very brave, and Francis knew it and loved him for it. Francis changed into Hamish then, and that was even nicer. Evan felt his friend's beautiful hands, cool on his smoldering arm, and opened his eyes to see them. It was only Altaf, his face shadowed in the dim light of an electric torch.

"Ah, you're awake. Sayed wrote that you'd had no antibiotic." Altaf opened the plastic container and drew one out.

Evan wouldn't take it. He had forgotten why he wouldn't take it, but it was something he had decided earlier in the night when he had been cooler.

"Here. Open your mouth for me — please." Evan looked blindly through Altaf, trying to appear less conscious than he was. He remembered now. Since he must die anyway, he had determined to muck up their plans by doing that as quickly as possible. Altaf pulled at his chin to insert the capsule, and Evan jerked his head away.

"You've decided to die on us, haven't you? You won't. You'll swallow this if I have to push it down your throat with my fingers. I took chances to get that doctor here." Altaf pressed Evan's cheeks near the jaw and forced his mouth open, pushed the orange capsule to the back of his tongue and closed his jaws again, stroking his throat with his thumb as Evan remembered doing for a distempered puppy. Altaf released him finally, and Evan coughed the pill back at him.

"What the hell is wrong with you? You won't make it, you know — it isn't that easy to stop breathing. I'll go out again and find the other kind and jab it into you with a needle. Why can't you save both of us the trouble?"

"No water," Evan croaked, "almost two days, no water." He felt his mouth contort like a weeping child's, and tears ran down his cheeks. He had lost it all now, the skirmish, the battle, the war.

"Oh, my God!" Altaf left him, taking the light, but returned in seconds to hold Evan's head and press a cup to his lips. At first Evan let the water run from his mouth, but then, as he had know it would, his body took over and he drank. Later, he swallowed the capsule.

Dikili: "Why are we making such an effort to avoid your journalist friend these days, Lindsay? I don't dislike him, you know; I only resented him when he wanted to monopolize you." Sharon buttoned the elegantly simple mint-green frock that set off her flaming hair.

"I'm afraid the avoidance is on my account. I've been surrounded by dependent males over the past several years; the next will be different."

"I know what you mean — he *is* immature," Sharon laughed breathily. Anger surged in Lindsay and was pushed aside, replaced by the wry recognition that criticism of Dirk was acceptable only from herself.

The breakfast chimes sounded, but Lindsay couldn't finish dressing. "Your friend," she began, "the one traveling parallel to us — will you see him again? I still hope to meet him."

"Possibly. His group isn't coming here, though or to Pergamum." Lindsay took the ash-blue pullover from under the checkered one and drew it over her head.

This was the last Muslim port, and the men, particularly Reg, would be discouraged. He had admitted last night to Lindsay that he was losing hope. "Insanity doesn't necessarily imply idiocy," he said. "I'm afraid Jones is right and she's decided not to risk it."

No, Sharon was not stupid — her currency conversion, for instance, was slow but accurate and she had absorbed a smattering of classical lore — but Lindsay thought she lacked the imagination to fear pursuit unless she actually saw it. She had leaned far out on the pinnacle on Delos, overlooking a sheer drop of hundreds of feet into the water. "Doesn't that frighten you?" Lindsay had asked. "I should imagine myself hurtling down."

"Oh, dear, no," Sharon laughed merrily. "My balance is good, and I don't expect a push from behind."

On their part too was Sharon's frenzied devotion. She read her Bible now as she waited for Lindsay to finish dressing. "Oh, Lindsay," she said rapturously, looking up from it, "we can never do enough for Christ Jesus." The inspiring words, though, had not come from Him, Lindsay saw, looking over her shoulder; Sharon was reading Leviticus.

"I made this myself," Altaf said. "I burned the first batch, but I don't think this is too bad."

The porridge that he was spooning into Evan was tasteless, but it felt marvelous sliding down his throat and into his empty stomach. That had begun to give him as much discomfort as the hand but was subsiding gratefully now, halfway through the porridge.

"I suppose, given Haneef, I should have expected it and not left you with him — he's not responsible. But why, what reason did he give you for denying you even water?"

"Why don't you ask Haneef?" The two, his cripples, his little madman and the speechless one, had become oddly close to Evan, unlike this man who spoke and behaved reasonably, yet was wedded to insanity.

"I'm not speaking to them. That sounds childish, I know, but they are like children, and my attention is very important to them. I got them both from prison, you know, oddly enough the same one from which you took your friend. They're devoted to me. Did you ask them for water?"

"Repeatedly. Look at the paper beside the water pitcher."

Altaf read it. "Idiots. It's known how the Russian died; the Kurds turned his body over to his people three days ago. You were foolish not to sign — with your blood splashed dramatically across it, it would have been worse than valueless."

"We all have our games. I'm beginning to understand Haneef's. Sayed wasn't involved, you know. He gave me some coffee and a cup of milk."

"He should have ignored Haneef," Altaf said irritably. "Oh,

the poor devil has no will left." He folded Haneef's creation into a paper airplane and sent it sailing onto a pile of debris in one of the corners. Evan felt a pang of regret and came near to asking that Altaf give it back. Found on his body, unsigned and blood-specked—

Evan imagined Francis reading it. "Not the most satisfactory of sons, but one could never fault his courage." Indulging himself in this bit of pre-posthumous self-dramatization, he must have looked smug. Altaf lashed out at him.

"You can't understand Haneef — or Sayed either — until you know what happened to them. You do know, I suppose, that they have no balls."

It was an American expression that Evan had heard and disliked; he was surprised to hear it from Altaf, usually tidy in his speech. "I should say that they're both lacking in sanity," he said stiffly, "hardly in courage."

"No, no. I mean that literally. They are both *castrati*."

"Good God. I'd no idea that was still done."

"It was resumed a few years ago — at the behest of that force for stability so beloved by your foreign office — the Emir. Centuries ago, Tariq was noted for its beautiful eunuchs; they served as concubines throughout the Middle East. The practice was revived for a different purpose — to deal with dissent, real, possible or imagined. The techniques used were different too, far more painful and slower. You've seen Haneef's wrists? He tried to claw himself to death."

"Oh, Jesus." And yet a spark of charm and beauty remained in the little wreck. Evan pushed away the hand bearing the spoon of oatmeal.

"Yes, distasteful, isn't it? Those Middle Easterners, I suppose you're thinking, always flogging and throwing rocks at people, and now this. You've got it wrong, I'm afraid. The Emir's technicians were imported from abroad, and the operation to which Haneef and Sayed were subjected has been taught to practitioners on three continents — by United States counterinsurgency experts."

He gave Evan a cigarette and lit it. "I suppose this wasn't the kindest time to tell you about it."

"I wanted to know. Were they political prisoners?"

"Yes. Haneef had taken part in an anti-government demonstration at his American university — the CIA provided names and photographs of all such demonstrators for the Emir — and he and his family were picked up when he came home on holiday. His father was an exporter — this is one of his apartments, incidentally, we've kept up the lease — and they accused him, falsely, of spying for Israel."

"What happened to him?"

"He, his wife and Haneef's two sisters simply disappeared. There's no possibility now that they're alive."

"And Sayed?"

"A brother-in-law in a suspect organization. His was regarded as a more serious case. They ended their attentions by burning his tongue out — through his cheeks, as you can see."

"How did you get them from prison?"

"Probably with less risk than you took — money from Sayed's brother-in-law who had escaped the country. I had known Haneef's family, and it was enough to buy what was left of both of them."

Evan felt oddly defensive, as if by being British he shared the guilt for these things. "Where are they now?"

"Downstairs, Sayed sleeping, Haneef praying. He does that five times a day, never fails. I wish I had his simple faith."

"Simple faith — oh, my God!"

"I suppose you regard Islam as backward, particularly the Shiites. I suppose—" The slightest touch of reluctant snobbery crept onto Altaf's face. "My family was not Shiite, incidentally."

"Then you'd best stay far from home." Evan told him about the schoolboys at Palat. "It isn't their backwardness that appalls one but their murderous conviction that they're the only ones holy enough to live."

It had been like an exchange of blows, and this one had hit Altaf unexpectedly hard. "I didn't believe it," he said and went silent, freshening their coffee. "Your friend Roud wrote an article that was reprinted here," he went on finally, "but I didn't believe him. Roud would seem to belong to an earlier century as well; he speaks of savages. I think he writes like one, implying it would be best for the West to ally with the Soviets for the explicit purpose of annihilating us all."

"He wouldn't have done — before the Tariqis imprisoned him and murdered two of his friends and various other innocents before his eyes. Simon had learnt a half dozen

191

Middle Eastern languages and planned to make his career here. Now he hates anything to do with it."

That would be worse now, Evan realized suddenly, worse still if Evan were killed. Simon, the dear old, utterly loyal bull in the china shop would be capable of doing something stupid and terrible to avenge him.

"Do you believe me? About Palat?"

"I'm afraid I do," Altaf answered. "I won't tell you that I don't find it disheartening. Though I understand it. They've been so terribly hurt so many times and for so long that they must strike out — sometimes at random."

"The mullahs?" Evan thought he had found a weak spot; Altaf drank wine, he knew, and was not praying with Haneef. "I'd had the impression that they were quite comfortable."

"They represent the hope of a downtrodden people."

"Those random targets of which you spoke, people like Simon and the Kurds and the Sunnis — they'll strike back. Hate spawning hate spawning hate." Evan sighed; his hand hurt, and Altaf, briefly reachable, had encased himself once more in dialectic. He had the look now of a young prophet, his eyes deep and liquid with vision, reminding Evan unpleasantly of — Sharon. They had *that* in common.

"I think that circle can be broken," he told Evan, taking their dishes from the table. "When you're rested, we'll talk about it."

Evan slept for a while and awakened to see Haneef occupying the camping stool, his eyes cast down. "Hello, Haneef." He started like a pet deer caught nibbling in a garden, his long lashes rising, and Evan's heart lurched with pity."

"Hello, David. No grudges?"

"No grudges."

"I'm glad. I bought something for you." Haneef peeled the wrapper and foil from a chocolate bar and gave it to him. "It's English."

"Mm. It tastes wonderful, thank you very much. Share it with me."

Haneef accepted back half the candy and nibbled at it. "You might like something else, some news that I heard. Sayed is very good with radios and fixed ours downstairs so we can hear almost everywhere. BBC this morning. One of your members of Parliament got into his car, right by the building, and was blown up. Pieces of MP and automobile all over everything."

Haneef's face was soft with pleasure from his story and the taste of chocolate in his mouth. Altaf believed the boy devoted to him, but Evan thought his first loyalty would be to death and the infliction of pain, only secondarily to Altaf or any living being.

"I don't like that news so very much."

"Oh, but that isn't what I meant to tell you. You're a hero in England now, isn't it funny, and all because of your crime. The announcer said that all the paintings you had up for sale were sold, some to dealers. The dealers are getting three and four times what you had been asking."

Evan was not displeased. Whatever critics had said, his work had been pleasant, rather pretty and wouldn't muck up people's houses. Its success now would create a better market for the new ideas buzzing about in his head. If, if he could get out of this—

"You will have lots and lots of money from them." God, he had never made a will, and Hamish would have nothing; Francis, who needed nothing, everything.

Evan must have been insane to think as he had done last night; he wanted not to die with a desperation deeper than any thirst, any pain he could imagine.

Pergamum: Max, Dr. Max Ross, had almost forgotten Asklepios and had failed to read last night's briefing in the cruise book because of an unproductive meeting with Reg and Hamish. The Asklepion at Pergamum took him completely by surprise. It had been a place given over completely to the practice of medicine, a kind of Mayo Clinic, among whose ruins, more than two millenia old, a soft-voiced local tour guide was leading him, his table companions and a score or so other Cobb's tourists. She was a homely little thing, squat, swarthy, and very bright indeed, another medical student; Max stayed as near to her as he could to catch her words.

"—a combination of primitive and amazingly sophisticated medicine, as we have seen. You are now in the cryptoporticus, whose use illustrates both sorts." It was a long, smooth underground passageway, dark and pleasantly cool after the midday heat above. "Patients were brought here after

193

completing their exercises. They would be a bit light-headed after running the course you have just walked over and not inclined to question auguries from a disembodied voice. Witch-doctor medicine, of course. Archeologists found how it was done; small tunnels from above ground convoluted to produce an unearthly tenor in the voice of prophecy.

"But sound modern psychology as well. Those promised recovery believed, and recovery began—"

She turned to lead them outside, and Max lost the next words. A few yards from the cryptoporticus, she stopped to point out a time-eroded relief in marble of two snakes drinking from a pan.

Max paused to touch it, and the group moved away from him. A little girl of seven or eight whom he had seen hanging about the fringes of other clots of tourists drew up to him, pressed a box into his hand and was gone in a swirl of full pallid dirndl.

It was identical to the one he had bought from Ali in Istanbul, the same candies pictured on its cover, but it was lighter, its weight not properly balanced. The cellophane wrapper was gone, and it was held together by pieces of transparent tape.

"Max." Reg had slipped back to him and spoke softly into his ear as Max began to slide his fingernail under the tape. "Don't open that. You and I will take it to the cryptoporticus, very carefully; it could be an explosive device."

Max felt a nasty inward jerk and moved slowly beside Reg to the mouth of the tunnel they had just left. It was empty now, the tourist group following theirs minutes away. "We'll leave it there," Reg said, "warn the others and notify the authorities. If it's only candy after all, I promise to take the shouts of laughter upon my shoulders alone."

Max knew it wasn't candy and was sweating as he entered the long passageway whose walls would absorb an explosive blast. He raised the box to his face suddenly, and his nose confirmed a whiff of corruption he thought he had caught from it. "Reg," he said sickly, moving back to the light at the entrance, "it isn't a bomb."

Reg swore softly and turned away as Max exposed the polyethylene bag containing the crushed and blackened fingers. He was holding it up to the light, studying the points of severance, when he heard voices outside. He dropped the box, tightened the wrapping around the fingers and thrust them into his pocket.

Hamish, Lindsay and Sharon appeared at the entrance. "Testing the acoustics," Reg said; no one believed him.

"That sweet little girl gave you a gift. What was it?" Sharon knew something was up — her smile was hungrier than usual.

"Yes." Dismayed to see the woman there at first, Max thought now he could muzzle her. "As Evan said, terror is their game, and this is their latest play at it; they want it broadcast. It's fortunate only the five of us are here. A leak would be mischievous but easy to trace."

She absorbed that stolidly. "But what *was* it?"

"Two fingers, Evan's. They were the ones worst broken—" Hamish reached out and grasped Lindsay's hand, his face bloodless. "Look," Max said, striving for cool professionalism, "however it was meant, it's good news. They were removed by a competent surgeon, a skin flap peeled from each to cover the wounds on his hand. That means he's been given medical treatment, that they're making an effort to care for him. Having seen what happened on the bus, I'd been afraid he would lose the whole hand if it wasn't seen to."

Lindsay was weeping for the first time. "I'm sorry," she said, unable to stop it. "I'm sorry."

Evan was light-headed still, as he found when he sat up too quickly, but he felt generally rather well, as if he were far into recuperation from a serious but defeated illness. His jailers had exhausted their cooking repertoire and served him tinned beans again for lunch, but that had been strengthening, and his stomach was behaving well.

He stood, steadying himself on the metal frame of the bed, Sayed watching. "May I look out the window?" Sayed gestured towards it, palm up. He lifted the gun though when Evan came near, and Evan made a wide, dizzy circle around him.

The window looked out forever, magnificently, onto a wide sea, but downward was quite hopeless: a cobble-stoned service area to an apparently unused warehouse whose blank brick wall closed itself against him. Memory of his early intention to jump from it made Evan queasy, and he looked up again out over the harbor.

Sayed made a noise in his throat and threw a lighted cigarette onto the floor beside Evan without being asked for it. He reached down, picked it up and smoked, watching Sayed who had returned to his book. If one shut out the hideous mouth, the face had an altogether different aspect: sad, even gentle. His hold on the machine gun was that of an unhappy child to a comforting toy — Evan had not seen him fire it and guessed suddenly with surprise but near certainty that he never had. Nor would he, unless under direct, immediate orders.

They were in or near a city; in the night Evan had heard the not-too-distant whoops of sirens. If he could get past Sayed, down the stairs and into the street, there would be people; Altaf and Haneef must go out sometimes—

Not now, though; Evan's knees sagged as he let go of the supporting window frame, and Sayed, gun and all, had to help him back to the bed. He read for a bit, his mind wandering from the Dickensian dinner party to the dinner group on the Alexandros, and then Haneef brought dinner: the tinned spaghetti, a wedge of white cheese and a glass of red wine.

"Wine?"

"They drink it," Haneef said disapprovingly. "I do not."

"What about hashish?"

"It's an intoxicant too, and I don't use it now; I try to practice my religion."

"You won't dine with me?"

"I ate early — I'm going to the films tonight."

"I thought there were Muslim strictures against those as well."

"Only against the indecent ones — with half-dressed women and all. This one is about war and soldiers, no women at all — lots of blood, if the previews can be believed."

Sayed returned, and took his place on the camping stool with a torch to read in the gathering dusk.

"Sayed, I should like to look out the window again." Sayed nodded agreeably. The antibiotic must have knocked out the fever altogether; rising was easy this time, and Evan got to the window with no dizziness at all. "You're not going to the films?" Sayed shook his head, not looking up from the book. "Is Altaf going?" Evan asked casually.

Sayed rested his cheek on his hand in a gesture indicating sleep — of course, Altaf had returned in the early hours of the morning. Perhaps Evan ought to try it now — or in a few minutes, to ensure that Haneef would be far away and Altaf well into sleep.

The ships and score or so small yachts in the harbor were lighted, and their reflections danced festively on dark velvet water. Sayed threw him another cigarette, and the raw dinner wine buzzed pleasantly in Evan's head.

He looked at Sayed, who seemed to have read something that annoyed him and didn't look nearly so passive as he had done in the afternoon. Evan felt a shrinking between his shoulder blades, imagining a gun blast hitting there if he had misjudged his man — or his dash for freedom could be ended another way. He remembered Sayed's long-legged, easy lope round the bus outside Priene. No, it was beyond him to chance losing his life now, at this moment; Evan would be stronger tomorrow, able to run faster.

He had gone back to the bed but was not asleep much later when Altaf appeared beside him. He was about to ask for a blanket, too cold now, with the fever gone, when Altaf took his left hand and wrapped something round his wrist.

"You're not going to like this, and I don't either, but Haneef told me you'd been up and about today." Altaf knotted a long, narrow linen strip onto the wrist, passed it through the metal grillwork of the bedstead and fastened it to the right wrist just above the dressings. "I wakened just now realizing that Sayed's been on guard for most of the past sixteen hours. He's got to have some rest, and I do too."

He was beginning the same trick on Evan's ankles now. The bindings were loose and not actually uncomfortable, but there was no way at all for Evan to get his hands together. Helplessness filled him — he ought to have made his break earlier — and fury. He was wearing shoes — his feet had been cold and his socks too filthy to wear — and aimed a kick at Altaf's fine, aquiline nose as he bent over the foot of the bed. Altaf dodged successfully and tied the foot securely beside the other.

"You're very angry. I understand, and I'm sorry this is necessary. There. You shouldn't be too uncomfortable; I think you can even turn, at least to one side or the other. Can you?"

Evan turned only his face so that it was away from Altaf and didn't answer. "So. Well, it's only for a few hours. You'll be free as soon as it's light, I promise. Good night, David." He stood for a moment, then went down the stairs. Evan ought anyway to have asked for the blanket.

He thought at first it was the cold that had awakened him, but it was the soft pad of bare feet upon ancient flooring. Someone touched his arm, and he stiffened.

"Don't be afraid. It's only me, Haneef." That wasn't at all reassuring in the dark, Evan's movements restricted to inches. Haneef untied his right wrist, though, and then the ankle; he was Cat's Eyes after all, working only by faint, deflected moonlight. He lay beside Evan then, close, and covered them both with a blanket. He was naked.

"I want you to make love to me."

"I don't think I can do that. I don't feel awfully well."

"I think you can. I think you're very strong."

"I don't want to do that; I have a lover."

"Tell me about her." The voice was sweet and quiet.

In his astonishment, he told the truth. "My lover is a man." And was glad — the lie was dead. "He is brave and good and very beautiful."

"I see. It's all right, I suppose, though I preferred women when I had a choice. It's all that's left to me now, and I've been told that soon I'll have no sexual feelings at all. The body changes. May I stay with you anyway?"

"Yes. Don't do that, though, please. Turn the other way."

He turned obediently, pressing his back against Evan's. Evan lay thinking about him for a long time. Then he turned and, driven by a terrible pity, was able to do what the boy had asked. The little madman kissed him on the forehead afterward and fell asleep first, with his arms wrapped around Evan.

When Evan awakened much later, he was shivering, bound to the bedstead again, the smooth slender body gone and the blanket as well.

Hall of the Grand Master — April 9: "You're left-handed, aren't you?" Haneef asked, holding the hand mirror before which Evan shaved. "I'm glad."

From Haneef, it was almost an apology. He had come at the first light to untie Evan, bringing a plastic basin of warm water, soap and the shaving things, items he had denied Evan earlier.

"You were in the news again this morning. Your father made a statement to the press."

The frenetically cheery actor's manner had returned suddenly; the news was not going to be good. "Tell me about it."

"He said he would not negotiate with us. Altaf is very sad about it, but he said we must keep to our deadline or it will all be for nothing."

"Never show fear," Evan remembered hearing on ITV from someone who had been held hostage in an airplane, "always act as if your situation were quite ordinary."

"Deadline?"

"You'll have a week."

Evan began to wash his body, and Haneef turned modestly away. What would Francis be thinking? What if Andrew or Monty were in his place? The response would be the same, Evan realized, perhaps made more easily.

But Haneef had tricked him before. "What exactly did my father say?"

"He was not very complimentary. He said, 'I will not dishonor the name of my son nor dim his courageous action in Tariq by submitting to criminal extortion.' Criminal, imagine! The English are so peculiar; they must see that the crime was yours and that we ask only reparation."

The style was without question Francis'. One week. One week to escape or—

"It's important to establish direct, personal communication with one's captors," the hijack victim had advised. "It's harder then for them to kill."

"It will be very quick, you know. I am to do it — Altaf and Sayed take no pleasure in such things. Because I love you, I will see that you feel nothing. One bullet, right here." Haneef touched the point at the base of his own skull at which he had shot the guide, Ahmad.

Evan studied him. That had been only half sadism, the other half meant to be reassuring. There would not be a lot to gain by "establishing communication" with *this* captor. Sayed appeared to replace him as guard. "Please tell Altaf I should like to speak to him when he has time," Evan told the departing Haneef.

Altaf finally came bearing breakfast, avoiding Evan's eyes and obviously eager to escape him as soon as possible. Altaf was going to be a reluctant assassin.

"Please wait," Evan said to his departing back. "I'd hoped we could talk again." He loved debate, and possibly Evan could inveigle him into one. "I've been thinking about what you said yesterday."

Altaf turned, met Evan's eyes and looked quickly away at the wall behind them. "Sit with me." He sat unwillingly at the foot of Evan's bed, looking now at a point somewhere near his chin. "I've been wanting to ask if you have connections with the PLO."

"We don't," Altaf answered mechanically. "One of our goals is, of course, a Palestinian homeland, but of the right sort."

"The right sort being a theocracy?"

"The other 'ocracies' have been singularly unproductive for my people." That had been more animated and addressed to Evan's face.

"Altaf, doesn't it trouble you that you'll be setting the scene for religious massacres like the one at Palat all over the Middle East? A holy war is a nasty thing to unleash — the holy ones can't see anyone else as human."

"Holy wars. Yes. Do you think they have ever stopped, David? They are merely fought on a larger scale, the religions given different names, like capitalism and Marxism, for instance. You should read the newspapers I grew up with in America." His subject was warming Altaf, bringing color back to his cheeks; at least a shadow of the young prophet had returned.

"Every so often some eccentric will complain, writing that General Pinochet or Mr. Somoza, for instance, is torturing people to death by the thousands with U.S. tools and support. Those in authority soon point out that the victims might possibly be Communists, and that makes it all right with everybody, because Communists are going to hell anyway. Holy wars? Of course!"

He stopped himself suddenly, looked at Evan as if just now seeing him and began, for the first time since Evan had met him, to laugh. "You are getting to know me too well, David. I'm going to leave you for a while to do some thinking. The escape of a clever war prisoner would not necessarily disgrace an army."

Evan finished his coffee and took the cigarette Sayed had lit for him to the window to look out over the harbor again. The sun was benevolent on bright, smooth water, and the large cruise ship that had arrived in the night was reflected almost perfectly upon it. It flew an American flag and looked vaguely familiar. There was another ship beside it, and behind them —

The Alexandros, dazzling him with her height and grace! In that instant, Evan realized Hamish was less than a mile away. He reached out with his mind to touch him.

14

Rhodes: Reg's disguise was not convincing. He was trying for the look of a race track tout on a spree of luck and might pass all right from the back, with his loud plaid jacket and impudent hat, but the white brows, flaring over tinted glasses, stood out like beacons.

"Eyebrow pencil?" Max suggested.

"No time. I'll need to do this in seconds." He repacked the glasses, jacket and hat inside his carrying case and stared at himself in the mirror. "If only Jones had got his man off sooner."

"Lindsay had told them last night that Sharon might meet her friend once more, and Reg had called the agent immediately. "He's at least half a believer now," Reg had said afterward. "He's sending a man to Rhodes tomorrow — he'll arrive just before noon, board the ship, where he'll keep himself scarce, then follow our group at each site like one of those hangers-on after a free lecture. And they've decided to arrest the woman at Luton rather than Venice."

"What if it happens tomorrow morning?"

"We'll have to cope," Reg had shrugged, "as we should have done before. I hope it won't be Rhodes, though; we'll need more than luck if she goes outside the old city and into the new."

Lindsay had worn the red and white checked pullover to breakfast. Reg had eaten with his usual maddening deliberation, and Max had contemplated pulling his chair from under him if he lingered over cigarettes and coffee. Reg had patted his mouth delicately with his napkin after his last bite of sausage and pushed his chair from the table.

"Oh, the hell with it," he said now to his reflection in the mirror, drew a small pair of scissors from his case and proceeded to trim of most of the glorious eyebrows. "Perhaps they'll grow back," he said sadly.

Someone rapped at the door. "Milly?" They had left her with Sarah at the beauty parlor below deck.

"No, Lindsay." Max opened the door, and she slipped inside, her cheeks pink with tension. "She's showering now, but I must hurry. We're to see the Street of the Knights together, and then she'll meet her friend. Something's brewing, all right. I said I'd like to be introduced, and we've made arrangements to meet at a cafe this afternoon, but she wants me out of the way this morning. She stopped at the cruise desk and bought me a ticket for the bus tour of the city, saying I mustn't miss it. How can I avoid going?"

"You'll have to go, Lindsay," Max said, "or at least get on the bus. We can't chance scaring her off."

"I want to be with you — " She agreed, though, before leaving them, to enter the bus and to stay on it until Sharon was out of sight.

They held a final briefing with Hamish in Hector Seven. "She might make a break earlier," he said. "Someone ought to be watching the gangplank now."

"No," Reg soothed, "Miss Shaw has arranged for the gangplank to be lowered at nine hours, not before." He took chalk of a poisonous aquamarine color from his pocket. "If we lose sight of each other at any time, watch for markers. I'll leave lines at hand level on every next building or so and at corners when she turns.

"No motor traffic is allowed inside the old city, but, should she go to the new one and be picked up by car, we'll first try for a taxi to follow her. Failing that, it will have to be the police — we'll give them a description of the car and its license. Hamish, how is your Greek?"

"Archaic, I'm afraid, but I think I can make myself understood. I've been studying this." He drew a yellow tourist dictionary from his coat pocket.

"The Turkish quarter in the old city is tricky as well," Reg went on. "There are dozens of small, narrow streets, beginning and ending at random, rather like a maze. We'll need to stay on our toes if she goes in that direction."

A door down the corridor slammed shut, and Sharon's breathy voice could be heard outside. She stayed with Lindsay as she had said she would across the hazardous highway that separated the harbor from the walled city, down to Socrates Street and all the way up the Street of the Knights. Max, Reg and Hamish kept in sight of each other but maintained their usual distance.

The guided tour ended at a moat, dry now and turned into a deer park. Across it, two buses waited for the tourists who had signed for them, and Sharon accompanied Lindsay to the first, waiting at its door until she was seated. Hamish turned as if to go back to the shopping area, Max took a few token steps after Lindsay, and Reg disappeared into the park's greenery. He emerged transformed in seconds; the scissors had done the trick, and Max wouldn't have recognized him at his present distance.

It was easy at first to keep him in sight. The city was lovely, small and prosperous, crowded to precisely the right degree. Two other large cruise ships, an American and a Norwegian one, were in the harbor, and the three sets of passengers were distinguishable only by the colors of their hand luggage. Several dozen small yachts were anchored there too, and their passengers were threading their way up and down Socrates Street along with the rest. In two or three weeks, the tourist population would double, and an individual could easily disappear among the swarm of pedestrians, but for now, following was easy.

They arrived at the south wall then to see Reg pass through its gate and into the new city. "Not a taxi in sight," Hamish said anxiously, surveying the stream of traffic on the highway dividing the two sections of Rhodes. They crossed it, catching the same traffic light that Reg had done; he was reading a magazine, slouched outside a news store in the first block off the highway.

Max and Hamish ducked into a shop across from it that featured bathroom fixtures in incredibly brilliant colors and had difficulty persuading the Turkish-speaking clerk that they were interested in neither the purchase nor the theft of the mauve wash basin against which Max had been caught leaning. They could see Sharon through the shop windows, still alone, picking up, skimming and replacing newspapers; the shopkeeper stood watching her, unannoyed; he thought her beautiful, no doubt.

She left the shop without buying a paper and turned back toward the old city, Reg pocketing his magazine and following. Max and Hamish misjudged their distance and were cut off by a changing stop light and a steady flow of fast traffic as Reg and Sharon disappeared inside the city wall. There was no sign of either in the thickening throng of tourists within the gate, and Max had begun to swear at himself hopelessly when Hamish saw the first chalk mark.

Reg had placed his markers regularly, and it was easy again for a while. They turned right, off Socrates Street, then left, then left again, onto narrower and narrower cobbled streets shaded by ancient plaster archways. The sounds, odors and colors rushing past were pleasant ones: birds, a housewife humming at her morning chores, a bar of rock music from an upstairs window — and flowers and flowers. But they continued twisting about in the pretty, vine-covered puzzle until Max feared he saw the same peacock-blue doorway they had passed minutes before. They were doubling their tracks, perhaps—

Reg waited for them, though, a few feet from the next turning, looking old and confused beneath the jaunty disguise. "She's gone in there," he said, indicating a narrow, white-washed archway. "It's a cul-de-sac, but there are seven houses inside — she was too fast for me."

Evan heard a woman's laugh on the stairway and then Altaf's angry voice. "I'd prefer to discuss it downstairs — or by telephone. I don't think your coming here was wise or safe for any of us."

The red-haired woman appeared then in the doorway, Altaf beside her. "I had to look at your glorious view once more — " She looked and saw Evan leaning against the window. He raised his eyebrows at her inquiringly, and she stared back for a moment with the repelled yet fascinated expression usually reserved for caged reptiles.

She turned back to Altaf then, arranging her face into the look she must regard as endearing. "I've been watching the newspapers, and I'm a little disappointed. There's a lot about Talbot and his very important family, but our demands are

205

hardly mentioned. To read the English language press, you'd think it was an ordinary, shoddy kidnapping, not a political act."

"What did you expect?" Altaf asked indifferently, not trying to hide his disgust at her intrusion. "The Islamic press is quite the other way."

"We're not trying to establish terror in Islam." Despite the challenge in her words, Sharon's manner was warm, almost flirtatious.

"Since we're speaking of disappointments," Altaf drawled, "I can't say that I'm pleased with your choice of target. We agreed that the first would be someone stupid and destructive, and this man isn't at all as you described him."

Sharon's eyes sparked. "He's a—" She stopped herself, not easily, and resumed the ingratiating smile. "What's done is done, and we have to make the best of it. I started to tell you that the fingers were delivered to Ross at Pergamum, but—"

"I'm sorry about that. Haneef stole them from the doctor, packaged them and arranged for their delivery. Sometimes I think he's improving, and then that ghoulish streak takes him—"

"Altaf!" The tone was archly shocked as if Altaf had indulged in some small naughtiness. "That could have been very good. Do you remember the Getty boy's ear? *That* was noticed. You've told me often enough that terror is our only weapon, and to create it, occasionally we have to do something a little bit terrible. But the Zionist Ross hid the package before anyone saw it."

"Zionist? Are you sure?" Altaf seemed momentarily shaken, then shrugged. "It doesn't signify. I chose him because people pay attention to doctors and because he's tall enough to be picked out in a crowd. He's served his purpose."

"He's a Jew and admits it, but, as you say, there's no harm done. I have a better idea — what I need is the other hand," she said ecstatically.

"What?"

"Talbot's other hand; this time we'll make headlines. Three busloads of tourists are leaving this afternoon for Lindos." She chattered on, ignoring Altaf's horrified repulsion. "When one of them opens his or her picnic lunch and finds a human hand inside, we'll have a story that can't be hushed up."

Evan was half-mesmerized as he might have been at a freak show, but not frightened. Haneef stood wide-eyed, his lips slightly parted. He would no doubt ally himself with Sharon — the prospect of cutting off anyone's hand, possibly even his own, would delight him. But Altaf would never tolerate it, and Sayed, holding the gun, sat in his place in the doorway.

"A woman," Altaf said wonderingly. "A woman who calls herself Christian. How can you even imagine such a thing?"

"Righteously." The smile was regal now. "Like Judith. Like Deborah."

"The prophetess among us," Evan murmured.

"Oh, Altaf, don't make it hard for me; God has told me what I should do, and it must be done."

"God told you to take this man's hand." Altaf spoke very calmly and distinctly as one might do to a mental case far from the reach of reason. "Are you sure you understood Him? It seems a rather bloody-minded command, not very holy."

Sharon made herself taller and mercifully stopped smiling. "The blood of the pervert shall be upon him; it's clearly said in the Bible, and in your Tariq, God's law is now actually practiced."

"Do you honestly believe that?" Altaf studied her clinically. "I suppose that you do, and it's time — past time — that you be set straight in the matter. The laws against sodomy are new and enforced only against political enemies — many of the mullahs have boys."

She flinched and paled, eyes and mouth rounding. "You're lying to me."

"Not at all — some have more than one." Altaf was enjoying himself, indulging a sadistic streak of his own, Evan thought, watching him smile at the girl's tormented face with the cool consideration a kind man might show one of the lower animals. "Enough now, the matter is closed, and I must ask you to leave us. Perhaps no harm was done, but it was frivolous of you to chance being followed here."

The girl stretched herself still taller, her face a mask of wounded determination. "I prayed that I shouldn't need to do this, but, since I must, I know God will strengthen me for it. I paid for everything, Altaf, I've supported you three for weeks now, and I'm taking command. You seem to have lost the will. Haneef," she turned to the boy. "I have only a little time to place the hand on one of those buses. Please get a cleaver or whatever it is you're going to use." The boy left them, Altaf ignoring his defection.

"As botched as you've made it," he said evenly, "I've chanced too much to let your psychiatric problems destroy this exercise—"

"Psychiatric problems—" Her eyes were dark coals in a paste-white face.

"They're obvious to everyone who knows you: you've arrived at this fixation because you can't face your own homosexuality." Evan was disappointed in Altaf, finding his analysis simplistic — one could see that she was strongly attracted to him — and annoying — Sharon was not one with whom Evan would care to share any label at all.

"You!" Her head snapped back and she gasped like a beached fish, fumbling around inside her handbag as if rescue lay within it. "Because I wouldn't jump into bed with you!"

"Good God! You'd never have been allowed there. I'd only known you a few minutes before deciding I'd rather bed a male wrestler — and I'm not gay. Come now." He moved toward her. "You may walk out by yourself or with my help." Altaf reached out to grasp her shoulders, snapped back a foot or two and threw back his head, roaring with rage, pain and astonishment. His face blurred then, a red circle appearing above his nose and spreading — he had hit the floor where he lay unmoving before Evan recognized the sound he had heard as a gunshot. Sharon removed a small, snub-nosed pistol from her handbag and pointed it at Sayed. Unnecessarily. He had let the machine gun slide from his lap to the floor, not in surrender, but to go to Altaf.

"Stay still, raise your hands," Sharon quavered, waving the pistol, but Sayed ignored her to kneel beside Altaf and turn him. Light reflected by the open eyes gave them a glitter, an illusion of movement, but Sayed's formless groan of grief said everything.

Haneef reappeared. "We don't have a proper implement — oh, but I seem to have missed a lot. He looks dead."

Sayed sat on the floor, tailor-fashion, rocking and cradling his friend and rescuer in his arms, and the gun's aim shifted from his face to Haneef's. "What do you plan to do about it?" Sharon asked, her voice pitched high.

"Oh, I am an organization man through and through, and it appears now that you command the organization. See, I brought you this." He held a kitchen knife, eight-inch blade pointed inward. "It's the sharpest we have."

Sharon bent over, the muzzle of her pistol shifting, between Haneef and Evan, lifted the machine-gun from the floor, stepped to the window and dropped it over. "I wouldn't know how to use it," she told Haneef; her speech had steadied, but she was dead pale and moved like a mechanical doll. "Have you a gun?"

"It's downstairs." It wasn't, and its bulge at the slim waist was evident.

"I think I ought to make sure. Put your hands high, Haneef, and turn all the way around, very slowly."

They stood between Evan and the doorway, and the knife, which Haneef had dropped, was too far away; he used Sharon's attention to Haneef to bolt for the opposite corner where the wine bottle lay. He picked it up by its neck and slammed it with all his force against the wall; it broke through the plaster but remained intact. Sharon had taken Haneef's pistol from him, thrown it too from the window and was almost upon him. The break in the plaster had revealed a beam, and Evan dashed the bottle against that; it shattered then, leaving a half dozen glass stilettos flaring from its neck.

"Sayed, Haneef, for God's sake, this woman is mad, she'll kill us all," Evan cried, but Sayed neither moved nor raised his tear-reddened eyes, while Haneef picked up the knife again but only stood beside the window, his eyes darting nervously back and forth between Evan and Sharon.

"Come on now, put down the bottle," Sharon said, stopping only a few feet out of its reach. "I don't want to kill you." Evan compacted himself into the corner, breathing slowly, saving himself. She raised the pistol and shot, hitting the bottle, but he was able to hang onto it, and four jagged points remained. He held it now between the gun and his heart.

He watched her forefinger tighten once more round the trigger and then loosen. "Oh, no. I won't let you make me kill you. I'll have that hand and keep you alive as long as I must." She backed away from him to the wall on which the discarded broom leaned and picked it up with her right hand, transferring the gun to her left.

Evan was able to dodge her first swipe with the broom's

working end, but it was hopeless — taller and heavier than he, possessed of two sound hands and a gun, she now had a four-foot reach over him. She was trembling, and sweat rolled down her face, but each feint came nearer. She reversed the broom suddenly and got in a sharp blow to Evan's nose, which bled copiously over his lower face and shirt.

Then Haneef started from his place by the window, and the knife flew from his fingers into the doorway. Evan turned to see his target, and the broom handle came down full on his right hand.

On the other side of the plaster archway was a courtyard common to seven dwellings, ornamented with stone cannonballs, fig trees, wild flowers and several alarmed chickens. The white-washed houses were low, very old and clean, their doorways and lintels painted in vivid colors. Two of them, on the sea side, had been built under and into an even older structure that towered thirty or so feet above them. It was stone, crenellated, like those the Hospitalers had built on the Street of the Knights, and very foursquare, direct and European in contrast to the rounded Eastern contours of the little houses beneath it. Max had seen a picture of it somewhere and thought it had housed, centuries before, the leader of the Hospitalers.

"It seems to be a dead end," he comforted Reg, "and we can hardly miss her when she comes out — unless — do you think these places exit into one of those alleys?"

The three had gathered among a cluster of low, leafy trees in the center of the courtyard from where they could watch the seven doorways, yet remain hidden. "Not the ones on the sea side," Hamish said. "I was looking at that castle one from the deck this morning — it's built into the city wall like part of the fortifications, and there's a long drop from the wall to the buildings on the other side."

They must first explore the four houses on their right, then, from which Sharon might escape unobserved. Max would take the first two, Hamish the next, while Reg covered them from the grove and watched the ones to their left; they had practiced a bird-like whistle to alert one another should one of them see Sharon.

Max, playing the intrusive tourist, peered into a small window outlined in lavender and caught the astonished and violated regard of a young mother nursing her child. No. The next door, scarlet, was half-open, and behind it two tiny old men smoked and drank coffee.

"*Kalimera,*" Max said pleasantly.

The larger, more wizened one rose and stared at him. "No Greek is spoken here," he said sourly, in perfect English. "Only Turkish." He closed the door firmly in Max's face. No again.

These four dwellings were contiguous, but a narrow pathway separated the fourth from the last house on their left. Hamish turned onto it and disappeared, presumably behind the fourth, the green-trimmed cottage, and Max had turned to follow him when a quick snap of a sound came from high behind him. Reg whistled, and Max hurried to him.

"That was a shot, Max, from up there." He gestured at the massive stone wall.

Either doorway might bring access. The first was open, and, inside it, an infant in a perambulator slept in the morning sun. The second, the orange one, was loosely latched; Max drew his pocket knife. "Should we wait for Hamish?" he asked Reg.

"I don't like that shot, Max. We'll leave our shoes outside, and he'll see where we've gone."

They slipped off their loafers, and Max lifted the simple latch easily and silently with his knife. The door creaked, though, as they eased it inward, and Reg, pressed against the adjoining wall, drew Evan's Luger. "No one here," he motioned to Max, who had backed himself against the opposite lintel. They stepped sock-footed into a small tiled entry, and Reg peered into a sitting room on their right.

The meaning of what they were doing hit Max so suddenly it knocked the breath from him. A gunshot. Somewhere inside was the crazy fanatic of a woman, the explosiveness of the youths from the bus and probably a whole nest of murdering conspirators. What in hell was he doing here? And maybe Evan was already dead, their risk for nothing. He followed Reg, though, because Reg expected him to follow and he had come to expect it of himself. They turned left into a cluttered kitchen and up a stairway at its end.

His first sight, through the doorless doorway, was the wild-eyed boy from the bus outlined by light from a large window and then Evan, bloodied and at bay in the opposite corner, the red-haired woman batting at him with a broom handle. Simultaneously, a knife flew toward them from the window, glancing harmlessly off Reg's shoulder, and the broom handle came down upon Evan, who fell back against the wall and slid down it onto the pile of trash where he had made his stand.

"Drop your weapons and raise your hands," Reg roared, directing the Luger at Sharon. She dropped the broom, tossed a small pistol down in front of her and lifted her arms soundlessly as Haneef had done. The scarred one, Sayed, sat on the floor unmoving, the head and shoulders of the third terrorist, obviously dead, on his lap.

"Max, go over them for guns, knives, what-have-you, then see to Evan. I saw a telephone in the entry, and we'll call the police—"

"Police!" screamed the boy at the window. In an instant, he grasped its crenellated frame and launched himself somehow up and out like a bird over the high sill; there was no other sound from him until the ugly, soft thump of his body against the ground beneath. Max got to the window without being aware of moving and, with Reg, looked down and down at him. Strangely, a broken machine-gun rested beside the boy's shattered right arm.

When they turned, Sharon had Evan.

She held him before her, her left arm across his chest under his arms and moved crabwise, facing them, toward the doorway. Her body was covered, but Evan's head drooped forward, leaving hers exposed — a clear shot, but Reg was setting his pistol down on the windowsill. Max saw his reason now: she had recovered her gun as they stared out the window and held it at Evan's throat.

"I don't need to tell you what I'll do if either of you move." She was deathly pale, her eyes enormous, face set and desperate; slowly the gun changed its angle. Reg would be first, then Max, finally Evan. Max, who was nearest but not near enough, tensed his body for the spring he would try regardless. Then Hamish appeared behind Sharon.

He bent down and out of Max's sight for a moment, then reappeared with Haneef's knife which had fallen there. He reached around Sharon then, his right hand whipping the gun up and out, his left driving the knife into her throat. The gun

212

sounded, echoing through the great room, a trumpet held by a time-worn angel was split in two, and bits of plaster floated down from the ceiling.

The red-haired woman struggled still for the gun, trying to wrestle it downward again toward Evan, but Hamish twisted it from her hand. "No," she choked, "the God of wrath protects me." The gun hand lowered and joined the other to grasp Evan whom she flung forcefully outward and down. Max reached him before he hit the floor and eased him onto the mattress opposite the window.

Sharon tried to speak again, but blood instead of words poured from her mouth. She flailed her arms more and more slowly, gradually subsiding against Hamish, her eyes fixed in fury and disbelief.

"God," Reg gasped, "that was close, that was very close. How is Evan, Max?"

He was stronger than he looked, his pulse weak but regular despite the blood loss, and his eyes moved beneath slitted lids as if he were trying to awaken. He began to choke on blood that had run from his nose down his throat, and Max raised him, hitting between his shoulder blades. The resulting cough eased Evan's breathing and sprayed Max's new shirt with red.

Hamish had disentangled himself from the dying woman and stood head bowed as if in defeat, his expression hidden. He would have heard the shot, Max realized, and, seeing the trail of blood from the corner, must have thought—

"Hamish, hear me," Max said briskly. "Evan is not dying, not seriously hurt. The blood comes from his nose, which may be broken, but his pulse is going like a metronome, and I think he'll be conscious soon."

The man who had saved them all raised his head; breathing convulsively, and then he focused on Max. "My God! I thought she'd shot him. Max, I needn't have killed her."

"Oh, yes," Reg said. "It had to be done. She had the strength of a maniac and would have killed us all if she'd got control of that gun again. We all owe you thanks, Hamish."

Max had moistened his handkerchief in a water pitcher beside the bed and was washing the blood-smeared face.

"Max," Evan breathed, his voice thin as a thread, "they've got you too."

"No. You're free, Evan, and safe." His eyes closed altogether then, and Max reached for a pulse, but Evan had forced himself awake before he found it.

"I don't know how you managed it," he said, "but I'm very grateful." His face showed no question, no guard, only a total, exhausted trust in Max. For a moment Max saw in him smaller, less vivid Alex, fragile after his long, late bout last year with measles. There were things to be made up to Evan, but new words, new action would cover them better than apology.

Evan saw the others then, and his sound hand reached out to grasp Hamish's. "You. And Reg as well—"

Reg saluted him, still holding the Luger on the surviving terrorist. "I don't think this chap is completely with us in his head," he said, "but I'm afraid to leave him to his own devices, and my arm's going stiff. Hamish, there's a telephone downstairs. Perhaps you could practice your archaic Greek on it with the police."

"What happened?" Evan asked. "Where are they all?" He managed to swing himself around on the mattress and, with Max's help, sat up. "Oh, God!" he whispered, catching sight of the blood-sodden woman stretched out before the door.

"The one I took to be their leader is dead too," Max told him.

"I know. She shot him. He was protecting me, oddly enough. And Haneef?"

"He left us," Max said, remembering the booted heel driving into Evan's hand, "via the window, I'm afraid."

"Oh, Jesus," Evan gasped. "Why? Why?"

"Reg said the word 'police,' and he screamed and almost flew out there."

"The poor little bastard." Tears slid astonishingly down Evan's pale, freckled cheeks. Then he saw Sayed, still holding the dead man, stood suddenly and went to kneel beside him. beside him. Reg was startled and brought the Luger closer.

"Sayed, listen to me. These police are not the same. Do you understand? I shall see to it that they don't hurt you. I want you to stand up now." One-handed, he detached Sayed's hands from the lifeless shoulders and helped him to lay the body out on the floor.

He was looking at Evan with the only expression Max had seen him wear — one of unmixed menace. He stood, though, and Evan, undaunted, drew a notebook and pen from his shirt pocket and put them in his hands.

"I want you to write something for me. We'll need your family's help to get you out of this, and I want a name and address." Sayed only stared. "Your brother-in-law, perhaps."

"Chelsea. I don't know the street," the scarred boy wrote in a normal, rather neat hand. "Ali Ahmad Nuri."

"Ah, there can't be too many of those — we'll find him."

Hamish reappeared and started back at Evan's nearness to the terrorist. "Evan," he said evenly, "step over here, please." Surprised, Evan obeyed. "I spoke to the commander of police, Reg. He has a little English, and, with my limping Greek, we got on famously; he's coming himself, immediately."

"There's something you've got to make him understand, Hamish," Evan said earnestly, motioning toward Sayed. "This man has hurt no one. He was with the others only because Altaf Yazdi had saved his life, and in no sense is he a terrorist."

Max looked away from Sayed's disfigured mouth and at his eyes, fixed spaniel-like on Evan, and Reg, seeing it too, let his gun arm relax. Three policemen arrived shortly, following their huge Greek commander. Max understood Reg's disinclination to involve them in the chase — those resplendent uniforms would have been visible for blocks.

Lindsay had hurried from the bus only to be commandeered by Milly and Sarah outside its door. They had invited her to shop with them. Later the three annoyed women would learn that Reg had urged it, pleading Lindsay's boredom with Sharon, actually wanting her away from the confrontation he hoped would come. The men were out of sight before she could finish her abrupt refusal, and she spent the next several minutes at a random, hopeless hunt. Having given up, she found herself unable to focus on the pretty streets of Rhodes and went back to the Alexandros.

She sat in the lounge now, watching small green waves lap against the side of the ship, her mind suspended. Dirk arrived beside her.

"May I?" She made room for him on the small divan. "You're still angry, though. Disgusted."

"No, I never had a right to be. There was something I had to do alone. It's finished now, and it's nice to have a bit of company."

"Something to do with Talbot, I suppose. You're in love with him, aren't you?"

She looked at Dirk directly, into the sad boy's eyes. "Evan? I like him awfully and respect him, but no, I've never been in love with Evan."

"Have you eaten?" She hadn't, and the line to the buffet lunch had disappeared; they would be removing the plates soon, and Lindsay was surprisingly hungry. She and Dirk gathered cold meats and cheeses and little pizzas and returned to the divan to nibble at them.

"My God!" Dirk jumped up, almost spilling his plate to the floor, and stared out the window onto the quay. Lindsay turned and saw the small victory procession, Hamish in the lead supporting a frail, bandaged Evan, followed by Reg and Max. She began to cry, and Dirk held her, stroking her head. The four disappeared into the ship.

Seeing Lindsay, Reg broke away from the others in the corridor and came to wring her hand. "We did it, young lady, the four of us; you and Max were right — at the last, she couldn't leave well enough alone."

"How is Evan?"

"There's no damage from the blow to his head — Max insisted that he be x-rayed in hospital, and they say that the hand has been competently seen to as well."

"Oughtn't he to have stayed there? He looks wretched."

"Max says he's dehydrated — he lost some blood from a broken nose — and wanted him to have a transfusion, but Commander Kokonis couldn't get him out of the city fast enough. He took Evan's and all of our depositions while we waited for the x-rays and then hustled us down to the quay. One of the patients — British — had recognized Evan, and the place was buzzing with it. The hospital's security is minimal, and I think Kokonis was afraid someone might have another go at Evan — large Middle Eastern population in Rhodes."

"I'd have thought he'd want to fly directly home," Dirk said.

"Max suggested that, but Evan insists upon finishing the cruise — he's quite mulish about it."

"I'd like to ring my paper and tell them he's safe," Dirk said. "Would that be considered premature, and is there anything that oughtn't be told? The loss of his hand, for instance?"

216

"His hand?" Reg cast a disappointed look at Lindsay. "Two fingers had to be amputated, but Evan had two hands ten minutes ago."

"Oh, I'm glad. I'd heard the whole hand was cut off and delivered to Ross at Pergamum. Your cabin-mate told me, Lindsay — very peculiar girl, that. She seemed absolutely horrified and yet was annoyed that I didn't want to send the story out immediately. I put her off with some nonsense about hearsay evidence." He watched Lindsay, wanting approbation.

"What about Sharon, Reg?" Lindsay asked levelly.

He looked back and forth between them. "I'm afraid Sharon is dead."

"How? What happened?" Dirk was astonished, but Lindsay felt neither shock nor sadness; perhaps it would come later, but now it was only as if some unneeded and unlovely object had been removed from her life.

Reg studied Dirk, who had somehow conjured up a notebook and pen and was beginning to scribble. He shrugged finally, as if deciding to get on with it anyway. "She had financed the terrorists and had chosen Evan as victim. She would have killed us all if — well, there was considerable confusion. The police came to the conclusion that Sharon and the terrorist leader killed each other." Reg's eyes were evasive, Lindsay thought; she believed it had happened differently.

"Regarding your story, Wilder, the police will brief the local press after the Alexandros lifts anchor. I suppose your calling it to London would do no harm, though — we'll be long gone from Rhodes before it can break there."

"What about the girl's involvement? Can that be told?"

"Yes. Her mother has been notified and is arranging to have the body flown back to America. I spoke to the poor woman myself after Kokonis' English ran dry. She was dismayed, of course, but I don't think terribly surprised. My only stricture, Wilder, would be that you imply, as Commander Kokonis is doing, that Evan has been flown directly home to an unspecified airport. Otherwise we'll be dogged by security problems for the rest of the cruise. There must be hundreds of aspiring Shiite saints out there who would leap at the chance to execute Evan for his crimes against Islam — in not allowing the other lot to kill him."

"I see. Oh, absolutely. Do you think he's safe here?"

"Yes, only passengers and cruise personnel will be allowed to board from here out — no visitors. A belated secret service agent ought to be somewhere on the ship right now, and Miss Shaw has been given a companion for the rest of the voyage — a fierce Greek policeman who will sit in the cruise office with an eye to the gangplank when we're in port."

"Where are the other terrorists?" Dirk asked.

"Evan is convinced that there were only four, including Sharon. Three are dead, and the fourth," he evaded, "is accounted for." He rose from the divan. "I'd best get about locating that elusive secret agent and let him know that four amateurs have done his job for him." He left them, holding himself straight, a hint of smugness on his kind face.

"And I'm going ashore to see about locating a telephone," Dirk said.

"I'll come with you."

"Lindsay, if you're coming out of concern for the story I'll send, you needn't. Sheer cowardice gives me an interest in keeping terrorists off the ship, and I shall do as I've been told."

They passed the cruise deck, inhabited for the moment only by a gorgeously garbed policeman.

"No, Dirk. We have two hours before sailing time, and I want to be a tourist again. With good company, for a change." His smile was brighter than the bright water, and he threw his arm around Lindsay. "That would have been quite a story," she said, "about Evan's hand."

"Yes. Not using it wasn't the sacrifice it might have been, though, since I had the job. I've been asking myself what I would have done if I'd still been unemployed. I'm not honestly certain."

"Are you still happy about it? The job?"

He grasped Lindsay's shoulders and turned her to face him. "Yes. It's all I know, really. I'm not that certain about my literary gift — nor my ability to put it to work. I shall probably go on and on writing things that you'll find trivial, even mean." It was all she wanted from him, the honesty. "I can promise one thing, though."

"What's that?"

"After today, I shall never write a word about your friend Talbot."

She laughed, took his hand, and they raced together across the busy highway and through the gate to the old city.

15

Corinth — April 10: "Hell. No beans — what kind of cruise is this?" Evan regarded his breakfast tray avidly and reached out for a piece of streaky bacon. He had been too tired for dinner, the intoxication of finding himself alive and free depleted, and had picked at it briefly, then curled himself beneath the covers of his bunk.

"Stay with me, Hamish." Hamish had squeezed in beside him, euphoric at the presence of the loved, whole breathing body touching his, but soon found that the slightest movement set Evan starting in his sleep — once he had hit the bad hand against the wall. Hamish kissed his face then and left him, and Evan went off as if drugged.

His pallor and sunken cheeks still troubled Hamish, but his appetite this morning hardly reflected them. "Not so much butter, please." Hamish was spreading it for him on a croissant. "More preserves — no, those raspberry ones. Ahh."

Max appeared and interrupted the feasting by thrusting a thermometer into Evan's mouth. "I've made the rounds," he told his silenced patient, "and everyone from the bus agrees not to press charges against your strange pet. A few expressed hope that your ordeal hadn't touched your brain, but I think any one of them would willingly perjure himself if you asked it."

"Thank you, Max," Evan said, relieved of the thermometer. Max read it with satisfaction and replaced it inside his black bag, taking a seat on Hamish's bunk. "It's awfully important to me to get him out of this, to get him somewhere he'll be safe—" With no charges against him, Sayed would be released in a week and sent to London on Evan's recognizance. "As important as anything I've ever done. How can I explain?" He finished his egg, pondering.

"Hamish, you were describing the Turkish children — how beautiful they are and bright and confident about life. Yet Turks are killing one another by the dozen each day. The killers — Sunnite, Shiite, rightist, leftist — must have been very like those children only a few years ago. And it's worse in the rest of the Middle East. I think what happens is—" Usually glib, he was fumbling for words, a study in earnestness. Hamish ached with love for him.

"Oh, I could almost draw it, but it's hard to say. All the pain they've inflicted upon one another over the centuries has created a prison of hate; they've trapped themselves inside it, and each act of revenge make the prison walls higher.

"Sayed is different. Terrible things have happened to him and to the people he loves, but he has never stepped inside the prison. He's more like the children — hardly beautiful, but — Max, how much could plastic surgery do for him?"

"I was looking at that yesterday — after things calmed down, of course." Flippancy gone, Max was serious, considering. "There are good bones there. I think the face can be restored to what it was. Something might even be done about his speech, depending on how much is left of the tongue."

"I should like to see to that. He's quite intelligent and sane, only battered. If he could be made to feel safe and the least bit sure of himself — it was what Altaf hoped for too — I think he's the sort who might make a dent in those walls. I'd give more than two fingers to know I'd helped him do that."

Evan addressed himself again to the cooling breakfast, a little embarrassed at his own intensity, and Max took his leave. Hamish followed him into the corridor.

"Max, what time were you supposed to call Sir Francis?"

"At eleven, when we dock at Corinth." Talbot had proposed flying his own plane to Athens yesterday to bring Evan home and had accepted Evan's refusal calmly but insisted that Max try to talk him around later. Max hadn't tried. "Does he know that his father refused to ransom him?"

"He knows — and accepts it as right and in character. I think the statement his father made to the press was the most attention Evan's ever had from the man. He — both of us —

want these next few days on the ship, though, to make plans and all, before dropping back into a world that we'll be facing differently. Max, let me ring Sir Francis."

"I'd appreciate that, Hamish. I confess, I barely understand him over the telephone."

Milly came out the door of Hector Six. "Come on, Max. You promised we'd have a look at Corinth before the buses leave for Mycenae. It's going to be nice to be married again," she told Hamish. "During Max's Eric Ambler period, I found that I missed it."

Evan had begun to dress himself when Hamish returned, having hard work with it, one-handed. "Let me help you."

"Ta, but no. It's a challenge of sorts, and the clean things feel wonderful. I'll need you to knot my tie tonight before we go down to dinner." He had slipped that in neatly — Hamish had hoped they would dine alone in Hector Seven. "Anyway, you'd best get yourself in order to go to Mycenae."

"Have you gone mad, Evan? I'll stay right here."

"You won't. I've been there, you know, and you'll like it so much. Mycenae isn't like Troy, all stripped and vacant. Those stone lions — perfect — whomp out at you — a thousand years older than the Delos one. I'll come along before I'll let you miss it."

"Lovely. The Muslim lunatic fringe will be delighted to hear it. I'm staying, and you are too."

"Please, Hamish. We have all the time in the world, you and I, but Mycenae won't come back to us so quickly."

That piece of persuasion ended any temptation offered by the stone lions. Hamish remembered thinking once along those lines — on the morning he had set out for Ephesus, Evan for Priene. He would imply he was going, to avoid argument, but return when the telephoning was done.

"You'll ring Simon," Evan called anxiously when he left. They had tried yesterday but got only Christina, who had cried.

"He hasn't been himself, Hamish," she had said. "I don't know what would have happened to us if Davie had died."

He was home now, waiting for the call Hamish had promised to make. "Did those animals hurt him?"

"No." The missing fingers would take some explaining later. "He was sorry for 'those animals.' In actual fact, he's having a damaged one sent home to minister to."

"Oh, Jesus!" Simon began to laugh, choked on his laughter and couldn't stop. Hamish talked nonsense for a while until he recovered himself. "May Chris and I run both of you home from Luton on Thursday?"

"That would be marvelous." Hamish decided to try it out now. "It will be only one stop — at Belsize Park. Davie's selling the cottage, and we'll be hunting for a larger flat in Hampstead."

"God, Hamish, I haven't had such fine news since — yesterday's. You'll be too tired Thursday, but Chris and I want to arrange some kind of celebration—"

Hamish made the second call with the pleasure of an avenger armed with a moral edge, finished it and returned to the Alexandros, the moral edge shrinking smaller at each step he took nearer Evan.

Miss Shaw was there when he arrived, cutting Evan's meat — a bit like having one's tea served by the prime minister. "I'll arrange to have your meal sent up immediately, Mr. Saunders," she beamed at him.

"Now that we're here together," Evan told her, "Hamish and I should like to apologize — about the chadri and all. We hated doing that to you."

"Nonsense. It was the only way it could have been managed and extremely clever of you both. I should have used one myself under similar circumstances."

"That would have created a less awkward impression."

She had a tinkling laugh, light and feminine.

Evan was a little sorry but very grateful that Hamish had foregone the lions of Mycenae. It was too soon to take his presence for granted, and Evan kept reaching out during their lunch to touch him and assure himself of it. He ate too much, as he often did when he was happy, finishing all the exotica left on Hamish's tray.

"Ought you to have lit into that octopus? It seems a little ambitious just now." Hamish lit him a cigarette. "I spoke to your father."

"You told him I wanted to finish the cruise."

Hamish, flushing, looked down at the carpet. "I'm afraid I told him a bit more than that."

What? Had Hamish berated him for not trying to ransom Evan? Evan would need to call and smooth things over, to let

Francis know that he understood about that. "You — lost your temper?"

"No, I think I was civil, anyway tried for it." Hamish lifted his eyes suddenly straight into Evan's. "What I told him was that you were coming home to my flat — our flat."

"So. So. It's done." Evan felt neither dismay nor relief, nothing.

"Evan, that isn't all of it. I bloody talk too much, always have done, and this time it just seemed to happen." His eyes were still on Evan's, direct but shy as if he expected to be punished. "I'm afraid, wanting it to have been, I let him think we'd been living together for some time."

"Oh." Warmth flooded Evan's chest, and he reached out to take Hamish's face between his hands, pressing it between the good and the bandaged one. "Wanting it to have been. I wished it too in that room I thought I'd never leave, wished we had had those years that I wasted — together."

"You're not angry?"

"God, no. I know what you were doing." He began to laugh helplessly. "Palat all over again. I girded myself for a great battle, prepared to endure anything — and you go off and fight it instead."

"More like Palat than that. One arrives and finds no enemy."

"What do you mean? What did he say?"

"I sprang my shattering revelation, and he said, 'I see,' in that vague, removed tone he has. 'Rather like Mortimer and *his* friend. Perhaps it runs in the family!'"

"Mortimer? *Uncle* Mortimer? Oh, bloody Christ!"

"Who is he?"

"Francis' younger brother — our only war hero. He was decorated several times, then killed late in the Battle of Britain. I'd no idea. What else did he say?"

"'Please tell David that we are all very proud of him. I've arranged to be at the place in Derby for the next fortnight and hope that he'll find a few days to spend with us there. You as well, Hamilton.'"

"He *didn't* call you 'Hamilton.'"

"Oh, but he did, and I was too nonplussed to correct him. I more or less agreed that David and Hamilton would arrive at Derby around the seventeenth of April."

Evan wished he had not eaten those last dolma and bits of

223

calamari; his stomach was beginning to churn along with his head. "Hamish, I've decided you were right, you know. For all Francis' kind words about faggotry running in the family, I think I'm none of *his* family at all. Aside from size and coloring, there's the handedness. It seems that every Talbot in recorded history was right-handed.

"I've decided too that it's no matter. He's treated me as his son in every important respect, and I owe him mine — not to try to change into something I'm not but — oh, to be decent, you know. I'm awfully glad you said we'd stop at Derby."

"Evan, are you all right? You're green."

"Awfully tired suddenly." He stood up and watched blue carpet tilt slowly toward him. Hamish caught him before the bad hand would hit the floor and helped him to the bathroom. His stomach and entrails were protesting the extremes of diet they had faced over the past days, and he had a few moments of swooning discomfort. He refused Hamish's support back to the bed but changed his mind once he got there and let Hamish undress him, going limp and languorous under the ministering hands. Naked and clean, his distress gone, tucked between crisp sheets, he felt safe and gay and good.

"You've overdone," Hamish fussed, "eaten indigestible things and too many of them. You'll stay in this bed all afternoon if I have to chain you to it."

"You won't need a chain if you'll stay with me." Hamish did and, enfolded in his arms, Evan let himself slide off toward sleep.

Also available from Alyson

Don't miss our *free* book offer at the end of this section.

☐ **ONE TEENAGER IN TEN: Writings by gay and lesbian youth,** edited by Ann Heron, $3.95. One teenager in ten is gay; here, twenty-six young people tell their stories: of coming to terms with being different, of the decision how — and whether — to tell friends and parents, and what the consequences were.

☐ **THE BUTTERSCOTCH PRINCE,** by Richard Hall, $4.95. When Cordell's best friend and ex-lover is murdered, the only clue is one that the police seem to consider too kinky to follow up on. So Cordell decides to track down the killer himself — with results far different from what he had expected.

☐ **A DIFFERENT LOVE,** by Clay Larkin, $4.95. There have been heterosexual romance novels for years; now here's a gay one. When Billy and Hal meet in a small midwestern town, they feel sure that their love for each other is meant to last. But then they move to San Francisco, and the temptations of city life create complications they haven't had to face before.

☐ **ALL-AMERICAN BOYS,** by Frank Mosca, $4.95. "I've known that I was gay since I was thirteen. Does that surprise you? It didn't me...." So begins *All-American Boys*, the story of a teenage love affair that should have been simple — but wasn't.

☐ **THE MOVIE LOVER,** by Richard Friedel, $6.95. The entertaining coming-out story of Burton Raider, who is so elegant that as a child he reads *Vogue* in his playpen. "The writing is fresh and crisp, the humor often hilarious," writes the *L.A. Times*.

☐ **CHINA HOUSE,** by Vincent Lardo, $4.95. This gay gothic romance/mystery has everything: two handsome lovers, a mysterious house on the hill, sounds in the night, and a father-son relationship that's closer than most.

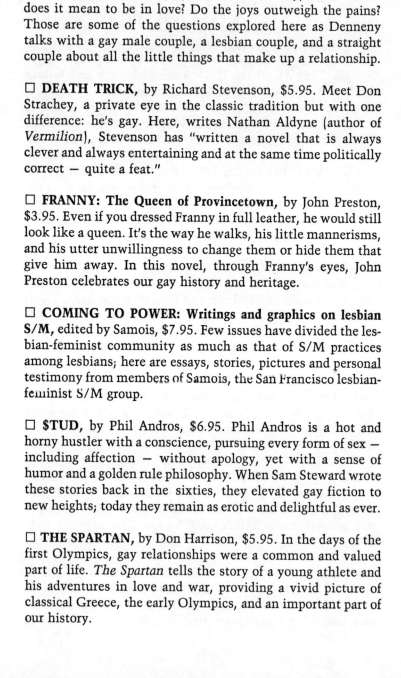

☐ **DECENT PASSIONS,** by Michael Denneny, $6.95. What does it mean to be in love? Do the joys outweigh the pains? Those are some of the questions explored here as Denneny talks with a gay male couple, a lesbian couple, and a straight couple about all the little things that make up a relationship.

☐ **DEATH TRICK,** by Richard Stevenson, $5.95. Meet Don Strachey, a private eye in the classic tradition but with one difference: he's gay. Here, writes Nathan Aldyne (author of *Vermilion*), Stevenson has "written a novel that is always clever and always entertaining and at the same time politically correct — quite a feat."

☐ **FRANNY: The Queen of Provincetown,** by John Preston, $3.95. Even if you dressed Franny in full leather, he would still look like a queen. It's the way he walks, his little mannerisms, and his utter unwillingness to change them or hide them that give him away. In this novel, through Franny's eyes, John Preston celebrates our gay history and heritage.

☐ **COMING TO POWER: Writings and graphics on lesbian S/M,** edited by Samois, $7.95. Few issues have divided the lesbian-feminist community as much as that of S/M practices among lesbians; here are essays, stories, pictures and personal testimony from members of Samois, the San Francisco lesbian-feminist S/M group.

☐ **$TUD,** by Phil Andros, $6.95. Phil Andros is a hot and horny hustler with a conscience, pursuing every form of sex — including affection — without apology, yet with a sense of humor and a golden rule philosophy. When Sam Steward wrote these stories back in the sixties, they elevated gay fiction to new heights; today they remain as erotic and delightful as ever.

☐ **THE SPARTAN,** by Don Harrison, $5.95. In the days of the first Olympics, gay relationships were a common and valued part of life. *The Spartan* tells the story of a young athlete and his adventures in love and war, providing a vivid picture of classical Greece, the early Olympics, and an important part of our history.

☐ **QUATREFOIL,** by James Barr, $6.95. Originally published in 1950, this book marks a milestone in gay writing: it introduced two of the first non-stereotyped gay characters to appear in American fiction. This story of two naval officers who become lovers gave readers of the fifties a rare chance to counteract the negative imagery that surrounded them.

☐ **REFLECTIONS OF A ROCK LOBSTER: A story about growing up gay,** by Aaron Fricke, $4.95. When Aaron Fricke took a male date to the senior prom, no one was surprised: he'd gone to court to be able to do so, and the case had made national news. Here Aaron tells his story, and shows what gay pride can mean in a small New England town.

☐ **YOUNG, GAY AND PROUD,** edited by Sasha Alyson, $2.95. Here is the first book ever to address the needs and problems of a mostly invisible minority: gay youth. Questions about coming out to parents and friends, about gay sexuality and health care, about finding support groups, are all answered here; and several young people tell their own stories.

Talk Back!

The Gay Person's Guide to Media Action

Lesbian and Gay Media Advocates

Get this book free!

When were you last outraged by prejudiced media coverage of gay people? Chances are it hasn't been long. *Talk Back!* tells how you, in surprisingly little time, can do something about it.

If you order at least three other books from us, you may request a FREE copy of this important book. (See order form on next page.)

To get these books:

Ask at your favorite bookstore for the books listed here. You may also order by mail. Just fill out the coupon below, or use your own paper if you prefer not to cut up this book.

GET A FREE BOOK! When you order any three books listed here at the regular price, you may request a *free* copy of *Talk Back!*

BOOKSTORES: Standard trade terms apply. Details and catalog available on request.

Send orders to: **Alyson Publications, Inc.**
　　　　　　　　PO Box 2783, Dept. B-35
　　　　　　　　Boston, MA 02208

— — — — — — — — — — — — — — — — — —

Enclosed is $_____ for the following books. (Add $1.00 postage when ordering just one book; if you order two or more, we'll pay the postage.)

_____

_____

_____

_____

_____

_____

☐ Send a free copy of *Talk Back!* as offered above. I have ordered at least three other books.

name: _____

address: _____

city:_____ state:_____ zip:_____

ALYSON PUBLICATIONS
PO Box 2783, Dept. B-35, Boston, Mass. 02208

This offer expires December 31, 1984. After that date, please write for current catalog.